FORGOTTEN GEMS

Astonishing stories of bloodcurdling horror
Mind-bending tales of the weird and supernatural
Magnificent stories of fantastic fantasy

MASTERPIECES of fantasy almost forgotten, tucked away in dusty volumes covered with cobwebs, resting in a creeking, dark library where bats sail through the musty air . . . gone, lost forever . . .

But wait! They've been found—recovered for those not afraid to venture into the unknown—reclaimed for *your* spine-chilling pleasure!

THE EDITORS

ALDEN H. NORTON is editor of three other anthologies of the supernatural. He was formerly editor of *Argosy* and *Adventure,* acting for many years as Associate Publisher of Popular Publications and in the field of science fiction, fantasy and horror was editorial director and editor of *Famous Fantastic Mysteries, Fantastic Novels, A. Merritt's Magazine of Fantasy, Astonishing Stories* and *Super Science Stories* among other titles. A skilled writer he has appeared in *The Saturday Evening Post.*

SAM MOSKOWITZ has been regarded for many years as probably the world's foremost authority on science fiction and fantasy, having published the only histories of the field *Explorers of the Infinite* and *Seekers of Tomorrow.* Working with Alden H. Norton as a consultant and co-editor on four weird anthologies have given him rising stature in the field of the macabre. His scholarly researches in the field of magazine publishing, are winning him a more secular appreciation. He is an editor and writer in the field of science fiction as well as an anthologist.

GREAT UNTOLD STORIES OF
FANTASY AND HORROR

Edited by ALDEN H. NORTON
and SAM MOSKOWITZ

With Notes by Sam Moskowitz

 PYRAMID BOOKS • **NEW YORK**

ACKNOWLEDGMENTS

The Dreams in the Witch-House by H. P. Lovecraft, Copyright 1933 by the Popular Fiction Publishing Company. Copyright renewed 1961 by August Derleth for Arkham. Reprinted by permission of the copyright owners.

GREAT UNTOLD STORIES OF HORROR AND FANTASY

A PYRAMID BOOK

First printing, October, 1969

Copyright © 1969 by Alden H. Norton

PYRAMID BOOKS are published by Pyramid Publications, Inc., 444 Madison Avenue, New York, New York 10022, U.S.A.

CONTENTS

INTRODUCTION

THERE ARE NO MORE loyal and dependable followers of literature in the world than the lovers of the weird, horrible and supernatural. They will come to the fictional well again and again and support anything of an offbeat nature they feel possesses real merit, yet few have been so shabbily treated through the years in terms of infinite repetition of the old standards in too many of the anthologies that have appeared.

The time is overdue to give them a fair shake and this anthology, *Great Untold Stories of Fantasy and Horror*, was conceived with that end in view. Few of the stories were to have appeared in an anthology of the horror before, and as few were to be familiar to even the long-term collector.

The goal was to find the stories of outstanding merit that had been permitted to disappear into the obscurity of some library reference file or the dusty shelves of specialist collectors.

The search is essentially hazardous. First, a dozen stories may have to be discarded before one is found that deserves to be revived. The anthologist must base his selections upon his own judgment, instead of enjoying the security of "experts" having already placed the stamp of approval on the stories. The time involved in locating and reading enough stories to fill a good-sized collection may not be good business in relation to the financial rewards to be expected. The reaction of the critics and reviewers now becomes unpredictable and they may not share the editor's high regard for the stories.

Against all these considerable deterrents must be balanced the thrill of discovery when after days and weeks of reading and searching, a hitherto forgotten gem is discovered. The feeling of creativity abounds as these discoveries begin to accumulate and are fashioned into a volume which adds to, rather than repeats, the library of great fantasy and horror.

That has been the objective of this collection and it is up to the reader to judge how close we have come to achieving that objective. The lead story was once a complete book in itself, influencing other writers and remembered by those who had been reading in the field for a long time. Today, the presentation of *A Study of Destiny* by Count Leigh de Hamong might just as well be a new story, thrilling the reader for the first time with a spine-chilling concept presented with horrifying directness. THE BLACK CAT magazine for 25 years was a familiar sight in the living rooms of America and Cleveland Moffett's enigmatic *The Mysterious Card* the most popular story it ever published. Today, few people remember THE BLACK CAT and fewer still *The Mysterious Card* but here again is a chance for readers to sample the qualities that made the fame of both so great in their time.

Winston Spencer Churchill is internationally regarded as one of the greatest statesmen of the century, and his multi-volumed histories of World War II and the English Speaking Peoples are among the bestsellers of our time, yet how many know that in his youth Churchill was a fiction writer?

The editors have discovered the short horror story *Man Overboard*, dating before the Boer War, which adds another dimension to the range of Churchill's remarkable abilities.

Time has a habit of obscuring even the works of the world-famous and in their day few authors were more popular than Robert W. Chambers, few more highly praised than was Norman Douglas for his remarkable study in character *South Wind*, and few more grippingly effective in narrative than the Hindu Sarath Kumar Ghosh, best-known for *1,001 Indian Nights*. It is almost a certainty that the reader is unlikely to have read three more effective masterpieces of the supernatural, horror and suspense than *The Messenger*, *An Unnatural Feud* and *Jungli Admi* by the respective three authors.

Huan Mee, author of *The Black Statue*, though a frequent contributor to popular British periodicals of the turn of the century, does not possess such landmark major milestones in his career as some of his more illustrious contemporaries but he was a story teller with a natural-born story teller's art as will be discovered in reading *The Black Statue* which is a horror story that could qualify as science fiction. Author of a relatively few stories, of which *The Seal of Solomon the Great* in this book is one, and author of a single hardcover book *The Strange Adventures of Mr. Middleton,* Wardon Allan Curtis deserves to be researched further because those stories of his that have been discovered display so skillful a rhetorical flair.

There are many women among the great names in weird fiction, but one who has been neglected is Clotilde Graves, novelist and playwright who under the non de plume of Richard Dehan wrote dramas of grim realism that must have pleased William Dean Howells in his time, yet under her own name indulged herself in a number of imaginative gems of ancient and evil supernatural sciences which must have provided her relaxation. One of them we reproduce here.

Most followers of tales of horror are familiar with Edgar Allan Poe, Ambrose Bierce, Nathaniel Hawthorne and Fitz-James O'Brien, but few would recognize the name of W. C. Morrow, a California author. Morrow's reputation rests upon a single volume of short stories which brought him short-term critical acclaim and then oblivion. Individually, the stories refuse to die, they keep popping up in magazines and in various references. *The Monster Maker* was first published in 1897, and is but one example of why Morrow's name belongs with the great masters of horror.

To round out the collection, it was decided to include one story by a recognized modern master H. P. Lovecraft for contrast. In common with a number of the authors in this collection, Lovecraft was destined for probable oblivion until championed by August W. Derleth in posthumous hardcover collections. Gradually his worth was recognized. There is no pretense that *The Dreams in the Witch-House* is a "forgotten" masterpiece, but there is the feeling that it has not yet received its just due as a remarkable modern deviant from the traditional tales of witchcraft, nor for its adroit use of theoretical science to make the unreal temporarily believable.

A STUDY OF DESTINY

Count Leigh de Hamong

It is possible that Count Leigh de Hamong was a very well-known personality in the year 1897, in which year internal evidence seems to indicate this short novel was first written and published, but it is certain that he is virtually unknown today. Sadly enough, so is his book. It appears in no bibliography of fantasy. No reference is ever made to it in serious studies of the weird and supernatural. Book publication was by Saxon & Co., London, England, in the 1890's to judge by the appearance of the edition and it is appropriately bound in black with the title laminated in white upon the twisting coils of a fork-tongued snake.

Here is a forgotten work if there ever was one, but it does not deserve to be forgotten because it is one of the most horrifying landmarks of fright ever written. Perhaps its chilling qualities have condemned it to near oblivion, for as the author stated in the introduction: "There are some persons who will probably think the story too horrible to have ever been published. My answer to that is, that the crimes that are every day committed through ignorance—or worse still, through thoughtlessness—of such matters as hereditary and prenatal influences, are far more horrible than any story the imagination could invent."

There is no question the author had a purpose in view, but he never let it interfere with his story. The action mounts steadily to the last, and when the final period is struck the story has come to its natural, terrifying conclusion, and not a single superfluous word is added.

There is one reference made by the acquaintance of H. P. Lovecraft, Muriel E. Eddy of Providence, Rhode Island, in the January, 1926, issue of WEIRD TALES that may conceivably relate to this remarkable story. Com-

menting on Lukundoo *by Edward Lucas White which had appeared in the November, 1925, issue of that magazine, she said: "It calls to my mind a story I read years ago (by a titled Englishman) entitled* The Hand of Fate," *and then goes on to give a description of the plot which is very close to* A Study of Destiny. *A book titled* The Hand of Fate *by Cheiro was issued by F. T. Neely in 1898 and appears to be the same story in an American edition.*

While Edward Lucas White in his book Lukundoo *published by George H. Doran Co. in 1927 admits that H. G. Wells' "very much better story, 'Pollock and the Porroh Man' was the source of his inspiration, re-reading could conjure a case for a much closer affinity to* A Study of Destiny."

I

IT WAS DURING the summer of 1889, that, accompanied by a rather antiquated archæologist, I found myself one morning trying to make a bargain with some Arabs for the use of a hut during our sojourn in El Karnak.

My companion was one of those extraordinary persons that one somehow expects to find travelling in a country like Egypt. He was a fragment of creation which refused to be ground by the wheel of life into the common mould of ordinary mortals.

By nationality he was a German, with an ancestry back to Noah, and with so many years upon his head, that his heart no longer measured time with regularity, and kept in lieu of palpitation a kind of dog-trot march which the Angel of Death seemed to quietly ignore. By profession he was Professor of Archæology. He knew every stone in the Great Pyramids, and he seemed without doubt to be personally acquainted with every mummy ever embalmed from the days of Cheops down to our present era of cremation. He was an attaché to the Mummy Department of great Museums—a man who worked for work's sake, and not sordidly for gold; and was so unusual in such matters, that people thought him quite mad, except of course when such insanity brought them more money than they could ever gain by the sanity of their own intellectual stupidity. His own country, "Das Vaterland," had not seen fit to recognize its child. It had many fossils, human and otherwise, but it is probable that it placed such value on its French Antiquities, that it failed to see the virtue of a study of dead Egyptians. Hence he had sought England—England was partial to mummies—she built coffers and cases for them, fine museums for them, she paid wise looking professors to label them chronologically, and then squabble for ages over the authenticity of their names—and England welcomed him, and became his scientific refuge.

At various times he was brought before the notice of the Government by his services to the British Museum, and on one occasion his knowledge of Egyptian jewels and relics enabled him to trace by the sale of a rare collection of such treasures on the Continent, a tomb previously unknown to Egyptologists, which was being slowly and steadily robbed by a band of Arabs. For this service to science any other man would probably have received a large reward, but in his case he was satisfied to be sent to Egypt in the worst part of the year to make arrangements for the future safe custody of the pillaged tomb. That work having been successfully accomplished, he turned his attention to the monuments of Thebes, and at the time my story opens, he had determined, single-handed and almost without capital, to search for evidence of another undiscovered tomb of unsurpassed magnificence which, he argued from certain data he had collected, existed in, or about Thebes.

As for myself, I had met the old man some years before in London, whilst dining one night in an old café close to the Museum. He was drawn to me by a ring that I wore. The ring had been found on the hand of a skeleton near Nineveh—a Persian relic consisting of three small chiselled scarabs, representing the Devil, the World, and Eternity. He took a wax impression of the ring, and found out that the scarabs dated back to the Sassasian period of Persia. Through this little incident we became fast friends. It was little wonder then, when we found ourselves fellow travellers in Egypt, that he laid his plans before me, and I agreed to spend the rest of my time with him in his researches among dried up mummies, broken idols, and buried tombs.

We had decided to make our headquarters at El Karnak, and so it was that on the morning my story opens we found ourselves making a bargain for a domicile with a respectable Arab citizen almost in the same spirit as one would with a London landlady.

It will be sufficient for the purpose of this tale, to dwell only upon the points of interest bearing directly upon it, therefore I refrain from detailing all minor experiences or elaborate descriptions of either El Karnak or Thebes.

On the morning after our arrival, fully equipped with a guide and all necessaries, we crossed the Nile and made our way towards that wonderful Valley of Death, the "Tombs of the Kings." It was scarcely dawn. There was only a long, luminous streak far away in the Eastern horizon sending out wide-spreading shafts of light like arrows to pierce the heart of departing night, driven hence like some fugitive before the fierce harbingers of the King of Day. Before us vaguely loomed a range of low hills, wrapped in that strange, chilling stillness that seems keenest about the hour preceding daybreak. In the jealous granite heart of the Necropolis were concealed the embalmed kings—kings perhaps before whom nations had trembled, and yet now their names are scarce spoken. The accumulated drift of centuries covers their greatness. Their glory has passed like the vanished rays of yesterday's sun. They are worse off than the unrenowned dead, who are soon forgotten—Kings that they were, they are doomed to be the prey of undying curiosity. They are rooted out of their resting places—they are bought and sold as merchandise—they are put in glass cases to be stared at, to be mocking fun for the ignorant, to have their limbs exposed, their deeds written and their follies recorded. And yet, in spite of the lesson, modern man would fain be great—either a devil or a god in his ambitious forgetfulness of the future.

It is impossible to adequately describe the sombre grandeur, the impressiveness of the scene environing these tombs. One can scarcely keep the heart from dread, and the soul from awe, at the keen sense of a desolation that enspells. On every side are crumbling ruins of catacombs and pompous monuments, solemn witnesses of past glory—sculptured sneers to the living—monitors no man heeds.

Here in this valley reigns a silence that contains within its stillness the elements of inarticulate eloquence, albeit the stones are tongueless, and the souls of the dead are voiceless spectres.

Away above the hills, one looks up to the limitless blue space of heaven, then back again to the darkness of the tombs, where sleep the Pharaohs—and the living heart quakes with fear, not of self, for self is as nothing here, but with a sense of that defiant mystery called life, and of that mystery of mysteries called death, that mortal seems so powerless to make, break, or control, and never yet solved.

Involuntarily we paused for a moment at the entrance. It seemed that here on the very threshold everything animate and inanimate resented man's intruding footsteps.

A large bat flew out of one of the neighbouring tombs and blinded by the light, dashed against our faces, gave vent to a sordine scream, and wildly disappeared in the direction of the night.

We thought we were alone—the first in the early morning to venture amongst relics of kingly splendours in the sanctuary of the dead. And yet it was not so. Scarcely a hundred paces apart we discerned the figure of a man—a young man, whose senses seemed deaf to sound, as it were, entranced by the wonderful stillness that pervaded the mysterious place. There was something unusual in his personality that at once claimed our attention. It was not the fact of his being there alone at this early hour, although that in itself was unusual, for El Karnak at this season of the year was deserted by tourists. There was a subtle something enveloping him. For are there not some persons whose atmosphere, whose every line and curve is the expression of their superior soul; whereas, are there not others as devoid of expression, as devoid of this quality, as they are soulless?

The stranger had taken off his cap, apparently in token of reverence in this ancient abode of the illustrious dead. As he stood there uncovered, one could not help noticing that his strongly marked and almost handsome face bore an expression of sadness and desolation that was strangely in keeping with the scene. Although an Englishman and in an ordinary tourist costume, there was something about him that harmonized with the weirdness of the valley and made him seem a part of the picture—a living example it might have been, of that strange invisible power called cohesion, that one sees in the Destiny of Nations, and does not care to admit in the individual Destiny of Man.

We approached him, intending to make friendly overtures, but to our surprise with a peculiar expression of distrust, without returning our salutation he walked rapidly away towards a more distant tomb, and as if perfectly familiar with the place, he entered it and was lost to our view.

From our guide we learned that he had been in the

vicinity some time; that he lived apart from everyone, and scarcely spoke to a human being unless circumstances forced him to do so. It was rumoured that he spent almost his entire time day and night, prowling about the ruins. His favourite haunt the Tombs of the Kings, where he was generally to be found. "But he is brave, brave as the lion," the guide went on to say, and then he told us how, but a month since, this man had plunged into the Nile, and saved a little native girl from being crushed by the paddle wheel of a steamer—"but"—and the guide lowered his voice in a mysterious way—"there is one thing the Englishman is afraid of," and with a writhing gesture of the hand, and emitting a sharp hiss, we knew that the stranger had some extraordinary fear of *a snake*.

We had reached the entrance of one of the large tombs, and the old professor forgot everything else in the enthusiasm of his work. By chance probably we had struck a tomb that was exactly in accordance with a chart he had carefully worked out, and his old face lighted up with joy, and became young again with the promised realization of one of his pet dreams.

During moments of great excitement, it was his habit to produce a little German pipe, and softly croon to himself as he rubbed and polished it with the sleeve of his old-fashioned black coat. On this occasion the bowl of the little veteran was polished till it shone like ebony, and I am certain that the sleeve of any other man's coat would have caught fire through the vigorous friction. With pride the professor confided to me that he had worn that same coat at his work for over twenty years. How it stood the wear is beyond my comprehension. In colour it was a rusty black, very shiny but very clean, for the professor had the peculiar knack of looking spick and span under all conditions. Even after a long tramp across the desert, I have seen him turn up at the finish without a hair out of place, and a freshness about his beardless face that would delude one into the belief that he had just made his toilet. He never ceased to taunt me over "the misfortune of having a heavy growth of beard," and exulted that Providence had spared him. I think he would have begrudged the five minutes required to shave, and waxed profane over the interruption to his work.

Although he had attained his seventieth year, he was agile and alert as a boy. True, he wore spectacles, but then one naturally does not expect a professor without them, particularly not an erudite Egyptologist. His gold-rimmed spectacles—his one extravagance—lent to his face a guise of profound learning that even seemed to impress our Arab guide, for the rascal did not attempt to impose upon us the usual yarns and lies which are as a rule launched upon tourists. He simply pointed out the places and objects of interest with a long, lean finger, and waited for the professor to explain.

We went from crypt to crypt, until at last the day came to an end, and we returned to our hut.

The professor was extremely pleased with his first day's work, but very suspicious of the Arab who had accompanied us. After our meagre supper as we sat chatting together, he pointed out to me many doubtful things in the Arab's behaviour. One instance in particular, when we had followed a passage, until it led us into a small chamber where the Arab had become positively insolent, because the professor insisted on tarrying to closely examine its formation. Cunning as the Arab was, he had not calculated on the tenacity of the man he had to deal with. Professor Von Heller had come to Thebes to fathom *something,* and neither a stone wall nor a horde of inimical Arabs would have in the slightest degree turned him aside, once he had arrived at the conclusion that it was his duty, in the interest of science, to proceed.

He determined, however, that we would go unattended to pursue our exploration on the following day, and his last words were to caution me to supply myself with plenty of matches: "For," he said, with a smile, "it is the custom of these tricky dogs, when an independent tourist refuses their guidance, to creep after him, and blow out his torch in the most bewildering part of the crypts; thinking that after he has spent a gruesome night in the society of mummies he will be only too willing to pay for guides in the future."

II

It was scarcely dawn when the professor, already dressed, awoke me, and informed me in his quiet, insistent way, that it was time to get up. Lazily and drowsily I complied. Whilst dressing, the voices of two men talking in Arabic in a half-whisper outside my window attracted my attention. I recognized one as our guide of yesterday, and the other as our Arab servant, who, by honest right, at that moment should have been preparing our breakfast. Something in the tones of the guide's voice—although I could not understand a word he said—impressed me with the idea that my companion and myself were the subjects of conversation.

Just at this juncture, the professor re-entered the room; instantly, his attention was also caught by the suspicious undertone of the voices. He understood Arabic. Giving me a sign of silence, he quickly crept to the window to listen. He jotted down in his ubiquitous note book every word, while a benign smile of satisfaction rose like a Nile moon over his face. In a few moments the conversation stopped, the guide departed, and our Arab servant, in the most acceptable broken English, announced breakfast.

Over our frugal meal, the professor confided to me that his suspicions of the previous day were too well founded. From the guide's words he had learned that we had been suspected of trying to find out too much, and that our Arab servant had been warned to give no information whatever in any way relating to the tombs. From the trend of their conversation there was no longer any doubt left in the professor's mind, not only that there was a tomb unrevealed, but that it was the most valuable quarry of all, and contained large quantities of jewels and relics. It was a concerted plan of the Arabs who knew the secret, to pillage it when an auspicious opportunity offered. Exactly what their attitude would be towards us when they found out that we had dispensed with their services, the professor had not gathered. The servant had been simply warned to look out for his own interests, as some day we probably would not return.

I must confess I felt a bit anxious as we made preparations to start. The professor had told me all kinds of stories, about torches being blown out in difficult passages, and people starving to death before their absence was discovered. But the genial old soul somewhat reassured me by saying, "I have prepared for such an emergency, and can foil even an Arab's cupidity," at the same time producing from his traveller's hold-all, two folding lanterns with dark slides and a small can of oil that he quietly slipped into his pocket.

Once more we started, and in order to divert the suspicion of the Arabs, we visited various other points of interest, before directing our steps towards the place we planned to reach. Barring the young Englishman, we were the only strangers in the vicinity. The season was far advanced, and everyone who could had fled to escape the intense heat. As for the stranger with the sad face, he was seldom to be seen. Occasionally we encountered him in passing through labyrinths leading from tomb to tomb, but each time he appeared deliberately to avoid us. We noticed that all the Arabs seemed to have some superstitious fear of him; they never went near him on any pretext, and even the little children, who usually beset every stranger for alms, crept away and left him alone. From his appearance and dress he was a gentleman, yet one could not see him without wondering at the nameless shadow that seemed always hanging about him—a shadow of gloom, of despair, of melancholy, of foreboding that it would be impossible to depict. One felt it.

When at last we reached the point where we had discontinued our investigations on the previous day, the professor lighted the lanterns, and without a word plunged forward into the all-encompassing darkness of the subterranean approaches to the more remote tombs. Occasionally he stopped and flashed the light on some piece of carving or inscription upon the walls, and I noticed at the beginning of every passage he carefully examined the left-hand side, and taking some wax from his leather geologist's satchel, he would take impressions of a small cypher or character that had completely escaped my notice. At first I thought that his object in making such observations was simply precautionary that we might be able to retrace our footsteps; but a little later he explained to me that in his enthusiasm he had not for a moment entertained a thought of danger; he had simply discovered some cypher that was not found in any of the other tombs, and which, he considered, was an important clue to the tomb of which he was in search.

Up to that moment we had not heard anything of the Arabs, nor were we molested in any way. But just when I had about overcome my apprehensions, the professor turned the dark slide of his lantern, and quietly drew me into a narrow niche hewn in the solid wall. The sudden darkness was intense; our eyes unable to adjust themselves reflected again and again the brilliant colourings of some of the figures and inscriptions we had seen in the light. The stillness was almost maddening, but suddenly it was broken by a slight pattering shuffle, and we became conscious of the naked body of an Arab crawling past us like a snake. It was some time before we ventured out, and when we did, it was to retrace our steps and return home for the day.

The professor spent the rest of the afternoon in arranging the different impressions he had taken. He placed them carefully according to the drawing he had made of the tombs, and when he had them symmetrically fitted, he called me to his side, and pointed out with a grim look of satisfaction, that every one of the marks led direct to that portion of the tomb where our guide had lost his temper on the day before. "And yet," the professor said, and he rubbed the little black pipe with a new vigour, "I would swear, after my examination yesterday, that there is nothing there but solid rock."

Just at this moment the young Englishman came up the street, and passed the doorway. He looked towards us, and that indescribable something in his face so attracted the professor that he forgot alike his chart and the wax impressions, and stepping to the door, watched the stranger go towards the ruins of the Temple of El Karnak. When the old man turned back to his charts, it was to think and not to work. His old withered hands listlessly pushed the wax impressions at random across the paper, even the little black pipe was forgotten, and I could see that the human mystery embodied in the person of the young man had a greater claim on his heart, than even that of time and Thebes which he had so determined to unearth.

Watching him sit there I gradually fell asleep in my chair, and after a long refreshing nap, I woke to find it near midnight, and the old man yet wrapt in profound meditation in the same position. Wishing to divert his thoughts, I touched him on the shoulder and suggested a walk before turning in for the night. He started at my touch, and assented by simply putting on his hat and mechanically following me out into the silent street.

We wandered aimlessly in the direction of the ruins of El Karnak. It was such a night as one can see only in Egypt, and that, too, but during certain seasons of the year. The stillness of death seemed to reign perpetually about this place; there was no breeze, no sound of man or beast—everything on earth seemed painfully hushed, while in the heavens a large pallid moon hung like the ghost of some dead world unrested and alone.

The heat was intense, a dull torrid heat that rose in filmy waves from the desert, that parched the lips, that swelled the veins like the kiss of a fever when one's strength is gone. The low whitewashed huts around the ruins were silent and grim. What insignificant kennels they were in the shadow of those majestic columns and sculptures, magnificent and stately, even in their dilapidation and decay! One could imagine the closed eyelids, the parted lips, the distorted limbs those squalid huts covered from the sky—covered, yes! that the spectres of the moonlight might not mock the miserable descendants of the past. Without uttering a word, we traversed court after court, gazed up at the massive pillars that rose like giants towards the unbroken silence of the sky. On every side were ruins, but what ruins!—majesty, grandeur, intellect, superb intellect—had designed and erected these monuments that even time's voracious teeth had failed to totally destroy—verily fitting sepulchres for kings.

Was it then indeed a wonder that those who had built these stupendous monuments to endure through centuries in witness of their mundane glory, their giant prowess, sought to preserve against the cruel ravages of time their dead, by swathing in bands of linen and embalming spices the hands that imperiously held sceptres or toiled, and the heads that devised or that ruled, and the bodies they had worshipped, hoping that they might also endure, if they could not live for ever?

And yet what vanity, for mortals to strive to cope with and thwart the inevitable—the law of Destiny—they could not keep the dead from decay, nor their temples from crumbling, nor their dynasties from devastation of usurpers. Strange and humiliating it is to our own era that we of to-day, have learned so little from the lessons of the past. Their religions are dead—their gods are broken—their dilapidated temples but monuments to folly. The mummies with all their spiced wrappings are powdered into dust, and more repulsive still, some worms have been cheated, while others have been fed like vampires. And yet, we with our boasted civilization, with our creeds and Christianities, we are consumed by a vanity that I question is not greater than theirs. We make no more gods of stone, but we make others less tangible—gods of ideas, gods of theories, gods that leave no visible ruins, except in the betrayed hearts of those who once were worshippers. Our various religions have built temples, it is true, but not like the temples of past faiths. We have no longer time to chisel the pictured story of our era thereupon, and we count, alas, their glory in the richness of their revenue. We make no visible sacrifices of blood and flesh—no, but in our selfishness and ambitious strife, our paths are strewn with more damning sacrifices. We substitute creeds for deeds—creeds that torture, that shackle, and blunt our consciences—that make us slaves to the egotism of some man-god, that in the end change and are futile and leave us wrecked and stranded in our disillusions.

And yet the law of Life and Death goes on the same—the flowers of the field bloom to fade and so do we. Children come and go as the buds on the trees, they laugh, they play, they look bright as the flowers, but like the flowers, they are hardly conscious of the inherited worm of disease that comes creeping to their heart's core, to blight and destroy them. Yet do we pay tribute to shrines—we pray to this saint, and that god, but the canker increases, we suffer, and the end comes. It is only when confronting a supreme moment that we realize how terrible, how inevitable is Destiny—only when we are helpless—when we are stunned by a something we cannot resist—then in half-cowardice the head is bowed, and the lips murmur, "Thy will be done," and yet the soul is in rebellion. Too late, too late!

We would disallow and cavil with the righteousness of the claim on man of that Destiny we recognize in nations—we would place ourselves on a pinnacle, and dream we see all because we see a little. Poor pigmies that we are, we say we will control when we are the controlled—the very most servants who obey without knowing the meaning of obedience. To pacify ourself each one makes an imagery of God to refuge his own irresponsibility. We feel dominated by the Infinite Who creates us, endows our being with thoughts, and feelings, and conscience, and spirit. Yet we fain do not imitate. We were born to reproduce and perfect our own species, see how woefully do we fulfil our mission—we transgress the God-given laws of nature, then idiotically wonder at their imperfections and cruelty when the inexorable penalties are exacted. In these transgressions we are worse than brutes. For we know evil, yet resist good. And yet, the world goes on, seed-time and harvest come and go. Nations rise and fall, and so do men, but they reck not what they sow in seed-time, or reap *"what they have not sowed."* The inscrutable law of Destiny is above all, around all, and in all, *is all.* It encompasses the beginning and the end—it is Truth and

Falsehood—the good and the evil and the consequences that follow. It is God the Infinite, man the finite—and love and good which is the mystery that conceals the purpose.

*   *   *

As I stood beneath those gigantic structures of the past, these thoughts ran through my brain. For the first time I fully realized the littleness of man and the greatness of that controlling law of Destiny which has been worshipped for centuries under so many names. I turned to my old friend, and was surprised to find that the effect on him had been similar. Once could read on his face his soul's surprise—see the breakdown of old ideas and orthodox beliefs. But, we had not learned the lesson. We had but opened the covers of the book. Men, like children, are fond of pictures. In a moment we would see one, an illustration, an etching from Fate's pencil, to be for ever engraven upon our hearts.

We had been advancing in silence towards the centre of that great "Hall of Columns," where the broken portion of the roof has still remained, when we were startled by a low sob that seemed to come from a corner of the ruins where the gathered shadows, even in daylight, are sombre and almost impenetrable.

It was more than a sob—it was a moan from behind clenched teeth—a moan that seemed more than human in its intensity—until it became the voice of pain that dashed itself from pillar to pillar, that echoed in our ears and chilled the hot blood that but a moment before was coursing through our veins. We stood rooted to the spot, possessed by a terror that is indescribable. We looked at one another, but our blanched faces frightened us in the light of the pallid moon that covered all with its ghostly shimmer. The awful silence that followed the cry seemed more than I could bear—I could hear the blood surging up my throat, singing past my ears, and stealing in upon my brain till every nerve and muscle grew paralyzed with fear. Again we heard that heart-rending cry, and in our excited senses we saw it—saw it in a thousand shapes and forms, crossing from under the shattered roof, breaking itself against the stone idols and broken gods, and moaning an anguish in our ears that made our very hearts stand still as we hearkened.

There could no longer be any doubt; it was the cry of a

soul in agony. Not an ordinary soul, but one of those sensitive, yet strong souls that shut themselves in with their sorrows, that cry only in the silence of the night when there is no one to share the Gethsemane of their anguish. Instinctively we started forward to help—to console, to do anything, in fact, to keep that sound from being repeated. But we had scarcely moved our feet in the soft sand, when from out of the shadows there appeared the apparition of a young man, the very man who had so often occupied our thoughts—whose mournful but handsome face we had remarked on our first arrival. Slowly, but with firm steps, he crossed to the centre and then stood still—still as the huge idol that lay across his path. His hair was thrown back from his brow, and his strong, manly face, marked by pain and gloom, stood out in bold relief against the enormous pillars that flanked him. His loose English shirt was open from throat to waist, while his hands were clutched on his breast as if ready to tear his heart out and dash it against the stones.

As he stood there, he seemed to look upward into the very eyes of Heaven; he was more than a man for the moment, he was a god, *questioning the mercy of a Greater*. But suddenly his whole appearance changed; he seemed to writhe with pain, and pressing his hands still tighter over his heart, he clenched his teeth to keep back the cry that even then was again rising from his very soul. He battled with it, but the agony was too great. It burst from him— burst through his clenched teeth, and with a moan like that of a hunted, wounded animal, he staggered forward and fell across the idol, as one dead.

In a second the old professor was leaning over the prostrate form, and with the tenderness of a woman he brushed the great drops of perspiration from the brow, rubbed the cold hands that lay motionless, and as there were no signs of life, he looked up anxiously at me, and then back again at the body lying there as inanimate as the broken idol at his side. But there was motion—a motion that caused us to almost hold our breath with suspense— there was something on the breast under the thin silk shirt that moved—something that somehow like a presentiment of evil, filled us with dread and dismay. Involuntarily I too had drawn near the sufferer, and put out my hand to raise the folds of the shirt. As I did so, I touched something that made me gasp with terror, something so horrible, so ghastly, that even now as I write, I can vividly recall the sensation. My hand had come in contact with a cold clammy something that lived there—it had moved under my touch, writhed, as if it were in torment. I looked closely. There was the head of a snake, with sightless eyes quivering beneath my fingers! One glance was sufficient, I staggered back and dropped senseless from the shock that my good friend thought would there and then prove fatal —but, resulted in making me keep my bed for weeks.

III

When I recovered consciousness I found myself alone with my old companion. With the greatest difficulty after this hideous episode he got me back to our abode, but days and even weeks passed before he mentioned what had happened after I lost consciousness. At last, one evening he told me that just as I fell, the stranger had revived and opened his eyes, and with a surprised, terrified look he hastily pulled his coat together over his breast, sprang to his feet and without one word disappeared among the ruins.

Even then, the professor would not credit what I averred I had seen. It was in vain that I tried to convince him. Finally, thinking to humour me he said, that such an eccentric individual might probably carry as a pet a snake, such as I described.

One night, as we sat talking the strange occurrence over, the individual in question came slowly towards our hut. For a moment we imagined he was going to speak to us —there seemed a glad look in his eyes on seeing me again—but instead of speaking, he slowly raised his cap, bowed, and passed on, once more in the direction of the ruins of El Karnak.

The professor was very pleased to get even that recognition. He had made up his mind that the mysterious individual would some day, in some way be instrumental in giving the key to the secret that he so earnestly desired to solve. He could give no actual reason for his conclusion, except that he felt that such would be the case. By some undefined intuitive force, his soul had already come in touch with the possibilities of the future. He felt confident of it, and yet, although it was his earnest desire, the assurance of the knowledge brought no happiness. Perhaps, his soul gazing into the future saw such trials and sufferings that it deemed the price too great for all it had to learn and irrevocably must endure.

My convalescence warranted our resuming our work at Thebes. Every morning we would cross the Nile, and sometimes not return to our hut till late at night. Again and again we met our strange friend in our wanderings, but he always appeared to avoid us; even the genial professor was gradually coming to the conclusion that we might as well try and form a speaking acquaintance with the Sphinx, when through a very simple incident, one morning the barrier was broken. How often it is so in life—when we have ceased to plan, we become successful.

For a long time the professor had been engaged in taking impressions from certain hieroglyphics he had found on the murals of the passages. By subsequently putting the segments together, he discovered that they formed a key, and by this he proceeded to make his way from passage to passage. On the day in question, however, he was baffled completely by what really seemed to be a simple character. The old man had tried again and again to make the sections fit, in order that he might be enabled to go on with his conceived plan. But there was something wrong, and after trying over and over again, he at last gave up the task, with a sigh of real despair. At that moment, however, the stranger stepped towards us from one of the passages. He seemed to take in the whole difficulty at a glance, and raising his hat to the professor he said, "Sir, if you will allow me, I will show you what is wrong." Without waiting for a reply he re-arranged the sections, and in a few seconds the difficulty was solved.

The professor's gratitude knew no bounds. He expressed himself in both German and English in the same breath, and was only checked when the stranger said quietly, "You are only at the beginning; you have not yet solved the difficulty." But the hope in the old man's heart was hard to kill. With gratitude and satisfaction, he again shook the young man's hand and turned to resume his work.

The stranger disappeared almost as quickly as he had come. But the ice had been broken, and the professor looked forward with joyful expectation to another meeting. He rubbed his hands with delight, as he thought how he had intuitively divined from the first, that this strange individual possessed the secret of which he was in quest. He pointed out to me with what perfect ease he had arranged the sections, a thing impossible without a previous knowledge of the meaning of the cyphers. "But where do your figures lead to, after all?" I enquired. The old man pointed to the odd-looking chart of cyphers before him. "The last one, that must contain the secret," he said, "is according to this, formed by the combination of the first seven symbols. We must be close to it here—let us look for it." So saying he picked up one of the lanterns and started forward. We were indeed close to the end. A few paces brought us to the same small chamber that we had visited on our first day with the guide, and to my amazement, we beheld, carved in the centre of the roof, the curious looking symbol for which we sought, and which was the counterpart of the one on the chart. With a look of satisfaction and triumph, the old man gave vent to his feelings by executing what, I am sure, he must have intended for a German version of a Highland fling. But the temperature of Egypt was not suited to such vigorous gymnastics, and the result was a quick collapse of the aged and honorable professor.

As soon as he had recovered from his exertions, he proceeded to examine the curious symbol. He could not interpret it as far as language was concerned, but he had no great difficulty in making out that, although having a distinct character of its own, it was in reality made up of the first seven signs. And yet he could not disguise the fact that he was no nearer the solution than before. It was true he had discovered something strange, something not discovered by other archæologists. But, after all, it was only a curious piece of carving in an empty chamber—a cypher without a solution, a door perhaps, without a key. It was in vain, he tried the walls for some opening or secret passage, in vain also that with his hammer he rapped on the floor, and the roof. All sounded the same. He but aroused echoes—echoes that mocked his hopes—echoes that died away in space and left him in despair.

It was a long time before he could bring himself to acknowledge that he was completely baffled, after all those days and weeks of toilsome research. He had sedulously worked up to the point when the signs he had discovered were obviously finger-posts, to guide through all those puzzling labyrinths, and subterranean passages, and that a sign made up of seven cyphers, if found, would undeniably be the open sesame to that secret tomb, the El Dorado of his dreams. Alas! the mysterious symbol, the coveted heptagon, was found in the most insignificant chamber, a mere blind room scarcely ten feet square, built of Thebian marble, marked by no other sign, word or hieroglyphic, except, that one strange carving in the centre. Yet the point of entrance to the great tomb, if any existed, remained inexorably hidden. Under great stress the old man once more searched every portion of the masonry, and his little faithful hammer noisily interrogated its surfaces. No use. I could see his eyes brim with tears, as he prepared to depart. He did not speak until we reached our hut and as he bade me good-night, I knew from the dejected tone of his voice that, for the first time in his life, he had altogether lost heart.

On the following morning, however, with renewed pluck, we started as before, again reached the catacombs, found the passages we had threaded the previous day, and after some difficulty once again we occupied the little chamber marked by that one significant symbol of seven. Again and again, the professor with his indefatigable pertinacity, tried by every means in his knowledge and power, to see if he could not wrest from these solid walls any clue to the secret passage that might lead to the goal, he hoped against hope to attain. Hour after hour passed without promise; the solid blocks of granite piteously echoed back, again and again, the metallic blows of his hammer, unrelentlessly refusing to yield their secret, until at last, worn out and exhausted, the poor professor threw himself down on the slabs, and abandoned himself for the moment to disappointment and despair. I could not bear to stay and be a witness of his grief, so I took my lantern, and made off into one of the adjacent passages on a little exploration tour of my own. I was careful to keep to the one passage, not daring to venture by myself into others, fearful I should get lost in their intricate labyrinths. I had scarcely gone any distance, when my foot struck against the naked body of an Arab, who was crawling away from the chamber in which I had left the professor. The man had evidently been surreptitiously listening to every word we had said, and in the one glance I got at his face, I recognized him as one of the gang from which on the first morning we had selected our guide. Fully expecting him to spring at me from the darkness, I quickly drew my revolver; but instead of attacking me, he mockingly laughed, and cursed all Christians as he made away and disappeared. Hastily retracing my steps after this occurrence, I was surprised and considerably startled to hear voices issuing from the chamber where I had left the professor alone. I rushed forward to protect him if need be, but, to my amazement, instead of finding him surrounded by villainous Arabs, I found him in the centre of the chamber, energetically shaking both hands of the young man who had already commanded so much of our attention, and profusely thanking him.

On my approach, my old friend, with voice trembling through emotion, told me in a few words, that the stranger had come of his own free will to act as our guide, and had offered to show us the very tomb we were in search of, which he and a few Arabs only knew.

"Yes," said the stranger, turning to the professor, "I will show you what you seek. Often have I desired to reveal my knowledge of the secret, but have waited until I could impart it to someone who would realize its historic and scientific value, and not regard it simply as a *treasure trove* to be pillaged. For this reason, I have, unobserved by you, watched you at work. I have even heard the words you have spoken to your friend. To-day, I have been so touched by your overwhelming disappointment, I could no longer refrain from telling you the thing you have toiled so faithfully to achieve, is now close at your hand. Do not thank me. Under different conditions, I probably would have used my present knowledge for my own advantage. The honour of the discovery would, however, be useless to me at this point of my calamitous career. But come, we have no time to waste in words—there is also danger in our being seen together, particularly in this place. Meet me to-night at the entrance to this crypt, and I will gladly reveal all to you."

IV

When night fell, faithful to the young man's instructions, we crossed the river from El Karnak to join him at the entrance to the tombs. I have often wondered since, why it was that both the professor and myself were more than usually impressed with the sweetness of the outside world. As we walked down that silent, mysterious valley to the "Tombs of the Kings" over and over again we instinctively remarked the brilliancy of the stars, the radiance of the moonlight, whereas, the lower we descended into the valley, the more we seemed to shrink from the task that lay before us. Whatever could it portend?

The hills that hid the resting-place of kings rose dark and sinister in the silence of the night and cut sharply against the sky. The entrance to the tombs now looked like black hungry mouths—vampire mouths—yawning for the bodies of the living or the dead, while the very air seemed to thrill with presentiments that we felt, but could not understand. During the latter part of our journey we did not speak, and it was a veritable relief, when at last we discerned our strange friend pacing to and fro before the appointed place of meeting.

His explicit instructions had been to carry no lighted lanterns, or do anything that might attract the attention of the Arabs, as we passed through El Karnak. We were also cautioned to guard well that we were not followed, and, the first question our new friend asked was, if we had been observed. We replied in the negative—as far as we knew, we had got through unseeen. Having satisfied himself that there were no Arabs skulking about the tombs, his caution dictated that we must all creep on our hands and knees, until we got some distance underground, before we lit our lanterns.

It was thus we started, our strange guide first, then the professor, and lastly myself. Slowly and noiselessly we went deeper and deeper into the tomb. At every turning, our guide waited for us, and led us safely from one passage into another. The darkness was intense, and the heat and closeness almost insufferable. The only noise that broke the silence, was when occasionally we disturbed some large bat, and heard the whisk of his black wings, as he flew past us and disappeared. Once we thought we heard voices behind us, but having waited some time without a recurrence of the sound, we came to the conclusion that our strained senses had deceived us, and cautiously proceeded.

At last our companion deemed it safe to light the lanterns, and with their help we soon reached the small chamber with the strange, mysterious symbol of seven.

Turning to the professor, our companion said, "Now, sir, you see that I have followed exactly the same route that you so carefully, and wonderfully worked out by those characters that you discovered. All your calculations were right up to this point, yet, it would have been impossible for you to have gone further by calculation, unless, by some lucky chance you had hit upon the secret. The Egyptians have always been famous for their intricate architectural devices. It will never cease to be the wonder of the world as to how the colossal stones that form the Pyramid of Cheops were ever placed in position. But what will you think, when I tell you that the wonder of this chamber is that one of its entire stone walls is in reality a swing-door, and a door, too, that the strength of a child might open, provided that the child knew the secret?"

So saying he looked upward at the strange symbol in the centre of the roof, and then following a certain angle, he placed his left foot in a slight mark of wear on the rock at his feet. With his right hand he barely touched one side of the wall, when to our astonishment, the entire side of the chamber swung round on its axis, leaving an opening on either side by which a person might easily pass through. We wistfully entered, and found ourselves in a chamber exactly corresponding to the one we had left.

Our companion went through the same process he had to open the wall, and with a slight noise the huge stone swung back into its place.

Passing through this chamber, we reached a narrow passage, which, in its turn, led us to the inside of an inverted cone, down whose sloping sides we were preparing to descend, when our companion called our attention to a huge block of stone resting on the edge of the cone, and balanced in such a way that the slightest touch would send it crashing to the bottom. "That stone," he said, "was placed there simply as a seal when the occasion required it; once it falls," he said slowly, "the tomb below will be sealed for ever."

In descending, we had to go round and round the cone, exactly like following the spiral threads of an immense screw. In doing this, we were forced to pass under the enormous stone several times, and I found it impossible to do so without experiencing a shudder of fear, lest it might be dislodged and fall. At last we reached the base of the cone, and stopped for a moment under a small arch, lost in amazement at the sight that greeted our eyes. We were standing on the threshold of the entrance of an immense tomb, larger even than that of the King's Chamber at Gizeh. It was of great height, and built in the shape of a seven-sided pyramid. The walls, floor, and roof were of polished Thebian marble, that reflected, and magnified in every direction the puny light of our lanterns. The bodies of seven mummies lay on raised stone platforms at the seven points of the chamber, and were so arranged, that the echo that was made by the mural of the chamber, at each point where the seven bodies lay, seemed to repeat the slightest whisper from one mummy to the other until, after circling round the seven, it ended where it started with redoubled volume.

It was the professor who unconsciously was the first to evoke this astonishing acoustic phenomenon. He had lingered an instant longer than had we, at the entrance, absolutely spell-bound. Reverently the old man had taken off his well-worn straw hat, and as he did so there fell from his lips, "Oh, God! How wonderful! how wonderful!" Mummy after mummy appeared to repeat the words, and as the seventh loudly emitted them, the old man clutched my arm for support, whilst his trembling lips involuntarily repeated the litany accepted of the dead—and again, this weird, mysterious echo, swung round the strange circle until it rebounded back to the professor, then floated upwards towards the roof and died away.

The effect in the sepulchral stillness prevailing here, can be more easily imagined than described. A sensation of awe, and reverence for the mighty dead completely possessed us. As we stood there, our modern race seemed made up of pigmies, our vaunted inventions as naught compared with the intellect and science of those dead Egyptians who had planned and erected all these marvellous structures.

But alas! what a sight of pillage and of vandalism was revealed to us as we proceeded!

Every sarcophagus had been burst open, except one, and even it had not quite escaped violation by the Arabs or probably earlier races who had invaded this wonderful crypt. Most of the mummies had been ruthlessly rifled. The linen bandages that had swathed the mummies had been indecently stripped completely off some, but more frequently they had been simply wrenched off the breasts, and the jewels and relics taken. Whoever the marauders had been, everywhere was evidenced extreme, reckless haste. Jewels and rings were scattered here and there on the floor, as though a whirlwind had swept over the place, and close to the entrance was the skeleton of a full-grown man, who had fallen with his avaricious hands full of jewels, and perished as he had fallen. The posture, and appearance, and proximity to the entrance, told its own tale—he had evidently been surprised, or overtaken by some calamity, and tried to escape with simply what he could grab, and red-handed, for some unaccountable reason had fallen, never again to rise.

The unopened sarcophagus was the special object of

interest to the professor. It stood apart from the others making up the seven, and occupied a position of distinction, almost in the centre of the tomb. It was unlike the others in shape, and was unembellished by any Egyptian characters, except one curious symbol, which the professor examined with avidity. Taking some tracings from his pocket, he scrutinized and compared with the symbol. At last, looking up triumphantly, he said, much agitated by his excitement:

"If what I think I have found here proves true, this will be the most valuable discovery of any heretofore made in connection with the history of Ancient Egypt." Growing more calm, he explained that the greatest puzzle to all Egyptologists had been, and to the present moment still was, the empty sarcophagus found in the Great Pyramid—the Pyramid of Cheops. He then in a few words told us that amongst the writings of Diodorus, in his description of the Pyramids dealing with the period of Cheops, he had clearly written:—" 'Although this king had intended this Pyramid for his sepulchre, yet it happened that he was never buried there. . . . For the people, being exasperated by reason of the toilsomeness of the work, threatened to tear in pieces his dead body, and with ignominy throw it out of the sepulchre; whereupon, when dying, he commanded his friends to bury him in another place.' "

"This curious sign," continued the professor, "is exactly similar to one found in the Great Pyramid, amongst the inscriptions relating to the First Dynasty; therefore, it is not illogical to conclude that this sarcophagus, before us, contains none other than the lost mummy of Cheops. We must return to-morrow," the professor was just saying—and simultaneously with the last words a slight, yet ominous sound startled us.

It might have been imperceptible, but for the echo of the tomb. It was at most only a slight sound, but one that struck terror to our hearts and sent a cold shiver through every nerve and vein. It came from the opening of the great cone through which we had passed. This was sufficient to tell us that we had been betrayed, and that in another second we would face a doom too terrible to even imagine.

Instinctively we rushed towards the opening by which we had entered. Too late! A mocking, fiendish laugh warned us of our danger. The next moment there was a low rumbling sound, and then a deafening crash that resounded like a thousand cannon about our ears. We realized that the stone had fallen and the opening was sealed for ever!

V

I will not dwell upon our feelings, it will be sufficient to trust to the imagination of the reader, to portray what agony the mere idea of being incarcerate, buried alive, would create. The greater the loss, the more quietly oftentimes it is borne, and it is the same, I expect, under pressure of any very great shock. The surprise of any new situation, be it misfortune or success, often robs the mind for the moment of its anxiety. The old professor, who twelve hours before had almost cried like a child when baffled in his purpose, now when face to face with such a terrible doom, was apparently as calm as if at that moment he was simply pursuing his daily work in the Mummy Department of the British Museum. In fact, the little German pipe even made its appearance—but not to be rubbed till it shone like ebony. Ah no! just to be fondly held with nervous fingers, as if two long-time friends were about to part.

As for our new companion, he said very little, but what he did say revealed in agonized tones the torture he was undergoing, for the terrible misfortune, he had unintentionally brought upon us. He would not rest until he had tried every possible plan of escape. But what escape could there be from such a prison, from a tomb under all the others; a place built for such secrecy, that it had baffled for centuries, every attempt at discovery. No, that last fiendish laugh from Arab lips must be the last sound of earth that we would ever hear.

Oh, God, how terrible! That constant march round and round our dismal prison; the pressing of our hands against the stones; eyes weary with the darkness; and hearts heavy with the want of hope! Occasionally, we started back, sick with fear, as our whispers summoned the weird echoes, and we heard the mimicry of our spoken thoughts return to us, as it were from the long dead lips of those stark mummies, who had lain so many centuries in this cold, dark tomb.

There was a well in the centre, a huge black hole plunging down into the bowels of the earth; just such an one as there is in the centre of the Pyramids at Cairo. Without hope we gravitated again and again to its edge, and held our lanterns over, as we peered down into its awful, limitless blackness, and wondered if help would rise to us from its boundless depths. Presently one of our lanterns went out. This reminded us that the hour approached surely when we would have no light. Like children we huddled together, terrorized through our own helplessness; and we lay down crushed, and quiet, by the side of that unopened coffer, which had lost the history of the mummy it encased.

In time we lapsed into absolute silence. We tacitly knew as hour after hour slipped by, that we should soon be in total darkness, and left without hope of rescue.

There are few, very few, who could possibly realize what such darkness means; or could imagine, the sensation of nameless dread that seizes the heart, and falls like an awful leaden weight upon the senses, and actually crushes one into the ground. What extraordinary visions and delusions pass before one's eyes under such conditions! At times strange lights, resembling coloured fire-flies, dance before the giddy senses, and then come whitish mists that grew out of the blackness, that took the shape of one's thoughts, that frightened one with distorted forms, absent faces and cherished fancies—that disappear to return—that return but to taunt, to tantalize, and again to vanish.

To add to the horror of the situation we soon began to realize that the temperature of the vault was considerably lower than that of our bodies. Possibly the extreme depression of our spirits affected our circulation; however, by degrees the cold seemed to penetrate and almost freeze the marrow of our bones. And this was not all—soon came the fear that there was yet another affliction in store for us, that would add to the misery of the darkness, to the coldness, to the captivity.

I could notice how terribly the cold seemed to affect our strange companion, as I heard him shudder and felt him shaking violently. I pulled my jacket off and threw it over him. Presently a slight moan was perceptible, a moan, something so like the one we had heard before, that I grasped the professor's arm. He too had heard it, and was sitting up to listen. Again we heard it slightly, but further off. We reached out to touch our unfortunate companion, but he had gone, and we could hear him creeping farther and farther away into a remote corner to suffer alone.

We had not the heart to light our matches, and drag him from his hiding-place. Instinctively we knew we could do no good, and so we had to lie and listen to the faint moans he unwillingly emitted from time to time. But his agony at last reached its crisis, and we groped our way across the vault, to find the spasm over, and the poor fellow lying exhausted on the stones.

Carefully and gently we raised him, and helped him back to the shelter of that unknown coffer, that somehow seemed to be our home in that dismal place. We had not alluded at any time to his suffering or its cause, and consequently we were rather surprised, when, of his own free will he commenced in a low voice to relate to us the following story.

VI

Placing himself against the unopened sarcophagus, in a weak voice he began: "I feel it is my duty at the present moment, to tell you the cause of my suffering, so that later on, you may more easily understand, that you can do nothing to either help or relieve. There is yet another motive that prompts me to speak—one which you may call a weakness, but a weakness that lurks in the breast of all mankind, namely, the desire to unburden the heart of every secret that has oppressed it, when the end draws near, when the tide of life is on the ebb, when the shoals, and the sands, and the weeds can no longer be sheltered by the ripples, or hidden by the froth.

"In a few hours I feel certain that my lips will be silent for ever. I am impelled to make this confession by a reason that my story itself will explain, but should it so happen by any extraordinary circumstance that you should yet escape, I ask you as a last act of kindness, to leave my body for ever in this place.

"In order that I may explain to you the strange events —that are as links in the chain of Destiny—that have irresistibly drawn me even into this very tomb, it is necessary that I recount certain circumstances that surrounded both my parents and my own early life.

"My father, Colonel Chanley, at about the time of my birth, commanded a very important garrison in the North of India, close to the frontier of Afghanistan. He had been for a long time in the Indian service, and was well known and feared by the natives in every quarter of the

country. He was a just man, but extremely stern, and
severe in his execution of justice. He was rather advanced
in life at the time of his marriage, and had been deemed
by his friends a confirmed bachelor. It caused considerable
comment when he suddenly announced his matrimonial
intention, and chose for his bride, the only daughter of
his old comrade Major Upham. My mother, though
young at the time of her marriage, was a woman who had
gained considerable experience in garrison life in India, and
consequently was well adapted to assume the numerous
social functions, that would later on devolve upon her as
wife of a commanding officer. Like my father, all her
ancestors for generations had been in military service, and
like him also, for the most part in connection with Indian
affairs. This may in some way have been responsible for
her haughty and imperious bearing towards the natives,
but on every possible occasion she took no pains to conceal her personal prejudices. People warned her again and
again, of the danger she was running by incurring the
hatred of such a race, but, neither warning, nor threat, had
the effect of causing a change in her feelings, or could
induce her to adopt a more diplomatic attitude. After her
marriage, she set herself deliberately to work to banish
from the surrounding country, all wonder-workers, miracle-
mongers, and such like, and so determined and antagonistic
was she in her zeal that she did not confine her task to the
more common fakirs, jugglers, and magicians, but went so
far as to carry her persecutions against the inoffensive
Yogis, and mystics, that are found in so many parts of
India.

"There was one, however, who, in spite of all her efforts,
she failed to either affect or dislodge. He was a man of
extreme age, a Yogi or Mystic of the highest order, who
dwelt far up in the mountains overlooking my father's
garrison. This man was believed by the natives to have
the extraordinary power of predicting disaster, plague or
death, weeks and even months in advance. His appearance
in any place or village was at all times responsible for
the entire cessation of labour or occupation of any kind.
When seen approaching, the entire population would turn
out to meet him, and in ominous silence would follow and
watch him walk, as it seemed, in a trance, until he reached
the centre of the village. Once there, he would pronounce
his prediction in a deep, sonorous voice, and as mysteriously disappear to the mountain whence he came.

"On account of the reverence with which he was regarded by the natives, this man of course should not have been interfered with, but yet at every opportunity my mother did not scruple to talk about the ignorant superstition of the natives, and cited the Yogi's claims to prophesy, as an example of the evil influence of such upon the credulous. And so things went on until within a short time previous to my birth. About the same time there was some trouble expected with the Afridis on the Afghan frontier, and a second regiment of soldiers were sent up to reinforce my father's command. It was a custom well observed in the garrison life in India, that on the arrival of a new regiment, an entertainment and ball were usually given to welcome the strangers to their new quarters, and on this occasion, it being the first entertainment of the kind that my mother had had the opportunity of giving since her marriage, she determined to do everything in her power to make it a memorable one in the eyes of her guests. Nothing was left undone to emphasize the event. It was arranged that the ball was to be held in the barracks, and the large building and the grounds around were gaily decorated with bunting and flags, until the entire place wore a festive appearance that must have been extremely gratifying to the new-comers.

"Everything went well, until about the middle of the ball, when a strange, wild figure emerged out of the night, and striding through the ball-room in the middle of the dancers, forced his way up to a dais on which my mother happened to be sitting, and in a deep sonorous voice proclaimed, as the last prediction he was ever destined to utter, that before the night would close, the garrison would be attacked and almost totally destroyed.

"During the excitement that ensued, the old man might have escaped, had not my mother pursued him into the very grounds and ordered the guard to place him under arrest.

"Returning to the ball-room, she restored festivities by ridiculing the prediction. The music struck up, and the dancing was resumed.

"Two hours later a small fire was discovered in one of the rooms, but was easily extinguished. A little later, however, the roof was found in flames, and as dancers, musicians, and spectators fled in alarm, the loud blast of a bugle was heard, and before the officers and men had time to even grasp their swords, many were speared, and struck down by a fierce band of Afridis, who, under cover of the darkness of the night, had crept in upon the unsuspecting revellers. For the first few moments, everything was wild confusion, but the soldiers speedily rallied, and after a stubborn fight, lasting for upwards of two hours, they drove the invaders back to the mountains and restored quiet, but not before a considerable number of the troops were killed and wounded.

"When morning broke, my mother urged an examination of the old man, who, all this time, had been confined in a cell. During his trial, the Yogi did not open his lips—not even when they had searched his habitation in the mountains, and returned with a paper covered with mystical signal, and having inscribed in its centre the exact moment of the attack. He was finally condemned on circumstantial evidence, as being in league with the insurgents, and marched out into the barrack grounds to be shot. I am ashamed to say my mother stood by my father's side to witness the Yogi's execution.

"Just before the command to fire was given, stepping forward to the old man, she asked him to confess freely, and fully the part he had played in the tragedy of the night. Drawing himself up to his full height, he said proudly, 'Madam, I have nothing to confess. Death to Yogis is nothing. We die to live. The crime that you are about to commit will bring its own punishment. As I do not desire to escape my fate, so shall you not be able to escape yours—or shall the child that you will soon bring into the world, escape his—remember! I have spoken. Kill me.'

"As she disdainfully stepped back, the word of command was given, the muskets blazed forth, and the old man fell riddled with bullets. At the same moment, high above the roar of the guns, there rang out an agonizing scream of fright and terror, and my mother fell back fainting into my father's arms. When the smoke had cleared away, it was apparent to everyone that something terrible had occurred to frighten her. Something seemed to have leaped from the grass and struck her, but what it was, no one seemed to know. 'Something has startled me,' was all the explanation she herself would give, and so they carried her back into the portion of the barracks that had escaped the fire, and she remained there for some months until, owing to her fright, I was prematurely born.

"Such was the story of my birth that I heard when I

mortal could last, and so each moment brought both fear and gladness in its train.

"I have often wondered since, why God created love, when the price we pay for it is at times even greater than the salvation of the soul. It is a little thing to lose one's rest hereafter, for the spirit can have no heartache. But to know what love is, and to lose what one has loved, to be compelled to live on and on through moments that are worse than eternities, to have a living body to care for, to clothe, to feed, while within there is a dead heart, is to my mind, a greater penalty by far, than the much paraded agony of the damned.

"But there are so few who have truly ever loved, so that words like these convey meaning to few, very few indeed. People as a rule but want, and desire, and lust to possess— they do not love! They misuse the word, and in their shallowness go to their school books for a meaning of its sacred sense. But to love truly, to love with heart and soul, with brain and body, is to be God-like, in the only human approach to Divinity—to the pure and faithful it is to create not one thing, but all things—a new Heaven, and a new earth. And in the fulfilment of dreams that be, to see the perfection of dreams to come.

"And it was thus with us. But we were children of earth, governed by the laws of cause and effect—doomed by the folly of others.

"One fatal morning the news came that my father had been killed, by accident. Such things custom calls accident or chance when they are evil, and puts down to the will of God when they are good.

"When my father's body had finally been laid to rest, in that peaceful churchyard in Devon, I found that the administration of his estate, and capital, lay solely in my mother's hands, during her life-time, with the exception of a tea-plantation in India, which he had lately purchased, and had bequeathed to me on my coming of age. My mother lost no time in exercising the legal powers, she was so unexpectly endowed with to prevent what she pleased to call a *mesalliance*. In vain I pleaded with her. In vain I protested. Come what would my mind was fully made up to marry Lucy, and I would go to the ends of the earth to accomplish my purpose. In her attempts to frustrate me she would not heed my entreaties; and I soon found I would have to resort to stronger means if I were to keep my resolution.

"In a few months I would attain my majority, and convinced that my mother determined to have me in her power by selling the property in India before I controlled it, there was nothing left for me but to go to India and endeavour to prevent all action in the matter.

"Not until the morning fixed for my departure for the first time did I tell her of my resolution. Everything was in readiness, the dog-cart had driven round to the door, when I entered her room to say good-bye.

"I had prepared myself for a scene, but certainly not for the tempestuous one that followed. When I told her, she at first simply attempted to dissuade me from going; then in turn she tried entreaties, then threats, and finally as I tore myself from the room, I heard her throw herself on the sofa and sob, 'Anywhere, anywhere, my boy, but to India!' There was something in those words that made me hesitate. I stopped and turned back to her; thinking to find her softened, I asked for the last time if she would consent to my marriage. But with the mere mention of the subject she lapsed again into the same hard woman of a moment before; further argument was useless, so saying 'Good-bye,' I turned from the room and without faltering was driven to the station.

"I had said farewell to Lucy the night before. She also had done all in her power to prevent me from going, and it was with a strange feeling of presentiment, and gloom, that I looked from the train in the direction of the vicarage, and saw, or fancied I saw, a white face among the roses at her window, and a little white hand that waved me a last farewell.

"I tried to console myself for leaving her by saying over and over again, that it was for her sake I had to go. 'I shall want money and position for her,' I thought; 'she must have everything the world can give her'—and yet my mother's words, 'Anywhere, anywhere, my boy, but India!' still echoed in my ears and filled me with gloomy presentiments and thoughts, that I tried in vain to banish.

"During the voyage I resolved that so soon as my business matters were settled, I would pay a flying visit to the place of my birth. I vividly remembered all my father had told me, and I tried to picture in imagination the rugged mountains, and that strange, tragic scene, that occurred before my birth. The desire to go there became irresistible.

"Reaching India, I proceeded to adjust the affairs in connection with the plantation which would be lawfully mine so soon. It was fortunate that such was the case, as it would expedite matters, and enable me to sell the plantation and return to Lucy immediately. But, ah, how little do we know what slaves we are in the hands of that same Destiny, that sent a Napoleon to the throne, and a Judas to destruction!

"Week after week passed, delay after delay came. A drunken soldier struck a sepoy—a riot ensued, and all Government affairs were at a standstill. On another occasion, by the miswording of a telegram, all transactions were for the time being stopped. All little things—yes, little things!—But alas, so potent! So fatal!

"And so it happened I came of age in India—came of age, an heir to property certainly, but what if I tell you that there was another heritage as well—a heritage for which I had not counted.

"On that morning, when my soul should have been jubilant, I woke as usual, woke to find the heat unbearable, even at that early hour, and as I threw aside the bed covering to relieve my oppression, I noticed a curious throbbing pain, in my left side, which I could not account for.

"Fatigued through pain, I fell asleep again, and dreamt, it seemed to me, the same dream over and over again. I thought my father came into the room; and stooping down, had whispered into my ear: *'The seed that is sowed must be reaped—it matters little by whom. Be patient, there is no law but that of God. Nature and destiny are servants thereto.'*

"I woke with the words ringing in my ears, woke, with that horrible gnawing pain, worse than before, and with a terrible fear and dread, of something, that I could not explain, and still less understand. Although my brain was much distraught during the day, I wrote a long letter to Lucy with the semblance of cheerfulness. She had astonished me in her last letter, by informing me, as a piece of news she thought would please me, that my mother had completely changed her attitude towards her, for which she expressed great joy; and that she had been at my mother's house several times, and was going again during the very evening on which she wrote, to talk about the future and me.

"My first thoughts were to prevent such visits. Her simple words filled me with misgivings. But the next moment I could not but feel ashamed of my filial disloyalty, so, I merely answered, that I was indeed surprised, at such a change on the part of my mother, and hoped that nothing would arise to cause her any regret. More I could not lend myself to write on that score, for my whole nature was in rebellion.

"Again and again I read my darling's letter, and as I paused and pondered over her sweet words, and sweeter thoughts, I was so happy that I forgot my dream, my forebodings of evil, and even the terrible gnawing pain in my side, which during some hours of the day caused me the greatest agony. I consoled myself with the thought that being now of age, I could dispose of the plantation in a short space of time, and return and hear those words of loving tenderness from Lucy's lips. Yes, I dreamed to claim her very soon as my wife.

"However, certain legal technicalities had to be gone through, and nearly six months expired before I could finally dispose of the property, and prepare to return.

"During all this time I suffered considerable pain, yet I sought no medical advice. I persuaded myself that it was probably the result of some strain, and that it would be better to wait, and get proper attention, when I returned to London. There was, however, something else that caused me greater anxiety. For a few months back, I had noticed a considerable change in the tone of Lucy's letters. They became more and more unlike the spontaneous expressions of love, and devotion, that I had at first received. Occasionally there would be one more in the former key, yet I could not but see that some change had taken place, and my heart grew sick with anxiety as to the cause. Presently word came from the rector that Lucy had been very ill, but, he thought, was getting better, and that there was no need for anxiety, or for my returning before my business was fully settled.

"I longed to take the next steamer, but, as everything was on the eve of conclusion, I was forced to wait, and tried to console myself by counting the hours and days, when I should be able to return to comfort Lucy.

"As a certain transaction, in concluding my business, had called me to within a short distance of the place of my birth; and finding myself after it was attended to free, and compelled to wait a week, before the steamer sailed, I determined to make the trip, as it would probably be the only opportunity I should ever have to do so.

"Alas! how little do we know what a single step in this

or that direction, may bring forth. And yet it is useless to repine. What is to be, will be. I had to go.

"I reached the place, made myself known, and was received with the greatest hospitality by the colonel and the officers at the barracks. As I intended to remain there but a day, on the following morning, accompanied by some of my new friends, I set out to see the various points of interest, such as forts, etc., constructed by my father during his command of the garrison.

"Again I heard the extraordinary story of the old Yogi, who was executed on the morning after the attack on the barracks. For, although years had passed, yet the story went the round of every regiment that was stationed there. Many and strange were the theories advanced as we rode along, as to what had so frightened my mother, or what my father and she had seen, as the old Yogi fell lifeless to the ground.

"Pulling up his horse as we passed under the ragged edges of a mountain, the colonel pointed upwards to a large cave just above an extraordinary plateau of solid rock, which, he said, had been the habitation of the old Yogi during my father's command. Jestingly I proposed that we should go there; the colonel took my proposal seriously, but personally declined to make the ascent with the excuse that his 'bones were too old for the climb.' The other two officers, however, jumped at the idea, so leaving our horses in the care of the colonel, we began to climb the steep escarpment.

"It was still early morning, and the dew of the night made the rocks and mosses so slippery and dangerous, we were forced to proceed with the utmost caution. At last we reached the wide rocky plateau facing the mouth of the cave, and for a moment stood enraptured with the magnificence of the view. All nature seemed to have combined to produce a wealth of scenery that could not be surpassed.

"Forest, and plain and mountain deployed around us, and like some grand panorama appeared to change, and grow, and then dissolve with every movement of the eyes. Above our heads, the rugged mountain peak rose into the very heart of heaven, while on every side Time had carved the rocks in strange, fantastic shapes, that would baffle the wildest imagination to describe.

"Stretched out below us we could see the barracks, and the soldiers moving about like busy little ants in the morning sunshine, while on our right lay a whitewashed fort flying the English flag, and with the black nozzles of its cannon like jealous eyes looking across the frontier.

" 'It would make a mystic of any man to live here,' said one of the officers, as he turned towards the cave. 'And see here, here is food to eat and water to drink.' And he pointed to where a spring burst forth through the very face of a large rock, surrounded by a perfect garden of edible herbs.

"Inside the cave we found everything as if its inhabitant had left it but an hour before. There was a rude couch in its furthermost corner, on which the skin of a large tiger was spread, and by its side was a rough set of shelves which contained a variety of books on profound subjects, that completely amazed us. At the extremity, far within, was a large cavity which apparently had been used for a temple. In the centre stood an altar and a stone figure of Siva—the Destroyer—which from its appearance must have been carved centuries agone. Before the god there still remained the withered stalks of herbs and flowers—probably the old Yogi's last propitiatory offering before that fatal night.

"On a table, rude as the other furniture, placed at the head of the couch, was a copy of the Vedas, an English Bible, and a slab, on which it was evidently the custom of the aged recluse to write down his thoughts. Tremblingly I took up the slab. I seemed to feel that my soul would read its death warrant, yet, I could not help but look.

"The first line was in Hindustani, which I could not decipher. Then came the words in English: 'No man shall escape his fate—did not even a God die that the scriptures might be fullfilled?'

" 'No man shall escape his fate!' Strange, I thought, that everywhere I turn is some warning of this kind accosting me. 'What can it mean?' I cried aloud, forgetful of my companions. In answer came a sigh, so weird, so strange, so audible, that even the soldiers stepped backwards in their fear.

" 'Come away!' exclaimed one. 'This place gives me the shivers, and besides, we can't keep the colonel waiting any longer.' And drawing me along by the arm, they prepared to leave. We had descended but a few steps when I recollected that I had forgotten my whip by the side of the couch, and returned for it, calling to the others not to wait, I would follow.

"Returning from the strong glare of sunshine into the

gloom of the cave, for a moment I could not see. When I did, my heart nearly failed me. I became conscious of the apparition of an old man looking at me from the couch, and as my eyes met his, he pointed with a long, lean finger to those words on the slab, which were still running like quicksilver through my brain.

"A sensation of fear possessed me. I blindly bolted out of the cave, my feet slipped on the rocks and mosses; in vain I clutched at the shrubs, and brambles, in my path. I tried to stop, but something seemed to pursue me. I could see the colonel far away in the path below. I could hear the voices of my companions shouting to me to take care. But my feet were slipping, the stones, mosses, and rocks were sliding from under me. I caught at branches, but they broke; my head was giddy, my senses sick with fear. I heard a huge rock I had dislodged, go crashing downwards into the abyss below, and with a wild scream for help, my body reeled over, and I remember no more.

"When consciousness returned, I found myself lying in the colonel's rooms in the barracks. They told me I had been there for three days. At first it was feared that the skull had been fractured, but when a thorough examination had been made by the surgeons, they found that together with a deep cut across the skull, the severest injury I had received was a complicated break of the right leg, sufficient to keep me on my back for eight weeks at least. 'But Lucy,' I thought, 'what of her? What will she think of this delay after all my promises to return?' and as I lay there day after day in agony, my thoughts were always of her, and of how she would bear the disappointment.

"After a long time, I was able to get my letters reforwarded to the garrison. The first one I opened was from the old rector, telling me the cruel news, that again, my darling was ill—so ill that she was unable to write.

"With a great effort, ill as I was, I rose and determined that I would start for England—even if it killed me. I remember that morning well. I had half dressed, when the pain in my side, which I had not felt for some days, returned with double fury. The surgeon came in at this moment, and when I was again placed in bed, he commenced an examination, and, I could see by the puzzled look on his face, that the agony I suffered, was beyond his comprehension. So things went on until the day came when the pain was beyond all endurance, and finally in the evening the flesh opened, and a peculiar growth began to make its appearance. The Army Surgeon from that moment refused to take charge of the case, so my good friend the colonel decided that there was nothing to be done, but to have me immediately removed to the nearest Military Hospital. An ambulance was finally constructed, and a band of natives engaged to transport me over the rough country to the nearest town. After a painful experience, I reached the hospital.

"The surgeons then held consultation after consultation. They admitted they had never seen anything like it before, but they persisted in calling it a tumour, so as a tumourous growth, with a Latin name, it was finally diagnosed. In spite of all their medical skill, the *thing* grew—I had never called it a tumour; to me it was a *thing*, undefined, horrible, and nameless. By the time the bones of my broken leg were sufficiently knit to travel, *it* had grown out of my side to the length of several inches. To complicate matters, it had grown from the inside, as it were, and had forced back the flesh, like the lips of a wound that it separated and kept apart. From its position between the ribs and the pelvis, the doctors argued that its proximity to the heart and other vital organs placed all chance of an operation out of the question. Yet hope kept alive within my heart, and looking forward to the superior skill of medical specialists in London, at last with a sigh of relief, I sailed for home.

"But I had not realized the full extent of the calamity that had overtaken me. I had but thought that *it* was some sort of growth of an unusual kind, and I felt certain, in spite of the decision of the hospital surgeons, that I would find some means in London or Paris, of having it removed. But the bliss of ignorance did not last long.

"One evening in the middle of the ocean, I was turning over some of my father's papers, and finding an old diary of his, written during his command on the Afghan frontier; I took it up on deck and commenced to read. Hour after hour passed as I perused the hopes, deeds, and dreams of the man who was responsible for my being. It was almost dark when I came to the passage, 'Oh how I should like to have a child—a son who would perpetuate my name.'

"A little later I read, 'I have married—more in order to have a child than to have a wife.'

"And so I read on and on, till I came to the terrible night of the ball, and the execution of the Yogi. 'At last,' I thought, 'I will know what caused my mother the terrible fright that resulted in my premature birth.' And bending over the faded leaves before me, I came to this passage:

" 'Oh, my God! What have I done? As the muskets rang out and the Yogi's body sank to the ground, there leaped from the grass at my wife's feet, a hideous black snake, that springing upward with an angry hiss, struck her on the side, and falling back into the grass, disappeared. Instantly I thought of the last words of the old Yogi. What if they had already come true, before the very breath had left his body! Again I thought of the child—the child I had wished for, had prayed for—the child that was living within her. Oh, my God! what have I done! what have I done! If a crime has been committed—if nature must be avenged, let the punishment, I pray Thee, fall upon me and not upon the child that is unconscious of the sin of the father.'

"I could read no more. The diary slipped from my hands and fell at my feet, but I did not move. My eyes instinctively, as in trouble, looked upward to the sky— but there was no God there for me. The night fell and the stars came out, but no God, no hope for me. The stars wandered on in their appointed courses—they could not change in their unwritten pathway through the sky—and as I watched them in my despair, again the words of the old Yogi passed before my eyes: 'No man shall escape his fate—did not a God die, that the scriptures might be fulfilled?'

"How long I sat there I do not know. *The seed that had been sown would have to be gathered.* There could be no doubt now as to what was my fate, and the discovery for the time being utterly unmanned me. A sharp pain in my side recalled me to myself. That pain had a new meaning to it now, which it would require all my fortitude to face. I pressed my teeth into my lips to keep back the cry of agony that rose from my very soul. And so I sat there waiting and fearing, as one would fear the stealthy approach of an invincible enemy.

"Suddenly my whole body grew cold and rigid with terror. There had been a slight movement in *the thing*— a little tremble—a quiver, but of life. The cold perspiration stood in great beads on my forehead. I could feel my heart cease beating, the blood chilled in my veins, and as I pressed my hands to my face, I shrank from their ice-cold touch.

"But there was a resolution forming in my mind—a thought, that a moment before I should have rejected with disgust. I had never seen *the thing*. I had never dared to look at *it*. Now, I would go to my cabin, and see my enemy, face to face. I reached for my crutches—softly I limped across the deck. It was midnight. Not a sound to disturb the silence of the ocean but the panting of the engines, as they forged their way across the deep.

"The lamp was burning in my state room—a little oil lamp, that gave a sickly yellow light. I took it down, and placing it where I could see well, I opened the loose silk shirt I wore, and looking into the mirror, one glance was sufficient to show me that my most deaded fears had been realized.

"Yes, *it* had begun to have life, independent of my life. Oh God! how my senses reeled when I saw the shape *it* had taken, the colour it had assumed. I staggered out of my cabin. I reached the deck, delirious with frenzy, sick with horror. Can you wonder at me, when those who have had some petty grief have put an end to their misery, that I should also at such a moment determine to end my accursed existences. It would be so easy, I thought—and accounted an 'accident of course.' Strange even at a moment like that, that one should consider the opinion of the world. And yet I did not think so much of ending my own life. My sole thought was to kill that *thing* and I looked upon my body more as one would look upon a stone—a stone to weight *it* down and drown *it*, and hold *it* to the depths of the ocean for ever and ever.

"I could so easily slip unnoticed over the side of the vessel, and be swallowed up for ever with my secret stigma. Yet, I dreaded people finding my body, and curious eyes wondering and speculating as to the growth and cause of the *thing*, and I feared too, ay, even more than all—that if I shot or destroyed myself with poison, that *it* might still live—and crawl about like a vampire on the dead body that had generated *it*—but, what matter, what matter, I should be insensible.

"I reached the stern of the boat. Everything was quiet. Leaning over I looked down into the fathomless black water, but Lucy's face reproachfully rose before me, and stopped me—her eyes gazed into mine—her arms held me back—and frightened of my cowardly intent, I crouched down on the deck under the shadow of a life-boat, and lay there till dawn.

"As I had sent no word of my departure from India, when I reached England, instead of going directly home, I went on to London and consulted several medical experts, before venturing to go down to Devon. But there was no hope: surgeon after surgeon examined and failed to diagnose. To kill *the thing* would be to kill me—to let *it* live, would be the same thing in the end. They listened to my story, but the wise men of science would not have believed it if they had not seen and examined *the thing* with their own eyes. Why *it* had not made itself manifest until I was of age, they could not understand, because legal and natural maturity are at variance. They agreed by common consent, in lieu of something better, it was attributable to the intense heat of India. But the chain of coincidence had been so strong, I knew instinctively that Fate ordained I should go to India. The doctors thought it would be some time before *the thing* would be fully developed, and its fangs might then be extracted, and I would live—but live with *the thing* for ever a companion.

"It was thus with hope completely dead that I returned home. I determined to see Lucy, to bid her good-bye for ever. Renounce my happiness, then go away to some quiet place, and strive to get the courage to end my life, or wait till it was ended for me, but never, never sow the damnable seed for some child to reap the infamy thereof. I racked my brains as to what plausible story I could tell her, as an excuse for leaving her again. I dared not tell her the abhorrent truth—I could not bring myself to do it. I could not seem to invent any subterfuge, so I counted each moment that brought me nearer to her; most harassed and uncertain as to the course I should pursue. The train entered the station, and with a heavy heart, I started out upon my mission—a victim branded by an obdurate heredity—a child of cruel Destiny.

"It was summer again. The hedges of the quaint old Devonshire road were full of blossom, and before I reached the vicarage, the perfume of the roses swept past and greeted me, charged with old memories. It was evening as I entered the garden—almost dusk. There was no face peering between the roses now, and so uncared for, and neglected they looked, that my heart almost failed me, for I wondered how long her hands had ceased to tend them.

"The porch was silent and deserted, the door was open,

and as no one answered my ring, I entered the hall and stood for a moment irresolute at to what I should do.

"The drawing room was empty, so was the study. On the desk, under an old-fashioned reading lamp lay the rector's notes for the following Sunday's sermon. In a nook of the desk, where the fond father's eyes could always see it, stood a little portrait of Lucy in the very dress in which I had seen her on that first morning in the garden. I snatched it up and kissed it, kissed it, till the tears rained down my cheeks, and I could scarcely see the picture. And yet, in a few moments I would have to part from her for ever—perhaps break her heart by what I had to tell her!

"At last I heard voices, hushed, subdued voices, up-stairs. I hardly know why I ascended. I went up the softly carpeted stairs, and stood for a moment on the landing outside a little room, within which stood a jar full of roses—the roses that I loved the most. I heard the old rector's voice in prayer, subdued words that I could scarce-ly catch, and which were every now and then, broken by a sob. I could now and again hear one word—yes, I could hear my name mentioned. Between deep, broken sobs, I heard the old man ask God to forgive me for the cruel deception I had practised. I could hear no more. Softly I entered. Lucy only saw me. In another second she was clasped in my arms, and in a strange faint voice I heard her say, 'Oh, I knew you would come. I did not believe them. They told me you would never return—that you had deserted me. But I knew that you would come back. Thank God! thank God!'

"She sank back, exhausted. The effort of speech had been too much. One look into her eyes told me that I had come too late. The long, lean arms of death had claimed her—she was his, not mine. Bending close to her I whis-pered, 'My darling, I never deserted you. What they told you was false, absolutely false. I love you now, as I have loved you always. You are mine in spite of Fate—in spite of death, Lucy, mine till the end of life, and time, and eternity.'

"A sigh of infinite love, of happiness, and a murmured 'Thank God,' and as the shadows of the evening closed in, the end came. And it was well.

"The old rector and I were left alone. From him in a few heart-broken words, I learned the cause of Lucy's anguish, and all she had suffered during my absence.

"My misguided mother had won her confidence—her love even, and after winning both, prompted by her pride, had crushed Lucy's heart, by her stories of my unfaithfulness, that rankled in the girl's devoted heart to finally kill her. Such was the end.

"And yet, my mother had committed this great sin, she contritely avowed to me that night of mourning, out of the great love she bore me—out of her accursed pride—her love of place and power—out of her jealous, selfish love for me! As she knelt before me suing for my forgiveness, I scarcely knew what I did, or what I said. I only remember in my frantic revolt, as I tore open my clothing and exposed the *writhing creature*, stirred by my mad passion, she shrank away with fear and loathing from the son of her pride, and without pity, I left her lying there the victim of her own iniquity, and went out into the night alone.

"Oh God! how I suffered for the days and months that followed. The coldness of the climate caused the *thing* to torture me with agony. I tried to die, ay, many times, but could not—dared not. Lucy's face would always come before me, her lips between mine and the death that I fain would drink. So, I have lived on, praying for the end; at last, I have not long to wait—it is close at hand. The physicians in London told me that they surmised that, in due course of development, the fangs or poison glands of the *thing* would grow, and all that could be done was to wait until that time, and have them then extracted. In the event of that being done, I might live, they thought, even to the term of mature manhood, of middle age. But such is not to be. A few days ago I noticed that the fangs were nearly ready to do their work—the coldness of this place will hasten matters, that is all. The seed that was sown is nearly gathered. I am not worse than others, for all inherit—some evil desires, some passions, some diseases, that are worse than death. One thing—I have had the moral courage to resist sowing blighted seeds of heredity. My strength was love for Lucy.

"I came here to live amongst these tombs that I might find the courage to face death. I have gained more, for I have learned a philosophy from my suffering, and from these dead Egyptians that is beyond death, and knows redemption, and promises reincarnation for the soul that has been purified of all that is carnal.

"As for my knowledge of this place, during my rambles

among these tombs, I too discovered those strange characters, and one day I was fortunate enough to find the
secret of the entrance through which we passed.

"I kept the knowledge to myself, hoping that when
death came, he would find me in this place where my body
might turn to dust undisturbed, without prying eyes to
question with their pitiless curiosity.

"My story is ended. My life soon will be. I do not rebel
now. A natural law governs that which seems too often
most unnatural. If evil is done, it must be atoned for, let
the thoughtless ones of the world remember. If we could
know, then we could change, for as the present is the
effect of a heretofore cause, so are our present actions
the cause of a hereafter effect. But we fain would torture
and punish those who would try to lift the veil, forgetting
that if we mortals are led ever so dimly, that the smallest
light might warn us in advance of dangers that there is
no escape from when we are once overwhelmed in their
midst."

VII

The effect of this terrible story, told in the gruesome
surroundings and blackness of the tomb, had, as might be
imagined, the most powerful influence on our minds.

As we lay there, we seemed to see that hideous *thing*
growing more and more angry every moment, until at last *it*
would bury its deadly fangs in the body on which *it* had
lived. And yet, strange as it may seem, the tale we had
listened to of sorrow and of suffering, and of rebellion, and
of noble resistance, had the effect of nullifying our own
agony of mind, and our dread for ourselves. Tender
sympathy possessed us. It is ever so in life—there is often
an anti-death to real death; the story of another's loss or
suffering has sometimes the effect of making us forget our
own. The influence of some strong soul going bravely
through personal suffering without complaint, enables others more weak ofttimes, to gather the fortitude to endure
even greater trials.

In silence we lay there after he had finished. In such
a moment, a clasp of the hand expresses more than all the
language of the lips . . . I question if either the professor
or myself had ever considered this problem of Destiny
in such a forcible way. Lamentable as it is, the education
of this practical age we live in does not encourage such

a vein of thought. We forge ahead in what we call progress, enlightenment, and elevation—why, then, should we be occupied with Destiny?

The laws of heredity are studied and practised in breeding cattle—yet spurned and neglected in human creatures. We mock at them, and cant about the inscrutable laws of God—mark you, not because we are a religious race, but that we may shirk our responsibilities and still be thought to be respectable. And so we live—or rather die—and it is only at our death that we deign to know; therefore, it is only at our death that we are truly alive.

Yet, we boast of our free will, and in our shameless ignorance we reproduce our species, we, who in our full knowledge, through carnal instinct damn, and worse than kill, our degenerate, afflicted progeny.

True, a man can say he is free to turn to the left or right by the action of his will, but in doing so he must not forget that his action is due to the conscious effort, whereas the unconscious is for ever at the wheel of Destiny.

Thoughts such as these trooped in myriads through my mind, in the awful silence that followed the story, as we speechlessly prepared for our own death, from which there seemed no possible escape.

With our last match we lit a pile of linen strips endued with bitumen, and strong smelling unguents, that had once swathed the head of a king's mummy. As the blaze weirdly leaped upwards, we perceived that we had for some unaccountable reason changed our positions, and were facing the entrance of the tomb, and looking towards the desecrated body of the seventh mummy, which had been so placed as if to guard all ingress and exit. We casually noticed that the wrappings had been entirely torn off the mummy's left hand, as it lay outside the broken sarcophagus, almost touching the floor. It was a trifle that distracted our attention for a moment and nothing more. The blaze would soon be gone. Jealously we turned towards it, believing it was the last gleam of light we would ever see; and, so we lay there regretfully watching it grow smaller and smaller, until it was finally spent, and there was nothing left, but a ball of fiery embers that glowed amidst the universal darkness. We drew a little apart from one another. There was no farewell spoken. A clasp of the hand was sufficient. The supreme moment was upon us. We waited for death, each man by himself.

It is more than probable that the professor instinctively

following his research to the last, had prepared to meet his doom with his eyes looking towards that seventh mummy, that occupied such a commanding position, but whether that was so or not, when the light died out, the old man suddenly startled us with an exclamation of surprise. In a husky voice he whispered, "See there! See there!"

Straining our eyes in the apparent direction his voice indicated, we descried a tiny spot of phosphorescent light, about the size of a thumb nail. Before I could move, Chanley had by a superhuman effort dragged himself across the stones and clutched it. In a voice trembling with emotion, he called out to us to fan into a blaze the embers of our exhausted fire. Our matches were all gone— if that little red spark could not be coaxed back to life, it would be impossible to obtain a light. Tearing up the wick of the lantern and fanning, whilst carefully feeding, the shreds to the embers, presently I succeeded in reviving a little glow, then a flickering flame, and with the additional help of some wrappings torn from the nearest mummy, once more a strong blaze shot up and illuminated the place.

In Chanley's hand was a large ring, a band of gold covered with inscriptions that encircled a curious flat stone of a greenish colour. His hands were trembling with nervous excitement, as he tried to examine and decipher the hieroglyphics. In the darkness, the stone was phosphorescent, emitting a pale uncertain shimmer. Placed near the light, it became almost black, and showed white lines that formed a strange-looking hierarchic design upon its surface.

With nervous voice Chanley turned and said, "There may be one chance left. The lines on this extraordinary ring contain a well-drawn plan of the passages radiating to and from this secret tomb, and from it I gather that there may yet be one way of escape open. What I am about to try is merely a venture. This ring tells of notches cut in the left side wall of the well. I will descend and try to find a passage which, according to this ring, should lead from this tomb to the outer world. Good-bye, comrades, in event some fatality claims me."

Chanley found the notches indicated without much difficulty, but it was with heavy hearts that we watched him disappear into that deep hole that seemed to have no bottom. As the professor had visited the well in the

Pyramid of Cheops, and as this one seemed exactly similar, it was with little hope that we could anticipate good results. The well in the Pyramid of Cheops, the professor had often told me, led nowhere, and was simply a source of marvel as to why it had ever been constructed. According to the testimony of the few who had ever attempted to descend, it was of an extraordinary depth, and the bottom was covered by a species of lizard not found elsewhere.

With hearts alternating between hope and despair, we fanned the blaze and tried to keep it alive, for the gloom of the place was now more terrible than ever. We would occasionally creep on hands and knees to the edge of the well to listen, but always to withdraw disappointed.

Minute followed minute, and still we waited.

We had fed the little beacon fire for the last time, for we were both weak and could do no more. When suddenly a slight sound like a gasp broke upon our ears, and before we had time to question whether it was a trick of our overwrought imagination or reality, Chanley climbed over the edge of the well and dropped exhausted at our feet.

His clothing was torn to tatters, and as he shook the water from his hair in the flickering fire-light I marked the haggard look of his face, and an expression in his eyes that could only have but one meaning. The supreme moment was upon him. His hour had come. He could scarcely speak. It seemed as if the muscles of his throat were becoming set and hard. "Quick, quick!" he said. "Listen! There are notches down the side of the well—climb down to a ledge of stone that has three passages. Take the left one. Creep on hands and knees till you reach a deep cavern filled with water. Have no fear, dive straight through—it leads to the Nile—it will bring you to safety. Leave me—leave me here."

His head fell back—he tried to smile, but his lips refused to move. The old professor, with tears streaming down his face, tried to raise him, saying as he did so, "You must come, my boy, you must come with us."

His hands meanwhile frantically tore his shirt open. Destiny had indeed been cruel and inexorable to the end. *The thing* was lying there, motionless—*it* had done its work—its fangs were buried in his flesh. With a last effort he raised himself; and taking our hands, said softly, "Remember—the seed that was sown is gathered—farewell!"

THE MYSTERIOUS CARD

Cleveland Moffett

THE BLACK CAT *was a magazine established in 1895 and published until 1923, which featured only short stories and sold for five cents. It bought a very large percentage of its fiction from relatively new authors, wooing them with perpetual contests, and popularized a clever, sometimes tongue-in-cheek story that made it highly regarded at the turn of the century.*

During its term of publication THE BLACK CAT *ran such highly regarded names (claiming discovery of some of them) as Jack London, Octavus Roy Cohen, Rupert Hughes, Ellis Parker Butler, Harry Stephen Keeler and many others but probably the most popular story it ever ran was* The Mysterious Card *by Cleveland Moffett in its February, 1896 number. Cleveland Moffett was a regularly selling professional even then and appeared in its February, 1896, number. Cleveland Moffet was a many distinguished magazines in both the United States and England. Perhaps his best-known work to fantasy collectors was* The Conquest of America, *a future-war story published by George H. Doran Co. in 1916. The* Mysterious Card *was the title story of a small book published by Small, Maynard and Company, Boston, in 1912 together with the sequel* The Mysterious Card Unveiled *from the August, 1896, issue of* THE BLACK CAT. *While the sequel was a satisfactory work as sequels go, the artistic effectiveness of* The Mysterious Card *is greatly enhanced when published alone.*

RICHARD BURWELL, of New York, will never cease to regret that the French language was not made a part of his education.

This is why:

On the second evening after Burwell arrived in Paris,

feeling lonely without his wife and daughter, who were still visiting a friend in London, his mind naturally turned to the theater. So, after consulting the daily amusement calendar, he decided to visit the *Folies Bergère,* which he had heard of as one of the notable sights. During an intermission he went into the beautiful garden, where gay crowds were strolling among the flowers, and lights, and fountains. He had just seated himself at a little three-legged table, with a view to enjoying the novel scene, when his attention was attracted by a lovely woman, gowned strikingly, though in perfect taste, who passed near him, leaning on the arm of a gentleman. The only thing that he noticed about this gentleman was that he wore eyeglasses.

Now Burwell had never posed as a captivator of the fair sex, and could scarcely credit his eyes when the lady left the side of her escort and, turning back as if she had forgotten something, passed close by him, and deftly placed a card on his table. The card bore some French words written in purple ink, but, not knowing that language, he was unable to make out their meaning. The lady paid no further heed to him, but, rejoining the gentleman with the eyeglasses, swept out of the place with the grace and dignity of a princess. Burwell remained staring at the card.

Needless to say, he thought no more of the performance or of the other attractions about him. Everything seemed flat and tawdry compared with the radiant vision that had appeared and disappeared so mysteriously. His one desire now was to discover the meaning of the words written on the card.

Calling a fiacre, he drove to the Hotel Continental, where he was staying. Proceeding directly to the office and taking the manager aside, Burwell asked if he would be kind enough to translate a few words of French into English. There were no more than twenty words in all.

"Why, certainly," said the manager, with French politeness, and cast his eyes over the card. As he read, his face grew rigid with astonishment, and, looking at his questioner sharply, he exclaimed: "Where did you get this, monsieur?"

Burwell started to explain, but was interrupted by: "That will do, that will do. You must leave the hotel."

"What do you mean?" asked the man from New York, in amazement.

"You must leave the hotel now—to-night—without fail," commanded the manager excitedly.

Now it was Burwell's turn to grow angry, and he declared heatedly that if he wasn't wanted in this hotel there were plenty of others in Paris where he would be welcome. And, with an assumption of dignity, but piqued at heart, he settled his bill, sent for his belongings, and drove up the Rue de la Paix to the Hotel Bellevue, where he spent the night.

The next morning he met the proprietor, who seemed to be a good fellow, and, being inclined now to view the incident of the previous evening from its ridiculous side, Burwell explained what had befallen him, and was pleased to find a sympathetic listener.

"Why, the man was a fool," declared the proprietor. "Let me see the card; I will tell you what it means." But as he read, his face and manner changed instantly.

"This is a serious matter," he said sternly. "Now I understand why my confrère refused to entertain you. I regret, monsieur, but I shall be obliged to do as he did."

"What do you mean?"

"Simply that you cannot remain here."

With that he turned on his heel, and the indignant guest could not prevail upon him to give any explanation.

"We'll see about this," said Burwell, thoroughly angered.

It was now nearly noon, and the New Yorker remembered an engagement to lunch with a friend from Boston, who, with his family, was stopping at the Hotel de l'Alma. With his luggage on the carriage, he ordered the *cocher* to drive directly there, determined to take counsel with his countryman before selecting new quarters. His friend was highly indignant when he heard the story—a fact that gave Burwell no little comfort, knowing, as he did, that the man was accustomed to foreign ways from long residence abroad.

"It is some silly mistake, my dear fellow; I wouldn't pay any attention to it. Just have your luggage taken down and stay here. It is a nice, homelike place, and it will be very jolly, all being together. But, first, let me prepare a little 'nerve settler' for you."

After the two had lingered a moment over their Manhattan cocktails, Burwell's friend excused himself to call the ladies. He had proceeded only two or three steps when he turned, and said: "Let's see that mysterious card that has raised all this row."

He had scarcely withdrawn it from Burwell's hand when he started back, and exclaimed:——

"Great God, man! Do you mean to say—this is simply—"

Then, with a sudden movement of his hand to his head, he left the room.

He was gone perhaps five minutes, and when he returned his face was white.

"I am awfully sorry," he said nervously; "but the ladies tell me they—that is, my wife—she has a frightful headache. You will have to excuse us from the lunch."

Instantly realizing that this was only a flimsy pretense, and deeply hurt by his friend's behavior, the mystified man arose at once and left without another word. He was now determined to solve this mystery at any cost. What could be the meaning of the words on that infernal piece of pasteboard?

Profiting by his humiliating experience, he took good care not to show the card to any one at the hotel where he now established himself,—a comfortable little place near the Grand Opera House.

All through the afternoon he thought of nothing but the card, and turned over in his mind various ways of learning its meaning without getting himself into further trouble. That evening he went again to the *Folies Bergère* in the hope of finding the mysterious woman, for he was now more than ever anxious to discover who she was. It even occurred to him that she might be one of those beautiful Nihilist conspirators, or, perhaps, a Russian spy, such as he had read of in novels. But he failed to find her, either then or on the three subsequent evenings which he passed in the same place. Meanwhile the card was burning in his pocket like a hot coal. He dreaded the thought of meeting any one that he knew, while this horrible cloud hung over him. He bought a French-English dictionary and tried to pick out the meaning word by word, but failed. It was all Greek to him. For the first time in his life, Burwell regretted that he had not studied French at college.

After various vain attempts to either solve or forget the torturing riddle, he saw no other course than to lay the problem before a detective agency. He accordingly put his case in the hands of an *agent de la sûreté* who was recommended as a competent and trustworthy man. They had a talk together in a private room, and, of course, Burwell showed the card. To his relief, his adviser at least showed no sign of taking offense. Only he did not and would not explain what the words meant.

"It is better," he said, "that monsieur should not know the nature of this document for the present. I will do myself the honor to call upon monsieur to-morrow at his hotel, and then monsieur shall know everything."

"Then it is really serious?" asked the unfortunate man.

"Very serious," was the answer.

The next twenty-four hours Burwell passed in a fever of anxiety. As his mind conjured up one fearful possibility after another he deeply regretted that he had not torn up the miserable card at the start. He even seized it,—prepared to strip it into fragments, and so end the whole affair. And then his Yankee stubbornness again asserted itself, and he determined to see the thing out, come what might.

"After all," he reasoned, "it is no crime for a man to pick up a card that a lady drops on his table."

Crime or no crime, however, it looked very much as if he had committed some grave offense when, the next day, his detective drove up in a carriage, accompanied by a uniformed official, and requested the astounded American to accompany them to the police headquarters.

"What for?" he asked.

"It is only a formality," said the detective; and when Burwell still protested the man in uniform remarked: "You'd better come quietly, monsieur; you will have to come, anyway."

An hour later, after severe cross-examination by another official, who demanded many facts about the New Yorker's age, place of birth, residence, occupation, etc., the bewildered man found himself in the Conciergerie prison. Why he was there or what was about to befall him Burwell had no means of knowing; but before the day was over he succeeded in having a message sent to the American Legation, where he demanded immediate protection as a citizen of the United States. It was not until evening, however, that the Secretary of Legation, a consequential person, called at the prison. There followed a stormy interview, in which the prisoner used some strong language, the French officers gesticulated violently and talked very fast, and the Secretary calmly listened to both sides, said little, and smoked a good cigar.

"I will lay your case before the American minister," he said as he rose to go, "and let you know the result to-morrow."

"But this is an outrage. Do you mean to say—" Before

he could finish, however, the Secretary, with a strangely suspicious glance, turned and left the room.

That night Burwell slept in a cell.

The next morning he received another visit from the noncommittal Secretary, who informed him that matters had been arranged, and that he would be set at liberty forthwith.

"I must tell you, though," he said, "that I have had great difficulty in accomplishing this, and your liberty is granted only on condition that you leave the country within twenty-four hours, and never under any conditions return."

Burwell stormed, raged, and pleaded; but it availed nothing. The Secretary was inexorable, and yet he positively refused to throw any light upon the causes of this monstrous injustice.

"Here is your card," he said, handing him a large envelope closed with the seal of Legation. "I advise you to burn it and never refer to the matter again."

That night the ill-fated man took the train for London, his heart consumed by hatred for the whole French nation, together with a burning desire for vengeance. He wired his wife to meet him at the station, and for a long time debated with himself whether he should at once tell her the sickening truth. In the end he decided that it was better to keep silent. No sooner, however, had she seen him than her woman's instinct told her that he was laboring under some mental strain. And he saw in a moment that to withhold from her his burning secret was impossible, especially when she began to talk of the trip they had planned through France. Of course no trivial reason would satisfy her for his refusal to make this trip, since they had been looking forward to it for years; and yet it was impossible now for him to set foot on French soil.

So he finally told her the whole story, she laughing and weeping in turn. To her, as to him, it seemed incredible that such overwhelming disasters could have grown out of so small a cause and, being a fluent French scholar, she demanded a sight of the fatal piece of pasteboard. In vain her husband tried to divert her by proposing a trip through Italy. She would consent to nothing until she had seen the mysterious card which Burwell was now convinced he ought long ago to have destroyed. After refusing for awhile to let her see it, he finally yielded. But, although he had learned to dread the consequences of showing that cursed card, he was little prepared for what followed. She read it, turned pale, gasped for breath, and nearly fell to the floor.

"I told you not to read it," he said; and then, growing tender at the sight of her distress, he took her hand in his and begged her to be calm. "At least tell me what the thing means," he said. "We can bear it together; you surely can trust me."

But she, as if stung by rage, pushed him from her and declared, in a tone such as he had never heard from her before, that never, never again would she live with him. "You are a monster!" she exclaimed. And those were the last words he heard from her lips.

Failing utterly in all efforts at reconciliation, the half-crazed man took the first steamer for New York, having suffered in scarcely a fortnight more than in all his previous life. His whole pleasure trip had been ruined, he had failed to consummate important business arrangements, and now he saw his home broken up and his happiness ruined. During the voyage he scarcely left his stateroom, but lay there prostrated with agony. In this black despondency the one thing that sustained him was the thought of meeting his partner, Jack Evelyth, the friend of his boyhood, the sharer of his success, the bravest, most loyal fellow in the world. In the face of even the most damning circumstances, he felt that Evelyth's rugged common sense would evolve some way of escape from this hideous nightmare. Upon landing at New York he hardly waited for the gang-plank to be lowered before he rushed on shore and grasped the hand of his partner, who was waiting on the wharf.

"Jack," was his first word, "I am in dreadful trouble, and you are the only man in the world who can help me."

An hour later Burwell sat at his friend's dinner table, talking over the situation.

Evelyth was all kindness, and several times as he listened to Burwell's story his eyes filled with tears.

"It does not seem possible, Richard," he said, "that such things can be; but I will stand by you; we will fight it out together. But we cannot strike in the dark. Let me see this card."

"There is the damned thing," Burwell said, throwing it on the table.

Evelyth opened the envelope, took out the card, and fixed his eyes on the sprawling purple characters.

"Can you read it?" Burwell asked excitedly.

"Perfectly," his partner said. The next moment he turned

pale, and his voice broke. Then he clasped the tortured man's hand in his with a strong grip. "Richard," he said slowly, "if my only child had been brought here dead it would not have caused me more sorrow than this does. You have brought me the worst news one man could bring another."

His agitation and genuine suffering affected Burwell like a death sentence.

"Speak, man," he cried; "do not spare me. I can bear anything rather than this awful uncertainty. Tell me what the card means."

Evelyth took a swallow of brandy and sat with head bent on his clasped hands.

"No, I can't do it; there are some things a man must not do."

Then he was silent again, his brows knitted. Finally he said solemnly:—

"No, I can't see any other way out of it. We have been true to each other all our lives; we have worked together and looked forward to never separating. I would rather fail and die than see this happen. But we have got to separate, old friend; we have got to separate."

They sat there talking until late into the night. But nothing that Burwell could do or say availed against his friend's decision. There was nothing for it but that Evelyth should buy his partner's share of the business or that Burwell buy out the other. The man was more than fair in the financial proposition he made; he was generous, as he always had been, but his determination was inflexible; the two must separate. And they did.

With his old partner's desertion, it seemed to Burwell that the world was leagued against him. It was only three weeks from the day on which he had received the mysterious card; yet in that time he had lost all that he valued in the world,—wife, friends, and business. What next to do with the fatal card was the sickening problem that now possessed him.

He dared not show it; yet he dared not destroy it. He loathed it; yet he could not let it go from his possession. Upon returning to his house he locked the accursed thing away in his safe as if it had been a package of dynamite or a bottle of deadly poison. Yet not a day passed that he did not open the drawer where the thing was kept and scan with loathing the mysterious purple scrawl.

In desperation he finally made up his mind to take up

the study of the language in which the hateful thing was written. And still he dreaded the approach of the day when he should decipher its awful meaning.

One afternoon, less than a week after his arrival in New York, as he was crossing Twenty-third Street on the way to his French teacher, he saw a carriage rolling up Broadway. In the carriage was a face that caught his attention like a flash. As he looked again he recognized the woman who had been the cause of his undoing. Instantly he sprang into another cab and ordered the driver to follow after. He found the house where she was living. He called there several times; but always received the same reply, that she was too much engaged to see any one. Next he was told that she was ill, and on the following day the servant said she was much worse. Three physicians had been summoned in consultation. He sought out one of these and told him it was a matter of life or death that he see this woman. The doctor was a kindly man and promised to assist him. Through his influence, it came about that on that very night Burwell stood by the bedside of this mysterious woman. She was beautiful still, though her face was worn with illness.

"Do you recognize me?" he asked tremblingly, as he leaned over the bed, clutching in one hand an envelope containing the mysterious card. "Do you remember seeing me at the *Folies Bergère* a month ago?"

"Yes," she murmured, after a moment's study of his face; and he noted with relief that she spoke English.

"Then, for God's sake, tell me, what does it all mean?" he gasped, quivering with excitement.

"I gave you the card because I wanted you to—to—"

Here a terrible spasm of coughing shook her whole body, and she fell back exhausted.

An agonizing despair tugged at Burwell's heart. Frantically snatching the card from its envelope, he held it close to the woman's face.

"Tell me! Tell me!"

With a supreme effort, the pale figure slowly raised itself on the pillow, its fingers clutching at the counterpane.

Then the sunken eyes fluttered—forced themselves open—and stared in stony amazement upon the fatal card, while the trembling lips moved noiselessly, as if in an attempt to speak. As Burwell, choking with eagerness, bent his head slowly to hers, a suggestion of a smile flickered across the woman's face. Again the mouth quivered, the man's head bent nearer and nearer to hers, his eyes riveted upon the lips. Then, as if to aid her in deciphering the mystery, he turned his eyes to the card.

With a cry of horror he sprang to his feet, his eyeballs starting from their sockets. Almost at the same moment the woman fell heavily upon the pillow.

Every vestige of the writing had faded! The card was blank!

The woman lay there dead.

AN UNNATURAL FEUD

Norman Douglas

*George Norman Douglas did not achieve very great
literary impact until he was over fifty, that coming with*
South Wind *published in 1917, perhaps his most widely
known work. His success was due primarily to his writing method, which despite the seeming contradiction
may be termed "romantic realism". His subject matter
could frequently be grim, more than brutal such as in*
An Unnatural Feud, *but his writing style had a rich, almost dreamlike quality to it that played a large part in
his acceptance by the literati.*

*He wrote at least three novels which may be adequate-
ly classed as fantasy and science fiction:* They Went
(1920); In the Beginning *(a dreamy fantasy of an un-
recorded early period of man that enjoyed more than
average popularity) and* Nerinda *(1929).*

An Unnatural Feud *was one of his earlier stories and
ranks easily as one of the finest things to come from his
pen. It was written on the Villa Daphne, Izola, Capri,
Italy, and was originally submitted under the title of*
Elfwater. *It was accepted by the famous Munsey fiction
editor Robert H. Davis and published in the December,
1908, issue of* THE CAVALIER, *and Douglas was paid
$45.29 or in British currency nine pounds six shillings.
When* FAMOUS FANTASTIC MYSTERIES, *a periodical spe-
cializing in the reprint of fantasy from old Munsey magazines appeared it was included in its April, 1942, issue,
with a "portrait" of the blind woman of the story by
Virgil Finlay that is a true masterpiece of pen and ink.*

*On a smaller scale the same elements of psychological
interplay that marked the destructions of a bishop's
morality in* South Wind *are present in this powerful
short tale.*

I

FAR AWAY, among desolate peaks, in that voiceless wilderness of stone and ice where the clouds linger, a horde of rivulets, bursting from patches of eternal snow, joined their waters and sped away. And the stream leaped downward through groves of bearded fir, or glided in a smiling flood over smooth meadows of foxglove and tigerlily and marigolds, caressing their roots with its eddies.

To the country folk who lived in the valley below, the stream was a living and a spiteful thing. They called it Elf-water. Its waves were dull, bluish, insipid to the taste, and fraught with unhealthy chills from the snows above—none cared to drink of them; and its shores were encrusted with fanciful stone shapes of grass and moss elves' work, like the ice-crystals on the window-panes in December.

And none cared to build houses near the water, or to own the fields on either side. For, sometimes, in the bluest days of midsummer, the stream suddenly swelled to a furious torrent and overleaped its flowery banks, drowning the lush meadows far and near "The elves!" the old folks would then whisper shaking their heads. They knew its elfish and wayward tricks, and some of them, maybe, still believed in such creatures. And the young men would come out to view the mischief, and gaze into the sunny sky and up at the hills, and talk together and look wise, secretly wondering.

Only one man could foretell the floods. He had lived on the Elf-water all his life. But he is dead long ago. His cottage is deserted; the roof has fallen in, the wooden beams are decayed, and green moss sprouts between the planks of his floor. He used to look up at the hills and see a small vapory cloud anchored against one snowy peak, and say nothing. Whenever they asked him to explain, he merely smiled, as if the Elf-water kept no secrets from him.

Meanwhile, the fair meadows were flooded, and the crops buried till only a few bright green tips showed above the seething foam. And up in the forest, where all should be still, the shriek of the torrent could be heard from afar. It thundered among the ravines and roared for freedom in its narrow prison, churning the boulders with hideous din and tumbling the tall pines, whose painted boles, loosened at the root, shivered and rocked like the limbs of some convulsed giant. The pale wood-flowers nodded helplessly in the tawny spray. The stream was unearthly in its rage.

And, then, with as little show of reason, its elfin wrath melted to a smile, and it shrunk back into a silvery thread of water, hushed and clear. It was ashamed of its freak, and weary.

But the harm was done, and only this one man's meadows were spared, for they lay out of reach of the wildest floods. They were remote from the valley by a many hours' climb—damp, sloping meads fringed by dark firs, on the shady side of the stream that rushed in a deep strid below the cottage. The people called them "elf-meadows," perhaps because, in times of flood, two or three tall columns of spray could be seen rising up from the gulf below and bearing some fancied resemblance to white elves or fairies.

The man had often watched these misty pillars swaying gracefully. He loved the Elf-water; he had learned to identify himself with all its moods. The ripple of its gray wavelets was the voice of an old friend, a friend of his boyhood—the sound that met his ears in the earliest morning and that charmed him to sleep at night; and he often thought of the days when, as a child, he used to hang over the dim forest pools and watch the bubbles and harken to rare music streaming upward from the depths. It was the pebbles dancing in the current; but to his childish ears it sounded like the faint songs of the water-fairies, disporting themselves on the crystal floor.

And, if by chance he dropped anything into the stream, the elves were sure to bring it to the surface again. Everyone, indeed, was agreed upon that point. Scythes and axes and sickles that had fallen into the deep pools, were always churned up again and found lying on the banks, "sharper than before," the owners said. And once, a heavy cart, loaded with hay, was overtaken by a sudden flood and borne away. Next day, wonderful to relate, they found it standing upright and unharmed on the bank. If there are no elves, who had done it?

Even the man's old mother was sometimes amazed at these things, although she generally scoffed at the mountaineers' beliefs. For she came from the green plains, far beyond the hills, where the folk are quite different. She laughed at the dull peasants and their ways.

She was no dreamer. She knew about everything and believed in nothing. They feared her, but she feared none.

She was calm and upright, and even-tempered, and prodigiously old—ninety years, maybe, or even a hundred. But she was lithe and strong, and her back was straight as a lance. Her husband had died long ago. She had lived in that lonely cottage with her son all his life.

II

"Will she live forever?" he often wondered. He hoped she would die, and that soon.

For these two hated each other. And yet, strangely enough, both were just and honest, and even kind, according to their lights. And they lived together, thinking that they were fulfilling a duty.

In that low-ceilinged room, with its wooden wainscoting stained and blackened by age, they often sat and looked at each other for many hours without speaking a word.

"You are your father's child," she would at last say, regretfully. She never reproached him with aught else, for he was a good son. And he never dreamed of vexing her, for she was his mother.

And then she would look at him again, and he would look back and say nothing.

What should he say? It was true enough; he was like his father in all things—short and heavy-chested, indifferent to cold and heat, with dark eyes, and crafty features that reflected in their harshness the crags and chasms of his home; slow to laugh, slow to speak, slow to decide, superstitious, gentle, but pitiless in resolve—a peculiar compound of strength and weakness. She would have wished to herself another son, tall, gay, ambitious, instead of this contented and crooked creature of the mountains.

And, perhaps, she thought of her own home in the rich plains, with their white-domed cities and laughing merchant-folk. Did she regret having exchanged it for a hard life among the mountains? Doubtless. But she was never heard to complain of her lot, and, much as people disliked her, none could find an evil word to say of her. She had a sense of duty and an unbending will such as would have driven her, in other times and places, to seek a martyr's death rather than yield in her conviction. She had served her husband faithfully up to the day of his death, and, although she had exacted blind obedience from the child, she never treated him with harshness.

But from his earliest youth he had never understood his mother, and after his father's death he smiled seldom. He soon learned to close the channels of his heart, to retire within himself, wondering and dismayed, and leaving unspoken many thoughts. Even in the olden days it had been a strange love that they bore each other. There was little charity in that house.

The old woman, accustomed to have her own way, treated him like a child long after he was grown to manhood, and such was his piety that he seldom ventured to cross her wishes.

Her mind was stronger than his, but he was warmer of heart.

"Why, then, do you not leave me and return to your own home?" he would sometimes ask. He longed for her to take him at his word, but she never left him. She evidently thought this a passing whim on his part; indeed—what vexed him most of all—she seldom entered seriously into any of his ideas, regarding him rather as an idle visionary whose fancies must be humored or—if mischievous—repressed.

"Leave you? Leave you, my son? And why leave you? My people are all dead. And what would befall you without me?" She seemed to doubt whether the man of fifty could provide for himself!

And, yet, she was not wholly insincere; there was something of pity mingled with her contempt. He was her son—her weak son, indeed; how else could he suggest such a thing?

"You drove *her* away!" he once dared to reply, trembling with rage "If she were here there would be no need for you to stay. Since that day I have suffered!"

He spoke of his lifelong grief, and wondered at his own boldness in thus reproaching his mother.

"These are foolish words, my son." She looked bravely into his eyes. "Foolish words."

But she feared inwardly, for he spoke the truth. The matter of the man's wife was the only one she dreaded to discuss with him—the old woman knew that she had made a mistake. But it was against her nature ever to acknowledge a fault, and she therefore affected to ignore his grief.

And, in truth, she could not easily bring herself to comprehend such an enduring affection.

"Twenty years have passed since then," she mused. "Why does he not forget?"

In this one thing the man had thwarted his mother—he had brought home a bride who was not to her liking. But the victory had sapped his energy, and he was too weak, or, maybe, too pious, a common enough story, to profit by it and bid the old woman begone. There followed a few short years during which the mother regained her power over her son and tormented in a thousand ways the young wife, who finally fled in despair, never to return.

The cottage remained the same, with its cool meadows and dark belt of forest, but the light of love was gone out, and an undying hatred kindled.

That terrible morning when he found himself deserted, the Elf-water was in flood, convulsed in its deep bed and howling in the hollow caverns that it had torn into the mountain's side. The man climbed up to a certain little knoll—there where the earth slopes away in a steep ledge above the thundering cataract, and where he had often sat with her who was now departed. The current below this point was so fast that it might well have carried away the strongest man. Had she perished in the water? Surely not. The water was his friend; it restored to him all that he ever lost.

He looked down the stream. There was sunshine and peace in the valley below, but here all was gray desolation and loneliness; the torn clouds stuck among the pines. And ever and anon a ghostlike pillar of spray rose up from the noisy depths and drenched the meadows. Sometimes one remained upright, swaying in the wind like a shrouded human form.

"She cannot be dead," he thought. "She will return."

In the course of time disquieting rumors of her, the absent one, had reached the valley. It was said that she well deserved all that she may have suffered, since she deserted a good husband for no cause.

But the man cared nothing for evil report. He knew the truth, and that the trouble had been all his mother's work. And each time he looked upon his mother's face—a hundred times daily—he was reminded of that other one who had suffered through her. But the old woman always knew the direction of his thoughts, and stared back at him fearlessly, though without unkindness. She knew her power over him, and exerted it freely, returning his look so steadfastly that he often felt the strength oozing out of his bones, as after a long illness.

Often they sat thus in that dark room, confronting each other. They stared for long, long hours, striving for the mastery. And never a word was spoken. He longed for her to yield—to confess with her eyes, at least. But she never admitted any fault; and there was nothing to be read out of her eyes, pale-blue, cold and lively as the ripples of a mountain river, and fringed with bristly white lashes. Her long curls dropped over them—for her oval forehead was overhung down to the nose with thick locks, white as driven snow—and stiff hairs curled over her lips and out of her nostrils. She had a strange, deep voice, gruff as a cracked bell, and a complexion clearer than a child's. Under its transparent skin could be seen the veins wandering about like little red rivers. And even in her old age she was taller than her son.

Likely enough she had been comely in her youth, but now she was grown monstrous.

She used to say: "Look you, what could you do without me? I must care for you like a little child. Do not I work for you, make your food and clothing?"

It was true enough, like everything that she said. He had grown idle and listless in latter years. But he thought: "How different it might have been! How happy I was, and how little would have contented me!"

Then he would sigh to himself, grief-laden, and the customary look of reproach, which she was awaiting, did not come. For he left the room silently with bowed head.

And as often as he returned he found her sitting upright on her bench beside the stove, with her long fingers working at her wool, ever ready to take up the mute challenge. To the man, thus peering into her glassy eyes, they seemed to swell till they dominated his whole being. He clenched his fists and looked away.

Sometimes, after such a struggle, a strange feeling of rage and power entered into him. It made his whole body tremble. He thought it was an evil spirit tempting him. It used to whisper in his ear, but he could not understand the words.

And, as the years went on, mother and son spoke less with each other. Silence and hatred lay heavy upon that home. The man's black, curly hair was already streaked with gray. The woman grew old—old, but she never changed.

III

"Will she live forever?" he wondered.

"Aye, we are a long-lived race," she said aloud. For even when he was yet a child she always guessed his thoughts as correctly as if he had spoken them out. "I am old—I have lost count of the time—but I shall live yet many years and work for you. Be thankful. We are a strong race—our blood is good—we live long—"

"Too long," he thought, and would have told her so, but the impious words stuck in his throat and choked him.

The old woman, meanwhile, fixed her eyes upon him, knowing his thoughts.

"Surely," she said, trying to sweeten the gruff tones of her voice into persuasive pleading, "surely you would not drive your mother out in her old age to die by the roadside?"

"Surely not," he replied, moved by a return of his natural piety. But, how different it might have been!

As he stepped out of the doorway he found, lying upon the threshold, a log of wood with some blood-stains upon it, and a bunch of gaudy feathers. They were those of a jay—doubtless the old familiar bird that visited the cottage at times. His mother must have killed it, after waiting for her opportunity all these many years. She hated it on account of its history, for it was the young woman, the absent one, who had caught and tamed it during her short life at the elf-meadow.

The man, although generally callous to the sufferings of the wild things of nature, was strangely affected, in his present exasperation, by the sight of these poor remains. His mother had chosen an evil moment. He carried in the feathers and held them before her eyes.

"Look!"

"I see."

"Why have you killed it?"

"Because it was thievish. And because I disliked it," she added truthfully. She was never so sure as now of her ascendency over him.

But he was enraged at the hard words. He thought of the absent one—it was as if a link between himself and her had been cruelly severed. He said fiercely:

"You killed it! Even as you killed her! This cannot endure!"

"All this is foolish talk. Will you never be reasonable?"

"Even as you killed her!" he repeated hoarsely. There was a tingling in his ears, and the veins in his forehead suddenly swelled.

Then the Evil Spirit came—it had come so often of late —and spoke to him. He understood what it said. It said: "Now!"

"You killed her! This cannot endure. One of us two shall die—even as she died! Ah! Do you understand? Do you confess? You killed her! And I will kill you!"

And, for the first time in his life, he seized her in a grip of steel and shook her till the white curls danced over her face. A rain of fiery sparks was falling before his eyes, and still he shook her, regardless of her shrieks. How light she was! She reeled under his arm, and he would assuredly have shaken the last breath out of her old body but that something in the touch of her cold, dry skin brought him abruptly to his senses again.

"Let me go!" she growled, as boldly as she could, gasping with rage and breathlessness. "Would you raise your hand against your mother? You are no man."

But he was inwardly glad, for the spell, he thought, was broken. He used to fear her, but now he had seen her weakness.

"She is only a woman—only a weak woman," he said.

Nevertheless, his energy soon melted away, and, as after his marriage, he lacked courage to bid her begone. He had felt his strength, but he feared to use it.

And the woman had felt her weakness, but she sought to hide it. She would show no signs of defeat. Yet, whenever she spoke to him, she was sensible of a strange twitching in her jaw, and a new tone in her voice—the sound of fear, which she tried to conceal, but could not. Therefore, she wisely ceased to speak altogether, and the man likewise preferred silence, since he foresaw that he could no longer reckon upon his self-control in the event of a dispute. Thus, neither daring to address the other, many days and many months would pass without a word being said, although they looked at each other from time to time in a way that left little to be misinterpreted.

In his dumb contest with those relentless eyes, the man was worsted. The old woman, without a word, gradually cowed him into submission and reestablished her empire. And the man now only clung with luxurious self-torture to the bitter-sweet remembrance of other days.

The absent one, at that distance of time, had become invested with a sacred and well-nigh supernatural character. He would not believe in her death. Surely she would return to him. His superstitious mind would have deemed it little of a miracle to have encountered her, in saintly guise, during his wanderings in the forest or on the banks of the stream where they had often lingered together. She was no longer a human creature, but a shadowy being crowned with a halo of immortality.

As for the old woman, she lived on for many years.

"Will she live forever?"

Aye, she was clearly fated to live forever, and he no longer cherished any hope.

He would repeat: "This cannot endure. One of us two must die!" But it endured.

"You are no man!"

It was true enough, like everything that she said. You are no man! He laughed at his own weakness—a bitter laugh. Should he kill her? He shuddered at the idea. Besides, he dared not.

Once, indeed, after an unhappy day and many hours of sleepless torment, the Evil Spirit came again and spoke to him in the same manner as before.

And he crept up to where she slept, hardly knowing what he was about to do. It was midnight. She lay with folded palms, half-reclining, in her accustomed attitude, on the bench beside the stove. She breathed softly.

But her eyes were not shut! They were open, and glowed like lamps in the dark. The man stepped back, awe-stricken.

"I see you," she said calmly, without moving so much as a finger—hated words, that haunted him ever afterward.

She was satisfied with her triumph, and said nothing; but the man's last spark of courage was crushed out of him. Thenceforth he walked with downcast head and averted look. Never again would he raise his hand, or even his voice, against her.

At times, to escape from his care, he descended into the valley and drank fiercely. But more often he wandered through the lonely forests, loudly praying for forgiveness, for guidance, and for release from those awful eyes that, vampire-like, sucked out the strength of his body. His soul was humbled to the dust. The trees, the rocks, and the wild waters were witnesses of his heartfelt supplications.

He prayed thus for many years. And, in the end, his prayer was heard.

IV

For the old woman grew blind. The blue fire faded out of her eyes. They became milky, as it were two white opals, though the flame still burned dimly within. For a long time she hid the change from her son, but he found out in the end, and thanked the Great Being who had heard his prayer.

"You wax blind, mother. Your eyes are filmy."

"Nay, you mistake; I see well," she answered, looking boldly toward him, for she knew that he was watching her.

She struggled on with an iron will. Whenever his glance fell upon her she must have felt it, for she at once stared back into his face, and so steadily that he often wondered whether he was indeed not mistaken. But her task became harder every day. And she began to fear mightily, for although her old body was healthy and tough as an oak, she foresaw that, with the darkening of her sight, her power over him would wane.

"The film grows upon you, mother."

"I think not. I see my wool," she croaked back. But slowly the crystal of her eye clouded to dull horn.

Again he insisted, "You see me less plainly than before," strangling, as best he could, the joy that quivered in his voice.

"I see you well enough."

But she saw him not at all! She was stone blind. And when her son spoke there resounded a horrible note of triumph and menace in his voice. She thought. "He will kill me if he discovers the truth," for thus she interpreted his crooked peasant nature.

Yet she still contrived to hide her fear, even as he hid his joy, casting about meanwhile for some new device to overawe him. At last she hit upon a cunning and bold deceit, worthy of her fearless mind.

"I am not blind! I see you—I see every hair on your head! And I look into your eyes—I pierce them through—"

He turned aside from her fixed stare.

"Is it possible?" he wondered.

"I see! This film, of which you speak, is in your own eyes! I can see into your very heart, and read your evil thoughts and wishes. Are you not ashamed?"

Such words she often repeated, and each time the man

heard them it was as though a lash had struck him. And he looked at her, endeavoring to read the truth out of her calm face, and his superstitious mind grew afraid.

"I see you!" she repeated, and she dissembled so well that he began to believe. His blood curdled with fear. Was it possible—?

He took to prowling stealthily as a lynx, hoping to avoid her glance and, by taking her unawares, to satisfy himself of her blindness. But she was too quick for him—her pearly eyes always discovered his whereabouts, and her words sank into his heart.

"I see you! I see everything!" she growled.

She had duped him!

But a nameless dread fell upon the man. He went out of the door and passed through the forest, and did not return for many weeks.

V

One sunless morning in the early spring he staggered home from the village. His gait was unsteady, but there was a steady purpose in his heart. The old woman lay in her accustomed attitude on the broad bench beside the stove. She never moved: she slept. She slept much in these latter days. The man crept nearer, craving to look into her face.

She slept on, and her sharp ears never heard his approach, for the Elf-water was in flood, writhing and screeching in its narrow channel till the cottage trembled with the fury of the water. As he bent down to look at her, the door was burst open by a sudden gust of wind. But she slept on.

He turned back to shut it, and, as he did so, he looked out upon the landscape. There was sunshine and peace in the valley below, but here all was gray desolation and loneliness; the torn clouds stuck among the pines. And ever and anon a ghostlike pillar of spray rose up from the noisy depths and drenched the meadows.

It was on such a morning, he remembered— How long he had waited! Surely she, the absent one, would come soon.

And he returned to look down upon the old woman, the cause of all. She slept on.

Then the Evil Spirit drew near and spoke to him. It said, "Now!"

And already his teeth were set to the work. But at that moment she awoke of her own accord, and opened her eyes. They were like disks of polished lead. And when she had done so, and never so much as took notice of him, he knew the truth. She was blind—blind as a stone. He stepped back a pace, breathing heavily with the weight of unexpected joy.

And then an immense wave of love and compassion swept out over him, submerging every other thought or feeling. He pitied her misfortune, and would fain have forgiven her all. He would love her doubly. He would humble himself in ministering to all the wants of her old age.

But the woman soon felt the human presence, and, in mingled fear and defiance, shrieked aloud, little dreaming what effect the words would have:

"I see you! I see everything!"

Hated words, that turned his love to very madness. It was as if a crimson flame leaped up before him, burning away the remembrance of all that was or had been. And he held her gently, and said—his words sounded like a lesson learned beforehand:

"Enough. Come."

"Begone, fool! Will you raise your hand against your mother? Leave me!"

But he only drew her nearer to him.

Then the truth flashed upon her, and her voice broke from its troubled depths to a scream that drowned the howl of the wild waters.

"Out upon you, monster! You wish to kill me, but I wish to live! Are you not satisfied with my blindness?"

She thought by this confession to appease his wrath. But it was too late—her words were lost.

Perhaps he would have obeyed if he had heard, for his piety was fervent. But he saw and heard nothing. There was a din in his ears as of crashing thunders, and a mighty curtain of blood swayed heavily to and fro before his eyes. He merely uttered that one word, "Come." It sounded dreamlike and distant, as though another man, not himself, were speaking.

The woman, undeceived as to his intent, struck out bravely with her arms, fighting like a mountain-cat; but he gathered energy from her resistance and picked her up as he would a child—for, though tall, she was thin and light—

and carried her out of the cottage and across the damp meadow. The Elf-water shouted for gladness.

He returned alone and sat still a while, pondering painfully. Slowly, reluctantly, one by one, the memories crept back, building themselves up into the hideous fabric of his crime.

"Ah!" He remembered it all. But a pallid fear shook him. What if she had not died? And if the Elf-water yielded her up again, even as it yielded up all else? If she were still alive—she was strong and active—

His teeth chattered, and his eyes remained fixed upon the half-open door, for he dreaded every minute to see her return with dripping garments to the accustomed seat, and then, turning, to confront him with that leaden stare. But, as she did not return, he finally crept across the meadows to the water's edge, peering into the misty depths below. Then he looked down the stream. There was nothing in sight.

And, then, suddenly, he saw, or thought he saw, a pale gray shape moving in the water far away. Soon it reached the shore and disengaged itself from among the boulders. It stood upright. How tall it was! Its garments were long and clinging, and it climbed slowly toward him, stumbling often among the stones. It seemed to be weak, for it paused at times to gather strength or to bethink itself. Was it a specter? Surely not. Surely it was his mother, escaped alive from the Elf-water.

The man raised his hand to his head, where the moist perspiration had gathered. He was unnerved with fear. But the shape had reached the narrow path, and, after resting a while, suddenly stretched out its arms, as though feeling the way, and seemed to drift straight toward him at a rapid pace. It had evidently decided. It came nearer.

He waited no longer. He was seized with a blind, unreasoning panic and fled upward, past the cottage, into the deepest shades of the dripping forest.

And there, sheltered under a huge fir, he remained many hours, terror-stricken. Evening closed in upon him. At last he reasoned away his fear and turned his steps homeward in a quieter frame of mind. And, yet, he could not rid himself of the notion that the horror was somewhere near at hand, lurking in the darkling shades.

And as he silently walked on, his alarms grew apace. Like a startled child he dared not turn his head, but walked faster and faster through the dark trees till, on the meadows, his pace increased to a run—a horrible, breathless race. He entered his home and looked around him, fearful of some unspeakable calamity.

The shape had arrived before him. It sat, upright and stern, on the accustomed bench, and its eyes—those awful eyes—stared at him with fixed determination across the darkened room. They seemed to say:

"One of us two shall die—"

He felt his hair raise itself under his thick fur cap. He would have fled, but his feet refused to move, and there began a strange throbbing in his head. He was constrained to stand still and gaze.

Aye! It was his own corporeal mother! Her clothes were dripping, and a little pool of water had collected on the floor. She remained immovable as a rock, save for an occasional spasm of shivering. She had apparently not yet heard him. There was a line of human suffering about the mouth, as of one who would weep, but cannot. And the man saw a small stream of blood oozing from a wound on her head. It trickled slowly and stained her white locks with crimson. At that sight there fled across his disordered mind a shadow, a fleeting mockery, of the former feeling of love and contrition.

But the old woman made a slight movement. She must have become aware of the human presence.

Then the man, by a last effort of will, tottered forth, vanquished. His temples ached fiercely; bereft of reason, he strayed into the gray twilight to the water's edge. And lo! not far away from a certain little knoll—there where the earth slopes away in a steep ledge above the thundering cataract—another frail white shape floated lovingly toward him. It enveloped him in its dewy shroud.

The spray fell in showers upon his burning head, but his arms sought the yielding form, and he fell prone into the void, meeting its chill caresses with a responsive kiss.

JUNGLI ADMI

Sarath Kumar Ghosh

Sarath Kumar Ghosh was a Hindu who set up residence in England and in 1904 published 1,001 Indian Nights, a work that became internationally renowned for its vivid, thrilling and colorful interpretation of Indian life. His short story Jungli Admi, *which was the lead story in the April, 1907, issue of* THE LONDON MAGAZINE, *if not altogether forgotten is little-known today, yet it must rank as one of the most ingenious and gripping stories ever written. The ordeal by which a condemned man must prove himself reminds one of Daniel and the Fiery Furnace, only in this case there is no divine intervention but only an utterly unique device to be utilized for salvation.*

It is completely safe to predict that, following its resurrection and reprinting in this volume, Jungli Admi *is destined to be anthologized frequently in the years ahead.*

A. Sarath Kumar Ghosh was introduced to the literary world by PEARSON'S MAGAZINE, *which ran six of the stories which later were to be collected as* Indian Nights Entertainment, *beginning in their January, 1902, number. At the time Sarath Ghosh was heralded as the only Hindu writer of English fiction and the editors were aware from the moment they first read his material that they had made an outstanding find.*

Ghosh was born a high-caste Indian who was raised in India. He received a scientific education as a youth and assisted his father in the writing of texts for Indian universities. His family sent him to England where he studied mathematics, science, economics and law. He was elected a member of The Royal Astronomical Society and was appointed Professor of mathematics and economics in the Calcutta University. Sir John Lubbock regarded him as an outstanding authority on Indian currency.

The decision to drop an anticipated legal career for literature came when a friend discovered a work of fiction by Ghosh in a waste paper basket and was so impressed by the power of the prose that he prevailed upon the young man to devote full time to literature.

Literary acclaim came to him before he was 30 and he went on to carve a respected niche for himself in the literature of India. It is of parenthetical interest to note that Ghosh continued to turn out popular scientific articles as well as fiction; a particularly interesting example was Life in Metals *in* PEARSON'S MAGAZINE, *July, 1902, dealing with the effect of fatigue, irritability, temperature, lack of use and chemicals on various metals.*

THE RAJA'S LIPS curled upwards in a smile of cynical scorn; then his blazing eyes flashed out in sudden wrath. "Captain Stourton, you are an English officer and a gentleman. Say, what has he deserved who breaks his plighted word?"

But his prisoner deigned no reply. Standing before his judge in the dim light of the inmost palace chamber, he knew that no word or plea could avert his fate. He drew himself up to his full height, and answered never a word. He inwardly felt that none would even know of that fate; for the two guards that held him were deaf and tongueless eunuchs. In that midnight hour in the harem of the palace he was at his captor's mercy.

"What has he deserved who abuses the sacred privileges of hospitality, and, like a thief at night, violates the sanctity of——" The curling lips formed a word his prisoner could not hear, though he vaguely felt its hidden meaning.

"What has he deserved who flings away his own honour, and brings shame upon the beard of his host?"

The young Englishman started. As in a nightmare, he began to realise the monstrous charge that was laid upon him. For the first time, its full significance began to dawn on him.

"It is false! I am innocent of your foul charge!"

The frown deepened upon the Raja's brow. He spoke in his own tongue. "Thou liest, O son of a dishonoured

father! My own eyes saw thee. Would that they were
burnt in the seeing! Enough! Thou shalt die the same
death as she!" He hissed the words in his captive's face,
and motioned to the eunuchs to bear him away.

They fell upon the prisoner, bound him with a triple
cord, carried him to the dungeon beneath the harem of the
palace, and there flung him upon the bare flagstones.

No escape was possible. He could not break through
the solid nine-foot walls of the cell, even if his limbs were
free. And, outside, he felt sure the enunuchs were keeping
ceaseless watch with drawn tulwars. If even by some
strange chance he escaped from the cell, they would catch
him outside, and lop off his head without a moment's
thought. His body, sewn up in a sack, would be flung
into the swift stream that flowed past the palace garden into
the deep ravine beyond. No man would know how he had
vanished from the face of the earth.

Would Muriel know? What cruel fate, perhaps worse
than his own, awaited her? Was she still in the palace,
or by some miracle had managed to escape?

Only a few hours ago, in her father's bungalow, their
bliss had been complete. Then, lover-like, they had strolled
out into the bright moonlight, not knowing they were going
to their doom. It was the canoe moored by the little stream
flowing past the compound that tempted them. Gliding
listlessly over the water, the bank had risen up on either
side; then, at a sharp bend, the canoe had shot under an
archway in a high wall, and passed into what seemed
to be an orchard.

New to the place, they did not know the exact course
of the winding stream, so could not tell what was this
orchard. Then, as they were well within it, the canoe
passed swiftly by champak-groves and jasmine-beds till a
garden-house had come in sight.

Before they realised their peril, the canoe was beside a
low balcony overlooking the stream. In the spirit of
mischief, like two children, escaped from school, they ran
the canoe aground and leapt ashore, when, with a merry
laugh, Muriel slipped away, and like Ginevra on her bridal
day, hid herself from her lover among the kuskus creepers
that flanked the balcony.

And then—and then, whilst yet Frank was looking
round for her, a face had appeared upon the balcony—a
face of transcendent beauty, of the clearest olive, such
as the loveliest Cashmeri might possess. The silken veil

was pulled well back over her head, showing the full contour of her face, her supple form lightly draped in the softest Dacca brocade. The moon, now risen above the distant hilltop, shone full upon her. Her startled eyes fell upon the intruder; her lips quivered in unspoken words; then, with a strangled cry, her arms were flung out towards him, bidding him begone, warning of some imminent peril. For a man to penetrate the harem of the palace the penalty was death. To gaze upon the Rani's unveiled face, death by slow torture. For the Rani herself to be caught holding converse with a man, death with ignominy.

Too late. A single clap of unseen hands, and a dozen eunuchs leapt to the bank from a room beneath the balcony and were upon the intruder. Hurling him to the ground, they bound him, gagged him, bore him away into the harem to his relentless judge.

And now, awaiting his death in the palace dungeon, he cursed the irony of fate. His whole thought was of Muriel; and yet he was going to his doom because of another woman!

*   *   *

"Be still! Do not move! The faintest sound—a gasp, a breath—and in vengeance thy own fate shall be worse than his. Be still. None has seen thee, save I!"

Like one petrified in horror, Muriel clutched at the creepers. The whispered words fell upon her dulled ear.

"Turn swiftly to the right, part the kuskus, pass through it. Run quickly though the winding steps that open behind into the chamber to which they lead. There, lie still among the cushions, piling the shawls upon thyself. Into the chamber I myself shall be borne—into my prison, awaiting the silken cord or the poison cup." And the Rani stood erect and still upon the balcony, now the triple veil drawn over her face. A yard to the right, Muriel clung to the creepers, transfixed in sudden horror, unable to move.

The tramp of feet upon the balcony, and the hot, panting whisper broke again from the Rani's lips, and came trickling into Muriel's frozen ear:

"Quick! They come! It is thy only chance!"

And even that instant the eunuchs reached the veiled form, lifted high their tulwars, kissed the hilt in salute, then signed to the Rani to follow them. But she stood motionless like a marble effigy, straining her ears. Was it

the rustling of leaves in the wind? Lo, the faint sound
had died away. She counted thirty beats of her heart—
just so long as it might take an affrighted woman to run
through twenty steps and a corridor. Then, bowing her
head, she walked between the eunuchs without a word.
Reaching the chamber, she sat down upon the cushions
on the divan, screening from view the pile of shawls behind. Her heart leapt to her mouth as she felt the shawls
quiver, tremble, then subside in stillness. But the eunuchs,
suspecting nothing, closed the door of the chamber and sat
down before it with tulwars in hand. Two of their number
went round to the balcony, and closed and sealed up the
private exit by the creepers. The Rani's chamber was now
a prison.

An hour later an old woman, doubled up, shrivelled up,
came to the door, and flung to the eunuchs the Raja's
signet-ring.

"To prepare her for the end!" she muttered.

The eunuchs, deaf and tongueless, cared nothing for
her words. But the ring they saluted with joined hands,
and gave it back to her, and opened the door.

She passed into the chamber, and cast herself at the
Rani's feet.

"These hands have nursed thee and served thee since
thou wert a babe; and since thy bridal—when the Fates
gave thee to a jealous husband—have I come here to serve
thee still. Say, O heart of my heart, is there naught in which
I can serve thee now?"

"Naught, my mother," the Rani answered in a level
voice, her eyes gazing straight before her, her head held
up high in unyielding pride.

"Then take this, and save thyself!"

The old nurse brought out from her bosom a long
dagger of the keenest Jaipur blade. She gave it to the
Rani, went to the door, saw that it was well closed, paused,
then glided back again.

"It shall be on the morrow, at earliest dawn! In the
forest beyond the garden-house and by the shere-kotee"
[private menagerie]. "I overheard the master say so to the
jemadar of the eunuchs."

Then, bringing her lips closer to her mistress's ear, she
hoarsely whispered:

"But Gunga Dass, my man, shall be there; he knows well
the tricks of the jungle. May benign Lakmée aid thee in

thy peril, and prove thy innocence! Pray to the goddess now!"

A moment after she was back to the door and was gone.

At the further end of the vast gardens and parks surrounding the palace was the beginning of a forest, to which an iron gate in the park-wall gave entrance. Amid the dense columns of peepul-trees, neems and sals, and flanked by a luxuriant growth of supple bamboos and pliant canes, there was a little open space in the forest, oval in shape, a hundred feet in length, fifty in width. It was surrounded by tall palisades fifteen feet high, and was covered all over with soft sand a foot in depth. The gigantic peepuls around stretched out their arms, and formed a canopy above the enclosure, casting it in dim, flickering shadows.

The enclosure had two gates to it, both iron-barred—one wide enough for an elephant to pass; the other, at the further end of the oval, scarcely five feet high, and opening into a dark gallery that led to a cavern under an adjacent hillock.

In front of the main gate there was a raised platform, and upon it a marble seat. Here the Raja was wont to sit and satisfy his jaded appetite for sport, witnessing in the arena before him dark deeds of senseless valour, of which not a whisper was permitted to reach the world beyond.

But now with sport there would be justice. It would be an appeal to the verdict of the gods. His victims should prove that they were guiltless of this unhappy intrigue, or die in torture and ignominy.

At earliest dawn in the dim twilight, they were taken to the enclosure—the English prisoner between two guards, his hands bound behind him; the Rani on the Raja's first elephant. The huge beast knelt upon the ground, and, curling up its trunk to form a rest for her feet, helped her lightly down.

Before the Raja's seat she stood a moment in unbending pride, her hands hidden at her breast in the folds of her sari, her face covered with the threefold veil. Her lips were sealed in silent scorn; no word or plea of innocence escaped them. Her life was in the hands of Lakmée. The goddess would save her by a miracle, if she chose.

At a sign from the Raja the main gate was thrown open. Inside the enclosure and close to the palisades there was already an iron cage, having been put there in the course of the night. To this the Rani was taken by two eunuchs. An attendant outside slackened a chain that came over the palisades to the top of the cage; the front of the cage, hinged along the bottom, fell off at the top and lay upon the sand. The Rani was placed inside, the chain tightened, and the front rose up again and closed the cage.

The Raja turned to his other victim.

"Thou shalt be placed within the arena with thy hands unbound, in perfect freedom." He waved his hand, and the eunuchs cut away the captive's bonds, and held him by the arm. "But thou shalt be made to face a foe against which triple steel would avail thee naught. When thou art killed, the cage shall be opened again; then *she* shall meet the same fate as thou. Her life hangs on thine. If thou canst escape death thou and she are guiltless."

"Name the foe," the captive curtly asked.

The Raja smiled grimly. "Thou shalt see," he said. At a signal from him, one of the eunuchs securely closed the main gate, and another went round to the far end and climbed up the hillock adjoining the palisades. Slowly and cautiously he lifted up, by an iron chain, the small gate between the enclosure and the gallery; then, going higher up the hillock, he thrust down a long bamboo spear through an opening.

An angry snarl, a muffled roar, and a flash of yellow shot through the gallery into the enclosure. It fell upon the sand, crouched low; then, in a gigantic curve, reached the middle of the arena.

A huge tiger!

Its thick fur quivered with pent-up force and vitality. A whole week it had lain in the cavern awaiting the Raja's fitful mood for sport; now it shook its limbs in joyous freedom. In the dim morning light just trickling in through the canopy above, it failed to notice at first the few people beyond the enclosure, and the iron cage within it, beside the palisades. Then suddenly its eyes fell upon it. One single leap, and it had spanned half the distance; another, and it stood before the cage, its forepaws upon the iron bars.

It thrust in its right paw, its left, and clawed the air. But the veiled form within stood silent and still, a span from the claws, scorning to recede a single step. The tiger closed its fangs upon a bar, gripped it above and below with its paws, and threw back its full weight upon the sand. The cage shook and creaked under the terrific pull. The thick chain holding the front of the cage tightened with a jerk at the end fastened to the palisades, cutting deep into the cross-beam above; then it held firm. It would have borne an elephant's pull.

The tiger released its hold, and bounded back into the arena a dozen paces; taking breath, it leapt full at the cage. The bars curved inwards under the shock; then, with a spring, regained their vertical form. Thus again and again the tiger leapt. It had not fed for forty hours; and now before its ravenous fangs was the tenderest of human flesh.

"Go in and save her!" A mocking laugh broke from the Raja's lips, its very irony serving well to disguise the bitterness of his heart. He had loved her deeply, albeit with a jealous love, till he had discovered this miserable intrigue—as he had thought—with a total stranger, and beneath his very eyes. Now he had trampled upon his heart under an iron heel. Her agony was great; his was greater. The stranger—he that was the cause of both—should suffer the greatest agony of all.

"Go in and save her, O accurst of Fate! But that none may say I am not just in my sport—or my vengeance—choose whatsoever weapon thou dost please from the jungle around thee. The beast is of the jungle, and has no weapon but of the jungle. Thus it shall be a fair match!" And in his eyes there burnt a fire of passion that was doubly fed by the agony in his heart.

But the words were still undried upon his lips when a wizened old man, hairy of face and limbs, emerged from the bamboo bush behind the daïs, and cast himself at the Raja's feet.

"Heaven-born, I am a jungli admi [wild man of the jungle]. Let me arm this youth with the jungle."

The Raja bowed his head, unflinching in justice as in vengeance.

"My word is passed. Arm this youth with the jungle."

Perchance, in his inmost heart, he clutched at this hope. Fate had sent this unknown man from the jungle; perchance Fate would choose him as the instrument of its verdict to prove *her* innocence. The old man vanished into the bush. Ten minutes after, he came back staggering under a load of supple bamboo rods and pliant canes. Quickly he set to work with his kugri. Taking a score of the rods, each six feet long and an inch thick, he wove them with the canes into the form of half a cone, tapering at the top; with another score he made the other half, so that, if the two were placed together, they would make a

complete cone, seven feet in diameter at the base, and
having a small opening at the top about two inches wide.
On the inner side of each half, about an arm's length from
the top, he fixed a stout strap made up of two pieces of
cane bound together by the tough outer bark of the
bamboo.

"This is thy shield," he whispered to the youth, taking
him aside. "Insert thy left arm over the first strap up to
the elbow and clutch the other strap with thy fingers."

Vaguely, as one in a dream, the young Englishman began
to realise its purpose. "And my lance?" he asked.

"This," replied the old man, thrusting into his hand a
mere bamboo rood, two feet long, and sharpened to a
point at both ends. The other looked at the fragile weapon.
To fight a tiger with that!

"It is enough," muttered the man of the jungle, "if
thou dost know how to use it and the shield. Strip!"

He took off the captive's boots and garments, all but the
trousers; even these he shortened just above the knees,
cutting off the pieces with his kugri. Thus clothed in his
own supple sinews and muscles, he allowed him to stand
for the fray.

Suddenly he laid a bony forefinger upon the captive's
brow, and peered into his face with beady eyes. The
captive's eyelids began to droop, and droop. He heard a
droning voice in his ear:

"Of the jungle, jungli; feet of iron, hands of steel; bones
of beaten brass, thews of molten fire; eyes of the eagle,
nostrils of the war-horse; the quickness of the sambur, the
courage of the wild cat, and the cunning of the hyena—
I make thee my brother jungli admi!"

The bony forefinger trickled down the white, glistening
body. The youth felt some strange iron flowing all down
his spine, some liquid fire surging through his very veins.
He was now of the brotherhood of the jungle.

"Awake! To the fray!"

The drooping eyelids flashed open. He sprang to the elephant that was standing by the gate of the enclosure, and
was lifted up to its back. The gate was thrown open, the
elephant thrust in half its body, and then stood still.
Poising a moment upon its back, the youth held the shield
in his left hand, extending the arm. Lo, the shield opened
out over his head like two fans. Then, running down the
sloping trunk, he leapt lightly on to the sand. The elephant
backed out behind him, and the gate was closed.

He was left to face the foe.

For a moment the tiger failed to understand this intrusion. Crouching upon the sand before the cage, fifty feet away, it turned its head and gazed upon its new victim. The man lowered his left arm before him, so that the two halves of the shield spread themselves out on his two sides like a pair of wings. The tiger was puzzled for a moment.

Slowly, with catlike tread, it came towards him. At six yards it stopped, surveying this strange creature; for the more ferocious a beast is, the greater is its suspicion of new things. The white, shining body, the flaxen hair, the blue eyes, and these greenish-yellow wings were all unwonted to its gaze.

It lay back upon its hind legs, with head erect. Then slowly the head came down. A swishing of the tail to the right, the left; a narrowing of the eyelids, a parting of the jaws, a short purr, a snarl, and it shot through the air in a huge curve.

That instant the man had dropped on his right knee. The left arm had been tilted up over his head and hooked at the elbow, the closed fist pressing against his chin. By that act the two wings had come down on either side, and completed the cone above him and all round him, the base resting on the sand.

The tiger fell upon it. A horrible creak and ominous grinding of pliant cane and yielding bamboo, the harsh sound of parting sand when an edged body is thrust into it, and the cone sank groaning into the arena under the tiger's weight. Six inches—nine inches—a foot it sank, then held firm against the hard ground beneath, flanked by the sand around.

That very weight had kept it together, for the pressure above had served to bring the two halves into closer contact. Nevertheless, upon the man's arm there was a shock as if it had parted asunder at the elbow. But for the rigid tension of the hard muscles the arm had parted, or the muscles snapped.

The tiger gazed bewildered a moment, looking for its vanished prey; then it espied it, beneath its own body. Down came its head to the side of the cone, its jaws opened wide, a huge fang fell sideways upon a binding cane and curled inwards into the gap between the bamboo rods, trying to snap the cane. But the gap, only an inch square, gave it no hold. The fang slipped over the cane again and again, merely sawing it on the outside. But even then might it not saw it away in time?

With a sinking heart the man realised that. He was now resting upon both heels, his knees upon the sand. His aching arm was above his head, held tight with the grimness of death, for he dared not slacken it an instant.

How could he make the tiger desist! If a single cane were snapped, then the rest were easy, for the break alone might suffice to enable the tiger to bite at the bamboo itself. Crouching as he was, he thrust his right arm under the left. He noticed the tiger's sawing jaw close against the framework. The soft flesh between the chin and the throat, a most sensitive spot, came into sight a moment, then went off again.

Breathlessly he waited. It came into view once more, and the sharp bamboo spear shot out from his right hand, and went an inch deep into its mark.

A roar of pain, the tiger flung off its head—shot clean off the cone. Five yards away it fell. There it crouched a moment, a thin stream of red trickling down upon its chin. It was to be an equal match after all between the man and the beast.

In that short respite the man extended his left arm. Already it was cramped and benumbed with pain. He rubbed it briskly with the other hand, dropping the spear. If he could only withdraw the arm altogether from the shield, just for a single moment! He glanced at the beast to see if he dared do it, and stiffened the arm instead with a jerk.

Even as it stalks its prey in the jungle, the tiger came slouching round in a long curve. Slowly the circle began to contract. When it started, its distance from the man was five yards; at the second circle it was only four. Thus it sought to wear down its victim.

Three yards, two, one, and the tiger suddenly stood up on it hind legs, and placed its forepaws upon the shield, even as it might stand beside a paralysed buffalo, and, placing one paw upon its back, smash in its skull with the other.

The yielding bamboos groaned beneath the terrific blow, curving down to within an inch of the man's upturned elbow. But for that saving inch the elbow itself had been smashed to a pulp. Then, by their elasticity, the bamboos regained their form. But the blow—this second round in the duel—had not been fruitless, for the man's right hand

received a jerk that for a moment made him fear that it
had been bodily wrenched off from the wrist, and in
the tiger's paw there was a hole from one side to the
other. For with his right hand the man had thrust up the
bamboo spear through the opening at the top of the cone,
and received the tiger's blow upon the spike.

With a snarl of rage the tiger snatched back its paw—
the slender spear creaked under the fierce tug—snapped
off four inches from the top. The broken piece, jagged
and barbed by the splintering, remained in the wound.
The tiger leapt back in frantic pain, hurled itself upon
the shield and beat it with its other paw; then, in impotent
rage, slunk off a while, lay down upon the sand, and tried
to bite off the embedded spear-end with its fangs.

But the man had lost half his weapon.

He now had only the other end of the spear. With that
he must kill the tiger, or himself be killed. For if that
also were broken off, he would be worn down by sheer
exhaustion, and, unable to hold the shield, be at the tiger's
mercy. Already his left arm was paralysed by pain; gradually all sensation was leaving it. When the beast had freed
itself from the spear-end, it would return to the charge,
and at one fierce onslaught break down the shield, or,
because of his own impotence, overturn it.

One only hope remained. He glanced at the tiger:
it lay a little to the left, about seven yards away. Slowly,
cautiously, he turned half round, released the left arm
from the shield, and inserted the right. Oh, if he could
only find protection from a corner! Then he would be safe
from all but a frontal attack.

But there was no corner: the arena was a complete
oval.

Yes, there was! Not quite, but very nearly. Glancing
over his right shoulder, he saw that the Rani's cage jutted
out seven feet from the side of the oval. If he could only
get beside it! Then he would be protected on two sides at
least; moreover, be near her at the moment of the final
round, when he must save himself and her, or both die.

Facing the tiger, he slowly raised himself from his knees,
lifting up the shield with him. Then gradually, by short
steps, he began to recede backwards, curving slightly to
the right towards the cage.

At the soft footfall the tiger looked up, growling. That
instant the man stood rigid and still. In the dim morning
light the beast saw the eunuchs' faces peering between the

palisades on the other side of its prey. Perchance it thought
that the sound had come from them. From the over-
hanging bough above a little fledgling myna fell upon the
sand before it. It picked it up in its injured paw and
turned it over, unharmed. In that action the spear-point,
jutting out an inch from the back of the paw, came upon
the ground, slightly thrusting out the broken end. Vaguely
the tiger's dull instinct realised its import. It had crunched
the broken end before; now it pulled it out bodily with
its fangs. The blood welled out from the wound, but the
acuteness of the pain was gone. The tiger was ready for
battle again.

But already the man had reached the side of the cage.
Profiting by the momentary distraction when the tiger was
tugging at the spear-end, he ran the dozen paces to the
sheltered spot, reckless of sound.

Two short leaps, and the tiger was upon him. Now it
was to be a fight to the death.

Like gladiators preparing for the last onslaught, each
seemed to realise that the end was nigh, that in this round
the one or the other would gain so distinct an advantage
as to ensure ultimate victory. By some strange animal
instinct the tiger seemed to understand that this was not
like the ordinary hunt it had been accustomed to in the
jungle to satisfy its daily hunger; rather, that it was in
the nature of a duel, in which its own life might have
to be staked against that of its foe.

The tiger stood before the shield, peered at the man
through the interstices, then suddenly, lowering its head,
arched its back and began burrowing in the sand. The
sand flew behind its hind legs in a shower, the bank in
front of the hollow began to subside. But realising the
possible peril, the man held on to the cone with both hands,
and put his full weight on it. Slowly it began to subside
also, in rhythmic time with each scoop of the tiger's paws.
Had the beast been gifted with human intelligence it would
have stood up on its hind legs, and lifted up the base
of the cone with its fore-paws. Instead, noticing its greater
slope owing to the sinking of its foundation in front, it
charged full tilt against it, embedding the other side of the
tough bamboo structure to an equal depth in the sand.
There the shield held firm in the corner formed by the
palisades and the side of the cage.

In baffled rage, unable to account for its failure, the
tiger leapt back, and charged again. Overshooting its mark,

it dashed itself against the palisades, and recoiled upon the top of the shield. There in mad fury it clawed the bamboos, thrust in its fangs at the little opening and crunched off the outer rim of cane. And the man shot out the spear into the opening, through the tiger's cheek, into the roof of its mouth. The stream of blood surged out after the spear as he jerked it back, and fell upon his upturned face in a shower.

Then a strange transformation came over him. So far he had been the hunted prey; now, painted red in the tiger's blood, he partook of the tiger's nature, and became the hunter. Was it sudden madness caused by that stupendous struggle, or perchance had the tiger's blood infected him with its own instinct of ferocity? So far he had acted purely on the defensive; now he would play with the beast even as a cat is wont to play with a mouse, or the tiger itself with a helpless nylghau.

The infuriated beast shot back a dozen yards, and crouched low for one fierce charge that should break down altogether its foeman's armour. That instant the man transferred the shield to his left arm, and sprang to his feet, lifting up the structure bodily before him. He stretched out his arm, and the shield resumed its former fan-like shape.

"Come on, you brute!" he yelled to the tiger in mad fury.

The beast paused in its leap. Startled by the human voice, it held back a moment, glared at the half-nude form; then, with a snarl of rage, sprang upon it like a bolt from a catapult.

But already the fan was closed, and the man upon his knee. With a yell almost tigerish he thrust out the spear as the beast fell upon the shield. Two inches into the tiger's body between the ribs it went. Recklessly he drove it further in by sheer force. With a snap it broke off at the wound, and remained buried three inches in the tiger's flesh, but in mad frenzy the man stabbed at the beast with the jagged end again and again.

"Take that, and that, and that!"

His weapon was now gone! But he failed to realise that. The lust of blood was upon him. He failed to realise that in the end he must die, not the beast. For in that agonising moment the balance of his mind gave way, and the man and the beast became alike.

But the beast was a tiger still, and a thrice-wounded

tiger. This time it did not leap off the shield. Instead, it clung on to it, clutched at the sides with both paws, and brought down its fangs to the small opening at the top. There in brute ferocity it crunched at the cane bindings, heedless of the repeated stabs from the splintered spear. Each fierce stab served but to madden it to greater fury and to nerve it to its last frenzied purpose.

Snap went the binding cane, the bamboo rods lay exposed. The huge fangs closed over three of them in a single bite. A terrific crunch, heedless that the palate of its mouth was cut open by the jagged ends, and the bamboos snapped off bodily. Another three, and then another. It was a gaping space nine inches wide.

With a roar of mingled rage and pain the tiger plunged its head into the gap. One fierce thrust, another, and the head was in up to the ears. The splintered ends caught it on the forehead and at the throat under the chin, peeling off the skin at each thrust. But the maddened beast grew more franctic with the pain. One more frenzied plunge, and the ears tore past the jagged ends.

The man slipped off his arm from the straps of the shield, else the beast had bitten off the elbow. He clutched the straps with both hands and clung on to them with his full weight. The tiger's face hung just between his hands; by stretching out its head to right or left it could lick his knuckles with its tongue.

And now the whole head and neck was within the shield. In despair the man abandoned the straps, lay back upon the sand, and clutched with both hands the base of the shield on the side of the tiger, drawing it towards him with his last effort. The other side of the base he left to the protection of the palisades. He saw the tiger's face a span from his face. Inch by inch the distance was lessening. Slowly but surely the ends of the splintered bamboos were curving inwards under the terrific pressure—or burying themselves deep into the tiger's body. Soon the saving space would be bridged, and then the beast would reach his head and crush it at a single bite.

He saw those terrible fangs, those iron jaws, keeping hideous time with the yellow, blinking eyes. Under their gaze his senses reeled. His frenzied madness of a moment ago forsook him; instead it was horror, fascination, that held him in their toils. He felt a spasm at his throat, a constriction at his heart. Something seemed to choke the breath from his lips; something rose up like a mist before his eyes, magnifying the terror they beheld.

He felt the tiger's horrible breath upon his face, his cheeks, his lips, and felt that a while later its terrible fangs would close over him and engulf him in death. In his dulled ear he heard the sound of creaking bamboo and bursting cane: to him it was like the sound of crunching bones and tearing flesh. Other sounds, faint as if from afar, trickled into his ear; but with his swooning senses he failed to realise their import. Some whispering voice seemed to be calling to him, bidding him awake—beseeching him in some vain and frenzied appeal. But he could not know the voice, even had it been that of his own beloved. For the torpor of death was upon him.

And then—and then—Fate, blind, senseless Fate, had had its cruel sport. In this last dream that seemed to him like the passage of death he saw a glittering thing flash before his half-closed eyes. It shot from the cage above, shone a moment in the air over the shield, then vanished from sight. He heard a soft thud close beside him, but knew not what it meant.

Vaguely, as still in the dream, he half turned his head. He saw the thing, but gazed at it helplessly, as an infant might at a shining thing. Then in his dulled senses the glittering steel began to grow and grow. Vaguely he stretched forth a hand, passed it through the loosened sand under the shield, and clutched at the object outside. Then, with the cold touch of the metal, his senses returned.

He drew in his arm, turned half round to the tiger's side, rested a moment upon one hand, and with the other, in one supreme effort, plunged the keen Jaipur dagger into the tiger's neck.

A terrific roar, choked off into a hiss by the gush of blood; the tiger shot up in the air, shield and all, fell back upon the sand, quivered, shook, clawed the air. The loosened shield fell off on either side. In its death-agony the tiger writhed; a tremor passed through its entire frame; the tail beat once, twice, thrice, then lay still. Stabbed through the jugular vein in that last desperate blow, the tiger had received its mortal wound.

The clank of chains, the rush of footsteps, and a dozen eunuchs burst into the arena. Two of them bore the man away; the rest escorted the veiled form in the cage back to the daïs.

But, standing before the daïs, she saw for the first time

the face of the man smeared with the tiger's blood, which she thought to be his own. With a strangled cry, a broken sob, she flung her arms around his neck and clung to him in the frenzy of love, despair, grief unutterable.

The Raja started in his seat as if a thunderbolt from the blue had fallen upon him.

"She is a perjured woman! Unveil her"—he motioned to the nearest guard—"then strike off her head."

There was a scream from the back of the daïs. The guard turned swiftly round, and saw the Raja's second elephant coming full tilt through the glade. The eunuch paused in doubt, but at his master's stern command stepped up to the veiled form and seized her veil. She released her arm from around her lover, and stood erect and still.

One rough pull, the veil parted along the seam at the brow, and came off in the eunuch's hand. He raised his sword aloft, poised it a moment above her head—then saw the maiden's face. With an inarticulate cry the sword dropped from the uplifted hand. And upon the Raja's face there was a look of wonder, of doubt, of insoluble mystery.

For the woman that stood before him unveiled was not the Rani, but an English maiden!

The second elephant, coming hot-footed from the palace, burst into the forest glade. An old woman, doubled up, shrivelled up, cast herself at the Raja's feet.

"My head be my sacrifice! It was this maiden, not the Jewel of the Palace, whom thou didst see last night holding converse with the youth. She had come to the harem to pay her salaam to the Jewel; I brought her there. This youth, her betrothed, came but to fetch her away." And she looked up to her master's face with unflinching eye, staking her own head upon this tale.

"And she?" It was scarce a whisper that broke from the Raja's lips. Some great conflict was raging within him.

But already a veiled form, arrayed in full regalia, was at the daïs. Kneeling before him, she lifted her veil so that he alone could see her face, proud and cold and haughty, but with unshed tears glistening in her eyes.

Then something burst in the tyrant's stubborn heart.

"It is well!" He stretched forth an arm and took her to the seat beside him, replacing her veil.

"Bear away the youth and the maiden to the palace on the first beast," he bade the eunuchs. "There minister to their wants. Then bear them to their home."

But the Rani slipped away from the musnud a moment, and, coming to the maiden, placed her arms around her neck.

"For the bridal, my sister!" she spoke into her ear.

For the nine rows of pearls that had been upon the Rani's bosom were now upon the maiden's.

THE MESSENGER

Robert W. Chambers

For 40 years, Robert W. Chambers was one of the most
popular and bestselling authors in America. Within a
decade after his death in 1933, he was virtually forgotten except for his short fantasies, which are considered now as when they formed the basis of his first
major success in 1895 as some of the finest ever written
by an American author.

There are more of them in more volumes than is
commonly realized, and gradually they are being
searched out and reprinted. It is hard to disagree with
Blanche Colton Williams, Ph.D., in her 1920 critique
Our Short Story Writers that "His best stories of rare
beauty and spirituality, are those of the supernatural.
They should live so long as theories of metempsychosis
last—the subject is as old as Pythagoras—and so long
as revenants return."

The influence of his volumes The King in Yellow and
The Maker of Moons on such master fantasts as Eden
Phillpotts, James Branch Cabell, A. Merritt and H. P.
Lovecraft is increasingly acknowledged.

The Messenger is a gem of a horror tale, published in
his collection The Mystery of Choice, issued in 1896, a
period during which he produced some of his most
superb fantasies. The locale is historical France, which
he had thoroughly researched.

Among American writers of supernatural, horror, fantasy and science fiction, Robert W. Chambers' name
deserves to be ranked with Edgar Allan Poe, Nathaniel
Hawthorne, Fitz-James O'Brien and Ambrose Bierce
and that statement is not intended to be a pious plati-
tude.

I

"THE BULLET ENTERED HERE," said Max Fortin, and he placed his middle finger over a smooth hole exactly in the center of the forehead.

I sat down upon a mound of dry seaweed and unslung my fowling piece.

The little chemist cautiously felt the edges of the shot-hole, first with his middle finger, then with his thumb.

"Let me see the skull again," said I.

Max Fortin picked it up from the sod.

"It's like all the others," he observed. I nodded, without offering to take it from him. After a moment he thoughtfully replaced it upon the grass at my feet.

"It's like all the others," he repeated, wiping his glasses on his handkerchief. "I thought you might care to see one of the skulls, so I brought this over from the gravel pit. The men from Bannalec are digging yet. They ought to stop."

"How many skulls are there altogether?" I inquired.

"They found thirty-eight skulls; there are thirty-nine noted in the list. They lie piled up in the gravel pit on the edge of Le Bihan's wheat field. The men are at work yet. Le Bihan is going to stop them."

"Let's go over," said I; and I picked up my gun and started across the cliffs, Fortin on one side, Mome on the other.

"Who has the list?" I asked, lighting my pipe. "You say there is a list?"

"The list was found rolled up in a brass cylinder," said the little chemist. He added, "You should not smoke here. You know that if a single spark drifted into the wheat—"

"Ah, but I have a cover to my pipe," said I, smiling.

Fortin watched me as I closed the pepper-box arrangement over the glowing bowl of the pipe. And then he continued:

"The list was made out of thick yellow paper; the brass tube has preserved it. It is as fresh today as it was in 1760. You shall see it."

"Is that the date?"

"The list is dated 'April, 1760.' The Brigadier Durand has it. It is not written in French."

"Not written in French!" I exclaimed.

"No," replied Fortin solemnly, "it is written in Breton."

"But," I protested, "the Breton language was never written or printed in 1760."

"Except by priests," said the chemist.

"I have heard of but one priest who ever wrote the Breton language," I began.

Fortin stole a glance at my face.

"You mean—the Black Priest?" he asked.

I nodded.

Fortin opened his mouth to speak again, hesitated, and finally shut his teeth obstinately over the wheat stem that he was chewing.

"And the Black Priest?" I suggested encouragingly. But I knew it was useless; for it is easier to move the stars from their courses than to make an obstinate Breton talk. We walked on for minute or two in silence.

"Where is the Brigadier Durand?" I asked, motioning Mome to come out of the wheat, which he was trampling as though it was heather. As I spoke we came in sight of the farther edge of the wheat field and the dark, wet mass of cliffs beyond.

"Durand is down there—you can see him; he stands just behind the Mayor of St. Gildas."

"I see," said I; and we struck straight down, following a sun-baked cattle path across the heather.

When we reached the edge of the wheat field, Le Bihan, the Mayor of St. Gildas, called to me, and I tucked my gun under my arm and skirted the wheat to where he stood.

"Thirty-eight skulls," he said in his thin, high-pitched voice; "there is but one more, and I am opposed to further search. I suppose Fortin told you?"

I shook hands with him, and returned the salute of the Brigadier Durand.

"I am opposed to further search," repeated Le Bihan, nervously picking at the mass of silver buttons which covered the front of his velvet and broadcloth jacket like a breastplate of scale armour.

Durand pursed up his lips, twisted his tremendous mustache, and hooked his thumbs in his sabre belt.

"As for me," he said, "I am in favor of further search."

"Further search for what—for the thirty-ninth skull?" I asked.

Le Bihan nodded. Durand frowned at the sunlit sea, rocking like a bowl of molten gold from the cliffs to the horizon. I followed his eyes. On the dark glistening cliffs, silhouetted against the glare of the sea, sat a cormorant, black, motionless, its horrible head raised toward heaven.

"Where is that list, Durand?" I asked.

The gendarme rummaged in his despatch pouch and produced a brass cylinder about a foot long. Very gravely he unscrewed the head and dumped out a scroll of thick yellow paper closely covered with writing on both sides. At a nod from Le Bihan he handed me the scroll. But I could make nothing of the coarse writing, now faded to a dull brown.

"Come, come, Le Bihan," I said impatiently, "translate it, won't you? You and Max Fortin make a lot of mystery out of nothing, it seems."

Le Bihan went to the edge of the pit where the three Bannalec men were digging, gave an order or two in Breton, and turned to me.

As I came to the edge of the pit the Bannalec men were removing a square piece of sail-cloth from what appeared to be a pile of cobblestones.

"Look!" said Le Bihan shrilly. I looked. The pile below was a heap of skulls. After a moment I clambered down the gravel sides of the pit and walked over to the men of Bannalec. They saluted me gravely, leaning on their picks and shovels, and wiping their sweating faces with sun-burned hands.

"How many?" said I in Breton.

"Thirty-eight," they replied.

I glanced around. Beyond the heap of skulls lay two piles of human bones. Beside these was a mound of broken, rusted bits of iron and steel. Looking closer, I saw that this mound was composed of rusty bayonets, sabre blades, scythe blades, with here and there a tarnished buckle attached to a bit of leather hard as iron.

I picked up a couple of buttons and a belt plate. The buttons bore the royal arms of England; the belt plate was emblazoned with the English arms, and also with the number "27."

"I have heard my grandfather speak of the terrible English regiment, the 27th Foot, which landed and stormed the fort up there," said one of the Bannalec men.

"Oh!" said I; "then these are the bones of English soldiers?"

"Yes," said the men of Bannalec.

Le Bihan was calling to me from the edge of the pit

above, and I handed the belt plate and buttons to the men and climbed the side of the excavation.

"Well," said I, trying to prevent Mome from leaping up and licking my face as I emerged from the pit, "I suppose you know what these bones are. What are you going to do with them?"

"There was a man," said Le Bihan angrily, "an Englishman, who passed here in a dogcart on his way to Quimper about an hour ago, and what do you suppose he wished to do?"

"Buy the relics?" I asked, smiling.

"Exactly—the pig!" piped the Mayor of St. Gildas. "Jean Marie Tregunc, who found the bones, was standing there where Max Fortin stands, and do you know what he answered? He spat upon the ground, and said, 'Pig of an Englishman, do you take me for a desecrator of graves?' "

I knew Tregunc, a sober, blue-eyed Breton, who lived from one year's end to the other without being able to afford a single bit of meat for a meal.

"How much did the Englishman offer Tregunc?" I asked.

"Two hundred francs for the skulls alone."

I thought of the relic hunters and the relic buyers on the battlefields of our civil war.

"Seventeen hundred and sixty is long ago," I said.

"Respect for the dead can never die," said Fortin.

"And the English soldiers came here to kill your fathers and burn your homes," I continued.

"They were murderers and thieves, but—they are dead," said Tregunc, coming up from the beach below, his long sea rake balanced on his dripping jersey.

"How much do you earn every year, Jean Marie?" I asked, turning to shake hands with him.

"Two hundred and twenty francs, monsieur."

"Forty-five dollars a year," I said. "Bah! You are worth more, Jean. Will you take care of my garden for me? My wife wished me to ask you. I think it would be worth one hundred francs a month to you and to me. Come on, Le Bihan—come along, Fortin—and you, Durand. I want somebody to translate that list into French for me."

Tregunc stood gazing at me, his blue eyes dilated.

"You may begin at once," I said, smiling, "if the salary suits you?"

"It suits," said Tregunc, fumbling for his pipe in a silly way that annoyed Le Bihan.

"Then go and begin your work," cried the mayor impatiently; and Tregunc started across the moors toward St. Gildas, taking off his velvet-ribboned cap to me and gripping his sea rake very hard.

"You offer him more than my salary," said the mayor, after a moment's contemplation of his silver buttons.

"Pooh!" said I, "what do you do for your salary except play dominoes with Max Fortin at the Groix Inn?"

Le Bihan turned red, but Durand rattled his sabre and winked at Max Fortin, and I slipped my arm through the arm of the sulky magistrate, laughing.

"There's a shady spot under the cliff," I said; "come on, Le Bihan, and read me what is in the scroll."

In a few moments we reached the shadow of the cliff, and I threw myself upon the turf, chin on hand, to listen.

The gendarme, Durand, also sat down, twisting his mustache into needlelike points. Fortin leaned against the cliff, polishing his glasses and examining us with vague, near-sighted eyes; and Le Bihan, the mayor, planted himself in our midst, rolling up the scroll and tucking it under his arm.

"First of all," he began in a shrill voice, "I am going to light my pipe, and while lighting it I shall tell you what I have heard about the attack on the fort yonder. My father told me; his father told him."

He jerked his head in the direction of the ruined fort, a small, square stone structure on the sea cliff, now nothing but crumbling walls. Then he slowly produced a tobacco pouch, a bit of flint and tinder, and a long-stemmed pipe fitted with a microscopial bowl of baked clay. To fill such a pipe requires ten minutes' close attention. To smoke it to a finish takes but four puffs. It is very Breton, this Breton pipe. It is the crystallization of everything Breton.

"Go on," said I, lighting a cigarette.

"The fort," said the mayor, "was built by Louis XIV, and was dismantled twice by the English. Louis XV restored it in 1739. In 1760 it was carried by assault by the English. They came across from the island of Groix —three shiploads—and they stormed the fort and sacked St. Julien yonder, and they started to burn St. Gildas—you can see the marks of their bullets on my house yet; but the men of Bannalec and the men of Lorient fell upon them with pike and scythe and blunderbuss, and those who did not run away lie there below in the gravel pit now— thirty-eight of them."

"And the thirty-ninth skull?" I asked, finishing my cigarette.

The mayor succeeded in filling his pipe, and now he began to put his tobacco pouch away.

"The thirty-ninth skull," he mumbled, holding the pipestem between his defective teeth—"the thirty-ninth skull is no business of mine. I have told the Bannalec men to cease digging."

"But what is—whose is the missing skull?" I persisted curiously.

The mayor was busy trying to strike a spark to his tinder. Presently he set it aglow, applied it to his pipe, took the prescribed four puffs, knocked the ashes out of the bowl, and gravely replaced the pipe in his pocket.

"The missing skull?" he asked.

"Yes," said I impatiently.

The mayor slowly unrolled the scroll and began to translate the Breton into French. And this is what he read:

> "On the Cliffs of St. Gildas,
> "April 13, 1760.

"On this day, by order of the Count of Soisic, general in chief of the Breton forces now lying in Kerselec Forest, the bodies of thirty-eight English soldiers of the 27th, 50th, and 72d regiments of Foot were buried in this spot, together with their arms and equipments."

The mayor paused and glanced at me reflectively.

"Go on, Le Bihan," I said.

"With them," continued the mayor, turning the scroll and reading on the other side,

"was buried the body of that vile traitor who betrayed the fort to the English. The manner of his death was as follows: By order of the most noble Count of Soisic, the traitor was first branded upon the forehead with the brand of the arrowhead. The iron burned through the flesh, and was pressed heavily so that the brand should even burn into the bone of the skull. The traitor was then led out and bidden to kneel. He admitted having guided the English from the island of Groix. Although a priest and a Frenchman, he had violated his priestly office to aid him in discovering the password to the fort. This password he extorted

during confession from a young Breton girl who was
in the habit of rowing across from the island of Groix
to visit her husband in the fort. When the fort fell,
this young girl, crazed by the death of her husband,
sought the Count of Soisic and told how the priest
had forced her to confess to him all she knew about
the fort. The priest was arrested at St. Gildas as he
was about to cross the river to Lorient. When arrested he cursed the girl, Marie Trevec—"

"What!" I exclaimed, "Marie Trevec!"
"Marie Trevec," repeated Le Bihan;

"the priest cursed Marie Trevec, and all her family
and descendants. He was shot as he knelt, having a
mask of leather over his face, because the Bretons
who composed the squad of execution refused to fire
at a priest unless his face was concealed. The priest
was l'Abbé Sorgue, commonly known as the Black
Priest on account of his dark face and swarthy eyebrows. He was buried with a stake through his heart."

Le Bihan paused, hesitated, looked at me, and handed
the manuscript back to Durand. The gendarme took it and
slipped it into the brass cylinder.
"So," I said, "the thirty-ninth skull is the skull of the
Black Priest."
"Yes," said Fortin. "I hope they won't find it."
"I have forbidden them to proceed," said the mayor
querulously. "You heard me, Max Fortin."
I rose and picked up my gun. Mome came and pushed
his head into my hand.
"That's a fine dog," observed Durand, also rising.
"Why don't you wish to find his skull?" I asked Le
Bihan. "It would be curious to see whether the arrow
brand really burned into the bone."
"There is something in that scroll that I didn't read to
you," said the mayor grimly. "Do you wish to know what
it is?"
"Of course," I replied in surprise.
"Give me the scroll again, Durand," he said; then he
read from the bottom:

"I, l'Abbé Sorgue, forced to write the above by my
executioners, have written it in my own blood; and

with it I leave my curse. My curse on St. Gildas, on
Marie Trevec, and on her descendants. I will come
back to St. Gildas when my remains are disturbed.
Woe to that Englishman whom my branded skull shall
touch!"

"What rot!" I said. "Do you believe it was really written
in his own blood?"

"I am going to test it," said Fortin, "at the request of
Monsieur le Maire. I am not anxious for the job, however."

"See," said Le Bihan, holding out the scroll to me, "it is
signed, 'l'Abbé Sorgue.'"

I glanced curiously over the paper.

"It must be the Black Priest," I said. "He was the only
man who wrote in the Breton language. This is a wonderfully interesting discovery, for now, at last, the mystery
of the Black Priest's disappearance is cleared up. You will,
of course, send this scroll to Paris, Le Bihan?"

"No," said the mayor obstinately, "it shall be buried in
the pit below where the rest of the Black Priest lies."

I looked at him and recognized that argument would be
useless. But still I said, "It will be a loss to history,
Monsieur Le Bihan."

"All the worse for history, then," said the enlightened
Mayor of St. Gildas.

We had sauntered back to the gravel pit while speaking.
The men of Bannalec were carrying the bones of the
English soldiers toward the St. Gildas cemetery, on the
cliffs to the east, where already a knot of white-coiffed
women stood in attitudes of prayer; and I saw the sombre
robe of a priest among the crosses of the little graveyard.

"They were thieves and assassins; they are dead now,"
muttered Max Fortin.

"Respect the dead," repeated the Mayor of St. Gildas,
looking after the Bannalec men.

"It was written in that scroll that Marie Trevec, of
Groix Island, was cursed by the priest—she and her descendants," I said, touching Le Bihan on the arm. "There
was a Marie Trevec who married an Yves Trevec of St.
Gildas—"

"It is the same," said Le Bihan, looking at me obliquely.

"Oh!" said I; "then they were ancestors of my wife."

"Do you fear the curse?" asked Le Bihan.

"What?" I laughed.

"There was the case of the Purple Emperor," said Max Fortin timidly.

Startled for a moment, I faced him, then shrugged my shoulders and kicked at a smooth bit of rock which lay near the edge of the pit, almost embedded in gravel.

"Do you suppose the Purple Emperor drank himself crazy because he was descended from Marie Trevec?" I asked contemptuously.

"Of course not," said Max Fortin hastily.

"Of course not," piped the mayor. "I only— Hello! what's that you're kicking?"

"What?" said I, glancing down, at the same time involuntarily giving another kick. The smooth bit of rock dislodged itself and rolled out of the loosened gravel at my feet.

"The thirty-ninth skull!" I exclaimed. "By jingo, it's the noddle of the Black Priest! See! There is the arrowhead branded on the front!"

The mayor stepped back. Max Fortin also retreated. There was a pause, during which I looked at them, and they looked anywhere but at me.

"I don't like it," said the mayor at last, in a husky, high voice. "I don't like it! The scroll says he will come back to St. Gildas when his remains are disturbed. I—I don't like it, Monsieur Darrel—"

"Bosh!" said I; "the poor wicked devil is where he can't get out. For Heaven's sake, Le Bihan, what is this stuff you are talking in the year of grace 1896?"

The mayor gave me a look.

"And he says 'Englishman.' You are an Englishman, Monsieur Darrel," he announced.

"You know better. You know I'm an American."

"It's all the same," said the Mayor of St. Gildas, obstinately.

"No, it isn't!" I answered, much exasperated, and deliberately pushed the skull till it rolled into the bottom of the gravel pit below.

"Cover it up," said I; "bury the scroll with it too, if you insist, but I think you ought to send it to Paris. Don't look so gloomy, Fortin, unless you believe in were-wolves and ghosts. Hey! what the—what the devil's the matter with you, anyway? What are you staring at, Le Bihan?"

"Come, come," muttered the mayor in a low, tremulous

voice, "it's time we got out of this. Did you see? Did you see, Fortin?"

"I saw," whispered Max Fortin, pallid with fright.

The two men were almost running across the sunny pasture now, and I hastened after them, demanding to know what was the matter.

"Matter!" chattered the mayor, gasping with exasperation and terror. "The skull is rolling uphill again!" and he burst into a terrific gallop. Max Fortin followed close behind.

I watched them stampeding across the pasture, then turned toward the gravel pit, mystified, incredulous. The skull was lying on the edge of the pit, exactly where it had been before I pushed it over the edge. For a second I stared at it; a singular chilly feeling crept up my spinal column, and I turned and walked away, sweat starting from the root of every hair on my head. Before I had gone twenty paces the absurdity of the whole thing struck me. I halted, hot with shame and annoyance, and retraced my steps.

There lay the skull.

"I rolled a stone down instead of the skull," I muttered to myself. Then with the butt of my gun I pushed the skull over the edge of the pit and watched it roll to the bottom; and as it struck the bottom of the pit, Mome, my dog, suddenly whipped his tail between his legs, whimpered, and made off across the moor.

"Mome!" I shouted, angry and astonished; but the dog only fled the faster, and I ceased calling from sheer surprise.

"What the mischief is the matter with that dog?" I thought. He had never before played me such a trick.

Mechanically I glanced into the pit, but I could not see the skull. I looked down. The skull lay at my feet again, touching them.

"Good heavens!" I stammered, and struck at it blindly with my gunstock. The ghastly thing flew into the air, whirling over and over, and rolled down the sides of the pit to the bottom. Breathlessly I stared at it, then confused and scarcely comprehending, I stepped back from the pit, still facing it, one, ten, twenty paces, my eyes almost starting from my head, as though I expected to see the thing roll up from the bottom of the pit under my very gaze. At last I turned my back to the pit and strode out across the gorse-covered moorland toward my home. As I reached the road that winds from St. Gildas to St. Julien I gave one hasty glance at the pit over my shoulder. The sun shone hot on the sod about the excavation. There was something white and bare and round on the turf at the edge of the pit. It might have been a stone; there were plenty of them lying about.

II

When I entered my garden I saw Mome sprawling on the stone doorstep. He eyed me sideways and flopped his tail.

"Are you not mortified, you idiot dog?" I said, looking about the upper windows for Lys.

Mome rolled over on his back and raised one deprecating forepaw, as though to ward off calamity.

"Don't act as though I was in the habit of beating you to death," I said, disgusted. I had never in my life raised whip to the brute. "But you are a fool dog," I continued. "No, you needn't come to be babied and wept over; Lys can do that, if she insists, but I am ashamed of you, and you can go to the devil."

Mome slunk off into the house, and I followed, mounting directly to my wife's boudoir. It was empty.

"Where has she gone?" I said, looking hard at Mome, who had followed me. "Oh! I see you don't know. Don't pretend you do. Come off that lounge! Do you think Lys wants tan-coloured hairs all over her lounge?"

I rang the bell for Catherine and 'Fine, but they didn't know where "madame" had gone; so I went into my room, bathed, exchanged my somewhat grimy shooting clothes for a suit of warm, soft knickerbockers, and, after lingering some extra moments over my toilet—for I was particular, now that I had married Lys—I went down to the garden and took a chair out under the fig-trees.

"Where can she be?" I wondered. Mome came sneaking out to be comforted, and I forgave him for Lys's sake, whereupon he frisked.

"You bounding cur," said I, "now what on earth started you off across the moor? If you do it again I'll push you along with a charge of dust shot."

As yet I had scarcely dared think about the ghastly hallucination of which I had been a victim, but now I faced it squarely, flushing a little with mortification at the thought of my hasty retreat from the gravel pit.

"To think," I said aloud, "that those old woman's tales of Max Fortin and Le Bihan should have actually made me see what didn't exist at all! I lost my nerve like a schoolboy in a dark bedroom." For I knew now that I had mistaken a round stone for a skull each time, and had pushed a couple of big pebbles into the pit instead of the skull itself.

"By jingo!" said I, "I'm nervous; my liver must be in a devil of a condition if I see such things when I'm awake! Lys will know what to give me."

I felt mortified and irritated and sulky, and thought disgustedly of Le Bihan and Max Fortin.

But after a while I ceased speculating, dismissed the mayor, the chemist, and the skull from my mind, and smoked pensively, watching the sun low dipping in the western ocean and moorland; a wistful, restless happiness filled my heart, the happiness that all men know—all men who have loved.

Slowly the purple mist crept out over the sea; the cliffs darkened; the forest was shrouded.

Suddenly the sky above burned with the afterglow, and the world was alight again.

Cloud after cloud caught the rose dye; the cliffs were tinted with it; moor and pasture, heather and forest burned and pulsated with the gentle flush. I saw the gulls turning and tossing above the sand bar, their snowy wings tipped with pink; I saw the sea swallows sheering the surface of the still river, stained to its placid depths with warm reflections of the clouds. The twitter of drowsy hedge birds broke out in the stillness; a salmon rolled its shining side above tide-water.

The interminable monotone of the ocean intensified the silence. I sat motionless, holding my breath as one who listens to the first low rumble of an organ. All at once the pure whistle of a nightingale cut the silence, and the first moonbeam silvered the wastes of mist-hung waters.

I raised my head.

Lys stood before me in the garden.

When we had kissed each other, we linked arms and moved up and down the gravel walks, watching the moonbeams sparkle on the sand bar as the tide ebbed and ebbed. The broad beds of white pinks about us were atremble with hovering white moths; the October roses hung all abloom, perfuming the salt wind.

"Sweetheart," I said, "where is Yvonne? Has she promised to spend Christmas with us?"

"Yes, Dick; she drove me down from Plougat this afternoon. She sent her love to you. I am not jealous. What did you shoot?"

"A hare and four partridges. They are in the gun room. I told Catherine not to touch them until you had seen them."

Now I suppose I knew that Lys could not be particularly enthusiastic over game or guns; but she pretended she was, and always scornfully denied that it was for my sake and not for the pure love of sport. So she dragged me off to inspect the rather meager game bag, and she paid me pretty compliments and gave a little cry of delight and pity as I lifted the enormous hare out of the sack by his ears.

"He'll eat no more of our lettuce," I said, attempting to justify the assassination.

"Unhappy little bunny—and what a beauty! O Dick, you are a splendid shot, are you not?"

I evaded the question and hauled out a partridge.

"Poor little dead things!" said Lys in a whisper; "it seems a pity—doesn't it, Dick? But then you are so clever—"

"We'll have them broiled," I said guardedly; "tell Catherine."

Catherine came in to take away the game, and presently 'Fine Lelocard, Lys's maid, announced dinner, and Lys tripped away to her boudoir.

I stood an instant contemplating her blissfully, thinking, "My boy, you're the happiest fellow in the world—you're in love with your wife!"

I walked into the dining room, beamed at the plates, walked out again; met Tregunc in the hallway, beamed on him; glanced into the kitchen, beamed at Catherine, and went upstairs, still beaming.

Before I could knock at Lys's door it opened, and Lys came hastily out. When she saw me she gave a little cry of relief, and nestled close to my breast.

"There is something peering in at my window," she said.

"What!" I cried angrily.

"A man, I think, disguised as a priest, and he has a mask on. He must have climbed up by the bay tree."

I was down the stairs and out of doors in no time. The moonlit garden was absolutely deserted. Tregunc came up, and together we searched the hedge and shrubbery around the house and out to the road.

"Jean Marie," said I at length, "loose my bulldog—he knows you—and take your supper on the porch where you can watch. My wife says the fellow is disguised as a priest, and wears a mask."

Tregunc showed his white teeth in a smile. "He will not care to venture in here again, I think, Monsieur Darrel."

I went back and found Lys seated quietly at the table.

"The soup is ready, dear," she said. "Don't worry; it was only some foolish lout from Bannalec. No one in St. Gildas or St. Julien would do such a thing."

I was too exasperated to reply at first, but Lys treated it as a stupid joke, and after a while I began to look at it in that light.

Lys told me about Yvonne, and reminded me of my promise to have Herbert Stuart down to meet her.

"You wicked diplomat!" I protested. "Herbert is in Paris, and hard at work for the Salon."

"Don't you think he might spare a week to flirt with the prettiest girl in Finisterre?" inquired Lys innocently.

"Prettiest girl! Not much!" I said.

"Who is, then?" urged Lys.

I laughed a trifle sheepishly.

"I suppose you mean me, Dick," said Lys, coloring up.

"Now I bore you, don't I?"

"Bore me? Ah, no, Dick."

After coffee and cigarettes were served I spoke about Tregunc, and Lys approved.

"Poor Jean! He will be glad, won't he? What a dear fellow you are!"

"Nonsense," said I; "we need a gardener; you said so yourself, Lys."

But Lys leaned over and kissed me, and then bent down and hugged Mome, who whistled through his nose in sentimental appreciation.

"I am a very happy woman," said Lys.

"Mome was a very bad dog today," I observed.

"Poor Mome!" said Lys, smiling.

When dinner was over and Mome lay snoring before the blaze—for the October nights are often chilly in Finisterre—Lys curled up in the chimney corner with her embroidery, and gave me a swift glance from under her drooping lashes.

"You look like a schoolgirl, Lys," I said teasingly. "I don't believe you are sixteen yet."

She pushed back her heavy burnished hair thoughtfully. Her wrist was as white as surf foam.

"Have you been married four years? I don't believe it," I said.

She gave me another swift glance and touched the embroidery on her knee, smiling faintly.

"I see," said I, also smiling at the embroidered garment. "Do you think it will fit?"

"Fit?" repeated Lys. Then she laughed.

"And," I persisted, "are you perfectly sure that you —er—we shall need it?"

"Perfectly," said Lys. A delicate color touched her cheeks and neck. She held up the little garment, all fluffy with misty lace and wrought with quaint embroidery.

"It is very gorgeous," said I; "don't use your eyes too much, dearest. May I smoke a pipe?"

"Of course," she said, selecting a skein of pale blue silk.

For a while I sat and smoked in silence, watching her slender fingers among the tinted silks and thread of gold.

Presently she spoke. "What did you say your crest is, Dick?"

"My crest? Oh, something or other rampant on a something or other—"

"Dick!"

"Dearest?"

"Don't be flippant."

"But I really forget. It's an ordinary crest; everybody in New York has them. No family should be without 'em."

"You are disagreeable, Dick. Send Josephine upstairs for my album."

"Are you going to put that crest on the—the—whatever it is?"

"I am; and my own crest, too."

I thought of the Purple Emperor and wondered a little.

"You didn't know I had one, did you?" she smiled.

"What is it?" I replied evasively.

"You shall see. Ring for Josephine."

I rang, and, when 'Fine appeared, Lys gave her some orders in a low voice, and Josephine trotted away, bobbing her white-coiffed head with a *"Bien, madame!"*

After a few minutes she returned, bearing a tattered, musty volume, from which the gold and blue had mostly disappeared.

I took the book in my hands and examined the ancient emblazoned covers.

"Lilies!" I exclaimed.

"Fleur-de-lis," said my wife demurely.

"Oh," said I, astonished, and opened the book.

"You have never before seen this book?" asked Lys, with a touch of malice in her eyes.

"You know I haven't. Hello! what's this? Oho! So there should be a *de* before Trevec? Lys de Trevec? Then why in the world did the Purple Emperor—"

"Dick!" cried Lys.

"All right," said I. "Shall I read about the Sieur de Trevec who rode to Saladin's tent alone to seek for medicine for St. Louis? Or shall I read about—what is it? Oh, here it is, all down in black and white—about the Marquis de Trevec who drowned himself before Alva's eyes rather than surrender the banner of the fleur-de-lis to Spain? It's all written here. But, dear, how about that soldier named Trevec, who was killed in the old fort on the cliff yonder?"

"He dropped the *de*, and the Trevecs since then have been Republicans," said Lys—"all except me."

"That's quite right," said I; "it is time that we Republicans should agree upon some feudal system. My dear, I drink to the king!" and I raised my wine-glass and looked at Lys.

"To the king," said Lys, flushing. She smoothed out the tiny garment on her knees; she touched the glass with her lips; her eyes were very sweet. I drained the glass to the king.

After a silence, I said, "I will tell the king stories. His Majesty shall be amused."

"His Majesty," repeated Lys softly.

"Or hers," I laughed. "Who knows?"

"Who knows?" murmured Lys, with a gentle sigh.

"I know some stories about Jack the Giant-Killer," I announced. "Do you, Lys?"

"I? No, not about a giant-killer, but I know all about the were-wolf, and Jeanne-la-Flamme, and the Man in Purple Tatters, and—O dear me! I know lots more."

"You are very wise," said I. "I shall teach his Majesty English."

"And I Breton," cried Lys jealously.

"I shall bring playthings to the king," said I—"big green lizards from the gorge, little gray mullets to swim in glass globes, baby rabbits from the forest of Kerselec—"

"And I," said Lys, "will bring the first primrose, the first branch of aubepine, the first jonquil, to the king— my king."

"Our king," said I; and there was peace in Finisterre.

I lay back, idly turning the leaves of the curious old volume.

"I am looking," said I, "for the crest."

"The crest, dear? It is a priest's head with an arrow-shaped mark on the forehead, on a field—"

I sat up and stared at my wife.

"Dick, whatever is the matter?" she smiled. "The story is there in that book. Do you care to read it? No? Shall I tell it to you? Well, then: It happened in the third crusade. There was a monk whom men called the Black Priest. He turned apostate, and sold himself to the enemies of Christ. A Sieur de Trevec burst into the Saracen camp, at the head of only one hundred lances, and carried the Black Priest away out of the very midst of their army."

"So that is how you come by the crest," I said quietly; but I thought of the branded skull in the gravel pit, and wondered.

"Yes," said Lys. "The Sieur de Trevec cut the Black Priest's head off, but first he branded him with an arrow mark on the forehead. The book says it was a pious action, and the Sieur de Trevec got great merit by it. But I think it was cruel, the branding," she sighed.

"Did you ever hear of any other Black Priest?"

"Yes. There was one in the last century, here in St. Gildas. He cast a white shadow in the sun. He wrote in the Breton language. Chronicles, too, I believe. I never saw them. His name was the same as that of the old chronicler, and of the other priest, Jacques Sorgue. Some said he was a lineal descendant of the traitor. Of course the first Black Priest was bad enough for anything. But if he did have a child, it need not have been the ancestor of the last Jacques Sorgue. They say this one was a holy man. They say he was so good he was not allowed to die, but was caught up to heaven one day," added Lys, with believing eyes.

I smiled.

"But he disappeared," persisted Lys.

"I'm afraid his journey was in another direction," I said jestingly, and thoughtlessly told her the story of the morning. I had utterly forgotten the masked man at her window, but before I finished I remembered him fast enough, and realized what I had done as I saw her face whiten.

"Lys," I urged tenderly, "that was only some clumsy clown's trick. You said so yourself. You are not superstitious, my dear?"

Her eyes were on mine. She slowly drew the little gold cross from her bosom and kissed it. But her lips trembled as they pressed the symbol of faith.

III

About nine o'clock the next morning, I walked into the Groix Inn and sat down at the long discolored oaken table, nodding good-day to Marianne Brupère, who in turn bobbed her white coiffe at me.

"My clever Bannalec maid," said I, "what is good for a stirrup-cup at the Groix Inn?"

"Schist?" she inquired in Breton.

"With a dash of red wine, then," I replied.

She brought the delicious Quimperle cider, and I poured a little Bordeaux into it. Marianne watched me with laughing black eyes.

"What makes your cheeks so red, Marianne?" I asked. "Has Jean Marie been here?"

"We are to be married, Monsieur Darrel." She laughed.

"Ah! Since when has Jean Marie Tregunc lost his head?"

"His head? Oh, Monsieur Darrel—his heart, you mean!"

"So I do," said I. "Jean Marie is a practical fellow."

"It is all due to your kindness——" began the girl, but I raised my hand and held up the glass.

"It's due to himself. To your happiness, Marianne"; and I took a hearty draught of the *schist*. "Now," said I, "tell me where I can find Le Bihan and Max Fortin."

"Monsieur Le Bihan and Monsieur Fortin are above in the broad room. I believe they are examining the Red Admiral's effects."

"To send them to Paris? Oh, I know. May I go up, Marianne?"

"And God go with you." The girl smiled.

When I knocked at the door of the broad room above little Max Fortin opened it. Dust covered his spectacles and nose; his hat, with the tiny velvet ribbons fluttering, was all awry.

"Come in, Monsieur Darrel," he said; "the mayor and I

are packing up the effects of the Purple Emperor and of the poor Red Admiral."

"The collections?" I asked, entering the room. "You must be very careful in packing those butterfly cases; the slightest jar might break wings and antennae, you know."

Le Bihan shook hands with me and pointed to the great pile of boxes.

"They're all cork lined," he said, "but Fortin and I are putting felt around each box. The Entomological Society of Paris pays the freight."

The combined collections of the Red Admiral and the Purple Emperor made a magnificent display.

I lifted and inspected case after case set with gorgeous butterflies and moths, each specimen carefully labelled with the name in Latin. There were cases filled with crimson tiger moths all aflame with color; cases devoted to the common yellow butterflies; symphonies in orange and pale yellow; cases of soft gray and dun-colored sphinx moths; and cases of garish nettlebred butterflies of the numerous family of *Vanessa*.

All alone in a great case by itself was pinned the purple emperor, the Apatura Iris, that fatal specimen that had given the Purple Emperor his name and quietus.

I remembered the butterfly, and stood looking at it with bent eyebrows.

Le Bihan glanced up from the floor where he was nailing down the lid of a box full of cases.

"It is settled then," said he, "that madame, your wife, gives the Purple Emperor's entire collection to the city of Paris?"

I nodded.

"Without accepting anything for it?"

"It is a gift," I said.

"Including the purple emperor there in the case? That butterfly is worth a great deal of money," persisted Le Bihan.

"You don't suppose that we would wish to sell that specimen, do you?" I answered a trifle sharply.

"If I were you I should destroy it," said the mayor in his high-pitched voice.

"That would be nonsense," said I—"like your burying the brass cylinder and scroll yesterday."

I looked at Max Fortin, who immediately avoided my eyes.

"You are a pair of superstitious old women," said I,

digging my hands into my pockets; "you swallow every nursery tale that is invented."

"What of it?" said Le Bihan sulkily; "there's more truth than lies in most of 'em."

"Oh!" I sneered. "Does the Mayor of St. Gildas and St. Julien believe in the Loup-garou?"

"No, not in the Loup-garou."

"In what, then—Jeanne-la-Flamme?"

"That," said Le Bihan with conviction, "is history."

"The devil it is!" said I; "and perhaps, monsieur the mayor, your faith in giants is unimpaired?"

"There were giants—everybody knows it," growled Max Fortin.

"And you a chemist!" I observed scornfully.

"Listen, Monsieur Darrel," squeaked Le Bihan; "you know yourself that the Purple Emperor was a scientific man. Now suppose I should tell you that he always refused to include in his collection a Death's Messenger?"

"A what?" I exclaimed.

"You know what I mean—that moth that flies by night; some call it the Death's Head, but in St. Gildas we call it 'Death's Messenger.' "

"Oh!" said I, "you mean that big sphinx moth that is commonly called the 'death's-head moth.' Why the mischief should the people here call it death's messenger?"

"For hundred of years it has been known as death's messenger in St. Gildas," said Max Fortin. "Even Froissart speaks of it in his commentaries on Jacques Sorgue's Chronicles. The book is in your library."

"Sorgue? And who is Jacques Sorgue? I never read his book."

"Jacques Sorgue was the son of some unfrocked priest—I forget. It was during the crusades."

"Good Heavens!" I burst out, "I've been hearing of nothing but crusades and priests and death and sorcery ever since I kicked that skull into the gravel pit, and I am tired of it, I tell you frankly. One would think we lived in the dark ages. Do you know what year of our Lord it is, Le Bihan?"

"Eighteen hundred and ninety-six," replied the mayor.

"And yet you two hulking men are afraid of a death's-head moth."

"I don't care to have one fly into the window," said Max Fortin; "it means evil to the house and the people in it."

"God alone knows why he marked one of His creatures

with a yellow death's head on the back," observed Le Bihan piously, "but I take it that He meant it as a warning; and I propose to profit by it," he added triumphantly.

"See here, Le Bihan," I said; "by a stretch of imagination one can make out a skull on the thorax of a certain big sphinx moth. What of it?"

"It is a bad thing to touch," said the mayor, wagging his head.

"It squeaks when handled," added Max Fortin.

"Some creatures squeak all the time," I observed, looking hard at Le Bihan.

"Pigs," added the mayor.

"Yes, and asses," I replied. "Listen, Le Bihan; do you mean to tell me that you saw that skull roll uphill yesterday?"

The mayor shut his mouth tightly and picked up his hammer.

"Don't be obstinate," I said; "I asked you a question."

"And I refuse to answer," snapped Le Bihan. "Fortin saw what I saw; let him talk about it."

I looked searchingly at the little chemist.

"I don't say that I saw it actually roll up out of the pit, all by itself," said Fortin with a shiver, "but—but then, how did it come up out of the pit, if it didn't roll up all by itself?"

"It didn't come up at all; that was a yellow cobblestone that you mistook for the skull again," I replied. "You are nervous, Max."

"A—a very curious cobblestone, Monsieur Darrel," said Fortin.

"I also was a victim of the same hallucination," I continued, "and I regret to say that I took the trouble to roll two innocent cobblestones into the gravel pit, imagining each time that it was the skull I was rolling."

"It was," observed Le Bihan with a morose shrug.

"It just shows," said I, ignoring the mayor's remark, "how easy it is to fix up a train of coincidences so that the result seems to savour of the supernatural. Now, last night my wife imagined that she saw a priest in a mask peer in at her window—"

Fortin and Le Bihan scrambled hastily from their knees, dropping hammer and nails.

"W-h-a-t—what's that?" demanded the mayor.

I repeated what I had said. Max Fortin turned livid.

"My God!" muttered Le Bihan, "the Black Priest is in St. Gildas!"

"D-don't you—you know the old prophecy?" stammered Fortin; "Froissart quotes it from Jacques Sorgue:

> 'When the Black Priest rises from the dead,
> St. Gildas folk shall shriek in bed;
> When the Black Priest rises from his grave,
> May the good God St. Gildas save!' "

"Aristide Le Bihan," I said angrily, "and you, Max Fortin, I've got enough of this nonsense! Some foolish lout from Bannalec has been in St. Gildas playing tricks to frighten old fools like you. If you have nothing better to talk about than nursery legends I'll wait until you come to your senses. Good morning." And I walked out, more disturbed than I cared to acknowledge to myself.

The day had become misty and overcast. Heavy, wet clouds hung in the east. I heard the surf thundering against the cliffs, and the gray gulls squealed as they tossed and turned high in the sky. The tide was creeping across the river sands, higher, higher, and I saw the seaweed floating on the beach, and the *lançons* springing from the foam, silvery threadlike flashes in the gloom. Curlew were flying up the river in twos and threes; the timid sea swallows skimmed across the moors toward some quiet, lonely pool, safe from the coming tempest. In every hedge field birds were gathering, huddling together, twittering restlessly.

When I reached the cliffs I sat down, resting my chin on my clenched hands. Already a vast curtain of rain, sweeping across the ocean miles away, hid the island of Groix. To the east, behind the white semaphore on the hills, black clouds crowded up over the horizon. After a little thunder boomed, dull, distant, and slender skeins of lightning unravelled across the crest of the coming storm. Under the cliff at my feet the surf rushed foaming over the shore, and the *lançons* jumped and skipped and quivered until they seemed to be but the reflections of the meshed lightning.

I turned to the east. It was raining over Groix, it was raining at Sainte Barbe, it was raining now at the semaphore. High in the storm whirl a few gulls pitched; a nearer cloud trailed veils of rain in its wake; the sky was spattered with lightning; the thunder boomed.

As I rose to go, a cold raindrop fell upon the back of my hand, and another, and yet another on my face. I gave a last glance at the sea, where the waves were bursting into strange white shapes that seemed to fling out menacing arms toward me. Then something moved on the cliff, something black as the black rock it clutched—a filthy cormorant, craning its hideous head at the sky.

Slowly I plodded homeward across the sombre moorland, where the gorse stems glimmered with a dull metallic green, and the heather, no longer violet and purple, hung drenched and dun-colored among the dreary rocks. The wet turf creaked under my heavy boots, the black-thorn scraped and grated against my knee and elbow. Over all lay a strange light, pallid, ghastly, where the sea spray whirled across the landscape and drove into my face until it grew numb with the cold. In broad bands, rank after rank, billow on billow, the rain burst out across the endless moors, and yet there was no wind to drive it at such a pace.

Lys stood at the door as I turned into the garden, motioning me to hasten; and then for the first time I became conscious that I was soaked to the skin.

"How ever in the world did you come to stay out when such a storm threatened?" she said. "Oh, you are dripping! Go quickly and change; I have laid your warm underwear on the bed, Dick."

I kissed my wife, and went upstairs to change my dripping clothes for something more comfortable.

When I returned to the morning room there was a driftwood fire on the hearth, and Lys sat in the chimney corner embroidering.

"Catherine tells me that the fishing fleet from Lorient is out. Do you think they are in danger, dear?" asked Lys, raising her blue eyes to mine as I entered.

"There is no wind, and there will be no sea," said I, looking out of the window. Far across the moor I could see the black cliffs looming in the mist.

"How it rains!" murmured Lys; "come to the fire, Dick."

I threw myself on the fur rug, my hands in my pockets, my head on Lys's knees.

"Tell me a story," I said. "I feel like a boy of ten."

Lys raised a finger to her scarlet lips. I always waited for her to do that.

"Will you be very still, then?" she said.

"Still as death."

"Death," echoed a voice, very softly.

"Did you speak, Lys?" I asked, turning so that I could see her face.

"No; did you, Dick?"

"Who said 'death'?" I asked, startled.

"Death," echoed a voice, softly.

I sprang up and looked around. Lys rose too, her needles and embroidery falling to the floor. She seemed about to faint, leaning heavily on me, and I led her to the window and opened it a little way to give her air. As I did so the chain lightning split the zenith, the thunder crashed, and a sheet of rain swept into the room, driving with it something that fluttered—something that flapped, and squeaked and beat upon the rug with soft, moist wings.

We bent over it together, Lys clinging to me, and we saw that it was a death's-head moth drenched with rain.

The dark day passed slowly as we sat beside the fire, hand in hand, her head against my breast, speaking of sorrow and mystery and death. For Lys believed that there were things on earth that none might understand, things that must be nameless forever and ever, until God rolls up the scroll of life and all is ended. We spoke of hope and fear and faith, and the mystery of the saints; we spoke of the beginning and the end, of the shadow of sin, of omens, and of love. The moth still lay on the floor, quivering its sombre wings in the warmth of the fire, the skull and the ribs clearly etched upon its neck and body.

"It is a messenger of death to this house," I said, "why should we fear, Lys?"

"Death should be welcome to those who love God," murmured Lys, and she drew the cross from her breast and kissed it.

"The moth might die if I threw it out into the storm," I said after a silence.

"Let it remain," sighed Lys.

Late that night my wife lay sleeping, and I sat beside her bed and read in the Chronicle of Jacques Sorgue. I shaded the candle, but Lys grew restless, and finally I took the book down into the morning room, where the ashes of the fire rustled and whitened on the hearth.

The death's-head moth lay on the rug before the fire where I had left it. At first I thought it was dead, but, when I looked closer I saw a lambent fire in its amber eyes. The straight white shadow it cast across the floor wavered as the candle flickered.

The pages of the Chronicle of Jacques Sorgue were damp and sticky; the illuminated gold and blue initials left flakes of azure and gilt where my hand brushed them.

"It is not paper at all; it is thin parchment," I said to myself; and I held the discolored page close to the candle flame and read, translating laboriously:

"I, Jacques Sorgue, saw all these things. And I saw the Black Mass celebrated in the chapel of St. Gildas-on-the-Cliff. And it was said by the Abbé Sorgue, my kinsman: for which deadly sin the apostate priest was seized by the most noble Marquis of Plougastel and by him condemned to be burned with hot irons, until his seared soul quit its body and fly to its master the devil. But when the Black Priest lay in the crypt of Plougastel, his master Satan came at night and set him free, and carried him across land and sea to Mahmoud, which is Soldan or Saladin. And I, Jacques Sorgue, travelling afterward by sea, beheld with my own eyes my kinsman, the Black Priest of St. Gildas, borne along in the air upon a vast black wing, which was the wing of his master Satan. And this was seen also by two men of the crew."

I turned the page. The wings of the moth on the floor began to quiver. I read on and on, my eyes blurring under the shifting candle flame. I read of battles and of saints, and I learned how the great Soldan made his pact with Satan, and then I came to the Sieur de Trevec, and read how he seized the Black Priest in the midst of Saladin's tents and carried him away and cut off his head, first branding him on the forehead. "And before he suffered," said the Chronicle, "he cursed the Sieur de Trevec and his descendants, and he said he would surely return to St. Gildas. 'For the violence you do to me, I will do violence to you. For the evil I suffer at your hands, I will work evil on you and your descendants. Woe to your children, Sieur de Trevec!' " There was a whirr, a beating of strong wings, and my candle flashed up as in a sudden breeze. A humming filled the room; the great moth darted hither and thither, beating, buzzing, on ceiling and wall. I flung down my book and stepped forward. Now it lay fluttering upon the window sill, and for a moment I had it under my hand, but the thing squeaked and I shrank back. Then suddenly it darted across the candle flame; the light flared and went out, and at the same moment a shadow moved in the darkness outside. I raised my eyes to the window. A masked face was peering in at me.

Quick as thought I whipped out my revolver and fired every cartridge, but the face advanced beyond the window, the glass melting away before it like mist, and through the smoke of my revolver I saw something creep swiftly into the room. Then I tried to cry out, but the thing was at my throat, and I fell backward among the ashes of the hearth.

* * *

When my eyes unclosed I was lying on the hearth, my head among the cold ashes. Slowly I got on my knees, rose painfully, and groped my way to a chair. On the floor lay my revolver, shining in the pale light of early morning. My mind clearing by degrees, I looked, shuddering, at the window. The glass was unbroken. I stooped stiffly, picked up my revolver and opened the cylinder. Every cartridge had been fired. Mechanically I closed the cylinder and placed the revolver in my pocket. The book, the Chronicles of Jacques Sorgue, lay on the table beside me, and as I started to close it I glanced at the page. It was all splashed with rain, and the lettering had run, so that the page was merely a confused blur of gold and red and black. As I stumbled toward the door I cast a fearful glance over my shoulder. The death's-head moth crawled shivering on the rug.

IV

The sun was about three hours high. I must have slept, for I was aroused by the sudden gallop of horses under our window. People were shouting and calling in the road. I sprang up and opened the sash. Le Bihan was there, an image of helplessness, and Max Fortin stood beside him, polishing his glasses. Some gendarmes had just arrived from Quimperle, and I could hear them around the corner of the house, stamping, and rattling their sabres and carbines, as they led their horses into my stable.

Lys sat up, murmuring half-sleepy, half-anxious questions.

"I don't know," I answered. "I am going out to see what it means."

"It is like the day they came to arrest you," Lys said, giving me a troubled look. But I kissed her, and laughed at her until she smiled too. Then I flung on coat and cap, and hurried down the stairs.

The first person I saw standing in the road was the Brigadier Durand.

"Hello!" said I, "have you come to arrest me again? What the devil is all this fuss about, anyway?"

"We were telegraphed for an hour ago," said Durand briskly, "and for a sufficient reason, I think. Look here, Monsieur Darrel!"

He pointed to the ground almost under my feet.

"Good Heavens!" I cried, "where did that puddle of blood come from?"

"That's what I want to know, Monsieur Darrel. Max Fortin found it at daybreak. See, it's splashed all over the grass, too. A trail of it leads into your garden, across the flower beds to your very window, the one that opens from the morning room. There is another trail leading from this spot across the road to the cliffs, then to the gravel pit, and thence across the moor to the forest of Kerselec. We are going to mount in a minute and search the bosquets. Will you join us? *Bon Dieu!* but the fellow bled like an ox. Max Fortin says it's human blood, or I should not have believed it."

The little chemist of Quimperle came up at that moment, rubbing his glasses with a colored handkerchief.

"Yes, it is human blood," he said, "but one thing puzzles me: the corpuscles are yellow. I never saw any human blood before with yellow corpuscles. But your English Doctor Thompson asserts that he has—"

"Well, it's human blood, anyway—isn't it?" insisted Durand impatiently.

"Ye-es," admitted Max Fortin.

"Then it's my business to trail it," said the big gendarme, and he called his men and gave the order to mount.

"Did you hear anything last night?" asked Durand of me.

"I heard the rain. I wonder the rain did not wash away these traces."

"They must have come after the rain ceased. See this thick splash, how it lies over and weighs down the wet grass blades. Pah!"

It was a heavy, evil-looking clot, and I stepped back from it, my throat closing in disgust.

"My theory," said the brigadier, "is this: Some of those Biribi fishermen, probably the Icelanders, got an extra glass of cognac into their hides and quarreled on the road. Some of them were slashed, and staggered to your house. But there is only one trail—and yet, and yet, how could all that blood come from only one person? Well, the wounded man, let us say, staggered first to your house and then back here, and he wandered off, drunk and dying, God knows where. That's my theory."

"A very good one," said I calmly. "And you are going to trail him?"

"Yes."

"When?"

"At once. Will you come?"

"Not now. I'll gallop over by-and-bye. You are going to the edge of the Kerselec forest?"

"Yes; you will hear us calling. Are you coming, Max Fortin? And you, Le Bihan? Good; take the dog-cart."

The big gendarme tramped around the corner to the stable and presently returned mounted on a strong gray horse; his sabre shone on his saddle; his pale yellow and white facings were spotless. The little crowd of white-coiffed women with their children fell back, as Durand touched spurs and clattered away followed by his two troopers. Soon after Le Bihan and Max Fortin also departed in the mayor's dingy dog-cart.

"Are you coming?" piped Le Bihan shrilly.

"In a quarter of an hour," I replied, and went back to the house.

When I opened the door of the morning room the death's-head moth was beating its strong wings against the window. For a second I hesitated, then walked over and opened the sash. The creature fluttered out, whirred over the flower beds a moment, then darted across the moorland toward the sea. I called the servants together and questioned them. Josephine, Catherine, Jean Marie Tregunc, not one of them had heard the slightest disturbance during the night. Then I told Jean Marie to saddle my horse, and while I was speaking Lys came down.

"Dearest," I began, going to her.

"You must tell me everything you know, Dick," she interrupted, looking me earnestly in the face.

"But there is nothing to tell—only a drunken brawl, and someone wounded."

"And you are going to ride—where, Dick?"

"Well, over the edge of Kerselec forest. Durand and the mayor, and Max Fortin, have gone on, following a—a trail."

"What trail?"

"Some blood."

"Where did they find it?"

"Out in the road there."

Lys crossed herself.

"Does it come near our house?"

"Yes."

"How near?"

"It comes up to the morning-room window," said I, giving in.

Her hand on my arm grew heavy. "I dreamed last night—"

"So did I—" but I thought of the empty cartridges in my revolver, and stopped suddenly.

"I dreamed that you were in great danger, and I could not move hand or foot to save you; but you had your revolver, and I called out to you to fire—"

"I did fire!" I cried excitedly.

"You—you fired?"

I took her in my arms. "My darling," I said, "something strange has happened—something that I can not understand as yet. But, of course, there is an explanation. Last night I thought I fired at the Black Priest."

"Ah!" gasped Lys.

"Is that what you dreamed?"

"Yes, yes that was it! I begged you to fire—"

"And I did."

Her heart was beating against my breast. I held her close in silence.

"Dick," she said at length, "perhaps you killed the—the thing."

"If it was human I did not miss," I answered grimly. "And it was human," I went on, pulling myself together, ashamed of having so nearly gone to pieces. "Of course, it was human; The whole affair is plain enough. Not a drunken brawl, as Durand thinks; it was a drunken lout's practical joke, for which he has suffered. I suppose I must have filled him pretty full of bullets, and he has crawled away to die in Kerselec forest. It's a terrible affair; I'm sorry I fired so hastily; but that idiot Le Bihan and Max Fortin have been working on my nerves till I am as hysterical as a schoolgirl," I ended angrily.

"You fired—but the window glass was not shattered," said Lys in a low voice.

"Well, the window was open, then. And as for the—the rest—I've got nervous indigestion, and a doctor will settle the Black Priest for me, Lys."

I glanced out of the window at Tregunc waiting with my horse at the gate.

"Dearest, I think I had better go to join Durand and the others."

"I will go too."

"Oh, no!"

"Yes, Dick."

"Don't, Lys."

"I shall suffer every moment you are away."

"The ride is too fatiguing, and we can't tell what unpleasant sight you may come upon. Lys, you don't really think there is anything supernatural in this affair?"

"Dick," she answered gently, "I am a Bretonne." With both arms around my neck, my wife said, "Death is the gift of God. I do not fear it when we are together. But alone—oh, my husband, I should fear a God who could take you away from me!"

We kissed each other soberly, simply, like two children. Then Lys hurried away to change her gown, and I paced up and down the garden waiting for her.

She came, drawing her slender gauntlets on. I swung her into the saddle, gave a hasty order to Jean Marie, and mounted.

Now, to quail under thoughts of terror on a morning like this, with Lys in the saddle beside me, no matter what had happened or might happen, was impossible. Moreover, Mome came sneaking after us. I asked Tregunc to catch him, for I was afraid he might be brained by our horses' hoofs if he followed, but the wily puppy dodged and bolted after Lys, who was trotting along the high-road. "Never mind," I thought; "if he's hit he'll live, for he has no brains to lose."

Lys was waiting for me in the road beside the Shrine of Our Lady of St. Gildas when I joined her. She crossed herself, I doffed my cap, then we shook out our bridles and galloped toward the forest of Kerselec.

We said very little as we rode. I always loved to watch Lys in the saddle. Her exquisite figure and lovely face were the incarnation of youth and grace; her curling hair glistened like threaded gold.

Out of the corner of my eye I saw the spoiled puppy Mome come bounding cheerfully alongside, oblivious of our horses' heels. Our road swung close to the cliffs. A filthy cormorant rose from the black rocks and flapped heavily across our path. Lys's horse reared, but she pulled him down, and pointed at the bird with her riding crop.

"I see," said I; "it seems to be going our way. Curious to see a cormorant in a forest, isn't it?"

"It is a bad sign," said Lys. "You know the Morbihan proverb: 'When the cormorant turns from the sea, Death laughs in the forest, and wise woodsmen build boats.' "

"I wish," said I sincerely, "that there were fewer proverbs in Brittany."

We were in sight of the forest now; across the gorse I could see the sparkle of the gendarmes' trappings, and the glitter of Le Bihan's silver-buttoned jacket. The hedge was low and we took it without difficulty, and trotted across the moor to where Le Bihan and Durand stood gesticulating.

They bowed ceremoniously to Lys as we rode up.

"The trail is horrible—it is a river," said the mayor in his squeaky voice. "Monsieur Darrel, I think perhaps madame would scarcely care to come any nearer."

Lys drew bridle and looked at me.

"It is horrible!" said Durand, walking up beside me; "it looks as though a bleeding regiment had passed this way. The trail winds about there in the thickets; we lose it at times, but we always find it again. I can't understand how one man—no, nor twenty—could bleed like that!"

A halloo, answered by another, sounded from the depths of the forest.

"It's my men; they are following the trail," muttered the brigadier. "God alone knows what is at the end!"

"Shall we gallop back, Lys?" I asked.

"No; let us ride along the western edge of the woods and dismount. The sun is so hot now, and I should like to rest for a moment," she said.

"The western forest is clear of anything disagreeable," said Durand.

"Very well," I answered; "call me, Le Bihan, if you find anything."

Lys wheeled her mare, and I followed across the springy heather, Mome trotting cheerfully in the rear.

We entered the sunny woods about a quarter of a kilometre from where we left Durand. I took Lys from her horse, flung both bridles over a limb, and giving my wife my arm, aided her to a flat mossy rock which overhung a shallow brook gurgling among the beech trees. Lys sat down and drew off her gauntlets. Mome pushed his head into her lap, received an undeserved caress, and came doubtfully toward me. I was weak enough to condone his offense, but I made him lie down at my feet, greatly to his disgust.

I rested my head on Lys's knees looking up at the sky through the crossed branches of the trees.

"I suppose I have killed him," I said. "It shocks me terribly, Lys."

"You could not have known, dear. He may have been a robber, and—if—not— Did—have you ever fired your revolver since that day four years ago, when the Red Admiral's son tried to kill you? But I know you have not."

"No," said I, wondering. "It's a fact, I have not. Why?"

"And don't you remember that I asked you to let me load it for you the day when Yves went away, swearing to kill you and his father?"

"Yes, I do remember. Well?"

"Well, I—I took the cartridges first to St. Gildas chapel and dipped them in holy water. You must not laugh, Dick," said Lys gently, laying her cool hands on my lips.

"Laugh, my darling!"

Overhead the October sky was pale amethyst, and the sunlight burned like orange flame through the yellow leaves of beech and oak. Gnats and midges danced and wavered overhead; a spider dropped from a twig halfway to the ground and hung suspended on the end of his gossamer thread.

"Are you sleepy, dear?" asked Lys, bending over me.

"I am—a little; I scarcely slept two hours last night," I answered.

"You may sleep, if you wish," said Lys, and touched my eyes caressingly.

"Is my head heavy on your knees?" he asked.

"No, Dick."

I was already in a half doze; still I heard the brook

babbling under the beeches and the humming of forest flies overhead. Presently even these were stilled.

The next thing I knew I was sitting bolt upright, my ears ringing with a scream, and I saw Lys cowering beside me, covering her white, set face with both hands.

As I sprang to my feet she cried again and clung to my knees. I saw my dog rush growling into the thicket, then I heard him whimper, and he came backing out, whining, ears flat, tail down. I stooped and disengaged Lys's hand.

"Don't go, Dick!" she cried. "O God, it's the Black Priest!"

In a moment I had leaped across the brook and pushed my way into the thicket. It was empty. I stared about me; I scanned every tree trunk, every bush. Suddenly I saw him. He was seated on a fallen log, his head resting in his hands, his rusty black robe gathered around him. For a moment my hair stirred under my cap; then I recovered my reason, and understood that the man was human and was probably wounded to death. Ay, to death; for there, at my feet, lay the wet trail of blood, over leaves and stones, down into the little hollow, across to the figure in black resting silently under the dark trees.

I saw that he could not escape even if he had the strength, for before him, almost at his very feet, lay a deep, shining swamp.

As I stepped onward my foot broke a twig.

At the sound the figure started a little, then its head fell forward again. Its face was masked. Walking up to the man, I bade him tell where he was wounded.

Durand and the others broke through the thicket at the same moment and hurried to my side.

"Who are you who hide a masked face in a priest's robe?" said the gendarme loudly.

There was no answer.

"See—see the stiff blood all over his robe!" muttered Le Bihan to Fortin.

"He will not speak," said I.

"He may be too badly wounded," whispered Le Bihan.

"I saw him raise his head," I said; "my wife saw him creep up here."

Durand stepped forward and touched the figure.

"Speak!" he said.

"Speak!" quavered Fortin.

Durand waited a moment, then with a sudden upward movement he stripped off the mask and threw the man's head back. We were looking into the eye sockets of a skull.

Durand stood rigid and the mayor shrieked. The skeleton burst out from its rotting robes and collapsed on the ground before us. From between the staring ribs and the grinning teeth spurted a torrent of black blood, showering and shrinking grasses; then the thing shuddered, and fell over into the black ooze of the bog. Little bubbles of iridescent air appeared from the mud; the bones were slowly engulfed, and, as the last fragments sank out of sight, up from the depths and along the bank crept a creature, shiny, shivering, quivering its wings.

It was a death's-head moth.

I wish I had time to tell you how Lys outgrew superstitions—for she never knew the truth about the affair, and she never will know, since she has promised not to read this book. I wish I might tell you about the king and his coronation, and how the coronation robe fitted. I wish that I were able to write how Yvonne and Herbert Stuart rode to a boar hunt in Quimperle, and how the hounds raced the quarry right through the town, overturning three gendarmes, the notary, and an old woman.

But I am becoming very garrulous, and Lys is calling me to come and hear the king say that he is sleepy.

And his highness shall not be kept waiting.

THE MONSTER-MAKER

W. C. Morrow

*That great, lamented magazine of the unusual, WEIRD
TALES, for more than 15 years ran a reprint department
in which they published masterpieces of the macabre
and in later years selections of the most popular stories
from their early issues. Four stories were reprinted by
W. C. Morrow, The Monster-Maker (December, 1928);
His Unconquerable Enemy (August, 1929); The Per-
manent Stiletto (August, 1939) and Over an Absinthe
Bottle (April, 1933). All four were from the author's
only collection of short stories, The Ape The Idiot &
Other People, published by Lippincott, Philadelphia, in
1897 and by Grant Richards, London, in 1898.*

*The persistence of the editor of WEIRD TALES, Farns-
worth Wright, in reprinting W. C. Morrow's stories
was a tribute to a Western author whose feel for the
macabre was one of the most infallible ever developed
in this country. Most of Morrow's stories are either
psychological horror or outright supernatural, but this
one, The Monster-Maker, is science fiction that qualifies
as a masterpiece of horror. The extraordinarily deft
handling of this theme before the turn of the century
is an achievement of the first magnitude. Strangely,
with the recent surgical triumphs of heart, kidney and
liver transplants, this story becomes more effectively believable year by year. Yet it is not a story of anticipating
surgical transplants, which today have so positive and
life-saving a connotation, but rather one of incredible
horror.*

A YOUNG MAN of refined appearance, but evidently suffering great mental distress, presented himself one morning at
the residence of a singular old man, who was known as a
surgeon of remarkable skill. The house was a queer and

primitive brick affair, entirely out of date, and tolerable only in the decayed part of the city in which it stood. It was large, gloomy, and dark, and had long corridors and dismal rooms; and it was absurdly large for the small family—man and wife—that occupied it. The house described, the man is portrayed—but not the woman. He could be agreeable on occasion, but, for all that, he was but animated mystery. His wife was weak, wan, reticent, evidently miserable, and possibly living a life of dread or horror—perhaps witness of repulsive things, subject of anxieties, and victim of fear and tyranny; but there is a great deal of guessing in these assumptions. He was about sixty-five years of age and she about forty. He was lean, tall, and bald, with thin, smooth-shaven face, and very keen eyes; kept always at home, and was slovenly. The man was strong, the woman weak; he dominated, she suffered.

Although he was a surgeon of rare skill, his practice was almost nothing, for it was a rare occurrence that the few who knew of his great ability were brave enough to penetrate the gloom of his house, and when they did so it was with deaf ear turned to sundry ghoulish stories that were whispered concerning him. These were, in great part, but exaggerations of his experiments in vivisection; he was devoted to the science of surgery.

The young man who presented himself on the morning just mentioned was a handsome fellow, yet of evident weak character and unhealthy temperament—sensitive, and easily exalted or depressed. A single glance convinced the surgeon that his visitor was seriously affected in mind, for there was never bolder skull-grin of melancholia, fixed and irremediable.

A stranger would not have suspected any occupancy of the house. The street door—old, warped, and blistered by the sun—was locked and the small, faded-green window blinds were closed. The young man rapped at the door. No answer. He rapped again. Still no sign. He examined a slip of paper, glanced at the number on the house, and then, with the impatience of a child, he furiously kicked the door. There were signs of numerous other such kicks. A response came in the shape of a shuffling footstep in the hall, a turning of the rusty key, and a sharp face that peered through a cautious opening in the door.

'Are you the doctor?' asked the young man.

'Yes, yes! Come in!' briskly replied the master of the house.

The young man entered. The old surgeon closed the door and carefully locked it. 'This way,' he said, advancing to a rickety flight of stairs. The young man followed. The surgeon led the way up the stairs, turned into a narrow musty-smelling corridor at the left, traversed it, rattling the loose boards under his feet, at the farther end opened a door at the right, and beckoned his visitor to enter. The young man found himself in a pleasant room furnished in antique fashion and with hard simplicity.

'Sit down,' said the old man, placing a chair so that its occupant should face a window that looked out upon a dead wall about six feet from the house. He threw open the blind, and a pale light entered. He then seated himself near his visitor and directly facing him, and with a searching look, that had all the power of a microscope, he proceeded to diagnosticate the case.

'Well?' he presently asked.

The young man shifted uneasily in his seat.

'I—I have come to see you,' he finally stammered, 'because I'm in trouble.'

'Ah!'

'Yes; you see, I—that is—I have given it up.'

'Ah!' There was pity added to sympathy in the ejaculation.

'That's it. Given it up,' added the visitor. He took from his pocket a roll of banknotes, and with the utmost deliberation he counted them out upon his knee. 'Five thousand dollars,' he calmly remarked. 'That is for you. It's all I have; but I presume—I imagine—no; that is not the word—*assume*—yes; that's the word—assume that five thousand—is it really that much? Let me count.' He counted again. 'That five thousand dollars is a sufficient fee for what I want you to do.'

The surgeon's lips curled pityingly—perhaps disdainfully also. 'What do you want me to do?' he carelessly inquired.

The young man rose, looked around with a mysterious air, approached the surgeon, and laid the money across his knee. Then he stooped and whispered two words in the surgeon's ear.

These words produced an electric effect. The old man started violently; then, springing to his feet, he caught his visitor angrily, and transfixed him with a look that was as sharp as a knife. His eyes flashed, and he opened his mouth to give utterance to some harsh imprecation, when he suddenly checked himself. The anger left his face, and only pity remained. He relinquished his grasp, picked up the scattered notes, and, offering them to the visitor, slowly said:

'I do not want your money. You are simply foolish. You think you are in trouble. Well, you do not know what trouble is. Your only trouble is that you have not a trace of manhood in your nature. You are merely insane—I shall not say pusillanimous. You should surrender yourself to the authorities, and be sent to a lunatic asylum for proper treatment.'

The young man keenly felt the intended insult, and his eyes flashed dangerously.

'You old dog—you insult me thus!' he cried. 'Grand airs, these, you give yourself! Virtuously indignant, old murderer, you! Don't want my money, eh? When a man comes to you himself and wants it done, you fly into a passion and spurn his money; but let an enemy of his come and pay you, and you are only too willing. How many such jobs have you done in this miserable old hole? It is a good thing for you that the police have not run you down, and brought spade and shovel with them. Do you know what is said of you? Do you think you have kept your windows so closely shut that no sound has ever penetrated beyond them? Where do you keep your infernal implements?'

He had worked himself into a high passion. His voice was hoarse, loud, and rasping. His eyes, bloodshot, started from their sockets. His whole frame twitched, and his fingers writhed. But he was in the presence of a man infinitely his superior. Two eyes, like those of a snake, burned two holes through him. An overmastering, inflexible presence confronted one weak and passionate. The result came.

'Sit down,' commanded the stern voice of the surgeon.

It was the voice of father to child, of master to slave. The fury left the visitor, who, weak and overcome, fell upon a chair.

Meanwhile a peculiar light had appeared in the old surgeon's face, the dawn of a strange idea; a gloomy ray, strayed from the fires of the bottomless pit; the baleful light that illumines the way of the enthusiast. The old man remained a moment in profound abstraction, gleams of eager intelligence bursting momentarily through the cloud

of sombre meditation that covered his face. Then broke
the broad light of a deep, impenetrable determination.
There was something sinister in it, suggesting the sacrifice
of something held sacred. After a struggle, mind had
vanquished conscience.

Taking a piece of paper and a pencil, the surgeon
carefully wrote answers to questions which he peremptorily
addressed to his visitor, such as his name, age, place of
residence, occupation, and the like, and the same inquiries
concerning his parents, together with other particular matters.

'Does any one know you came to this house?' he asked.

'No.'

'You swear it?'

'Yes.'

'But your prolonged absence will cause alarm and lead to
search.'

'I have provided against that.'

'How?'

'By depositing a note in the post, as I came along,
announcing my intention to drown myself.'

'The river will be dragged.'

'What then?' asked the young man, shrugging his
shoulders with careless indifference. 'Rapid undercurrent,
you know. A good many are never found.'

There was a pause.

'Are you ready?' finally asked the surgeon.

'Perfectly.' The answer was cool and determined.

The manner of the surgeon, however, showed much
perturbation. The pallor that had come into his face at
the moment his decision was formed became intense. A
nervous tremulousness came over his frame. Above it all
shone the light of enthusiasm.

'Have you a choice in the method?' he asked.

'Yes; extreme anæsthesia.'

'With what agent?'

'The surest and quickest.'

'Do you desire any—any subsequent disposition?'

'No; only nullification; simply a blowing out, as of a
candle in the wind; a puff—then darkness, without a trace.
A sense of your own safety may suggest the method.
I leave it to you.'

'No delivery to your friends?'

'None whatever.'

Another pause.

'Did you say you are quite ready?' asked the surgeon.

'Quite ready.'

'And perfectly willing?'

'Anxious.'

'Then wait a moment.'

With this request the old surgeon rose to his feet and stretched himself. Then with the stealthiness of a cat he opened the door and peered into the hall, listening intently. There was no sound. He softly closed the door and locked it. Then he closed the window-blinds and locked them. This done, he opened a door leading into an adjoining room, which, though it had no window, was lighted by means of a small skylight. The young man watched closely. A strange change had come over him. While his determination had not one whit lessened, a look of great relief came into his face, displacing the haggard, despairing look of a half-hour before. Melancholic then, he was ecstatic now.

The opening of the second door disclosed a curious sight. In the centre of the room, directly under the skylight, was an operating-table, such as is used by demonstrators of anatomy. A glass case against the wall held surgical instruments of every kind. Hanging in another case were human skeletons of various sizes. In sealed jars, arranged on shelves, were monstrosities of divers kinds preserved in alcohol. There were also, among innumerable other articles scattered about the room, a mannikin, a stuffed cat, a desiccated human heart, plaster casts of various parts of the body, numerous charts, and a large assortment of drugs and chemicals. There was also a lounge, which could be opened to form a couch. The surgeon opened it and moved the operating-table aside, giving its place to the lounge.

'Come in,' he called to his visitor.

The young man obeyed without the least hesitation.

'Take off your coat.'

He complied.

'Lie down on that lounge.'

In a moment the young man was stretched at full length, eyeing the surgeon. The latter undoubtedly was suffering under great excitement, but he did not waver; his movements were sure and quick. Selecting a bottle containing a liquid, he carefully measured out a certain quantity. While doing this he asked:

'Have you ever had any irregularity of the heart?'

'No.'

The answer was prompt, but it was immediately followed by a quizzical look in the speaker's face.

'I presume,' he added, 'you mean by your question that it might be dangerous to give me a certain drug. Under the circumstances, however, I fail to see any relevancy in your question.'

This took the surgeon aback; but he hastened to explain that he did not wish to inflict unnecessary pain, and hence his question.

He placed the glass on a stand, approached his visitor, and carefully examined his pulse.

'Wonderful!' he exclaimed.

'Why?'

'It is perfectly normal.'

'Because I am wholly resigned. Indeed, it has been long since I knew such happiness. It is not active, but infinitely sweet.'

'You have no lingering desire to retract?'

'None whatever.'

The surgeon went to the stand, and returned with the draught.

'Take this,' he said, kindly.

The young man partially raised himself and took the glass in his hand. He did not show the vibration of a single nerve. He drank the liquid, draining the last drop. Then he returned the glass with a smile.

'Thank you,' he said; 'you are the noblest man that lives. May you always prosper and be happy! You are my benefactor, my liberator. Bless you, bless you! You reach down from your seat with the gods and lift me up into glorious peace and rest. I love you—I love you with all my heart!'

These words, spoken earnestly, in a musical, low voice, and accompanied with a smile of ineffable tenderness, pierced the old man's heart. A suppressed convulsion swept over him; intense anguish wrung his vitals; perspiration trickled down his face. The young man continued to smile.

'Ah, it does me good!' said he.

The surgeon, with a strong effort to control himself, sat down upon the edge of the lounge and took his visitor's wrist, counting the pulse.

'How long will it take?' the young man asked.

'Ten minutes. Two have passed.' The voice was hoarse.

'Ah, only eight minutes more! . . . Delicious, delicious!

I feel it coming. . . . What was that? . . . Ah, I understand. Music. . . . Beautiful! . . . Coming, coming. . . . Is that—that—water? . . . Trickling? Dripping? Doctor!'

'Well?'

'Thank you, . . . thank you. . . . Noble man, . . . my saviour, . . . my bene . . . bene . . . factor. . . . Trickling, . . . trickling. . . . Dripping, dripping. . . . Doctor!'

'Well?'

'Doctor!'

'Past hearing,' muttered the surgeon.

'Doctor!'

'And blind.'

Response was made by a firm grasp of the hand.

'Doctor!'

'And numb.'

'Doctor!'

The old man watched and waited.

'Dripping, . . . dripping.'

The last drop had run. There was a sigh, and nothing more.

The surgeon laid down the hand.

'The first step,' he groaned, rising to his feet; then his whole frame dilated. 'The first step—the most difficult, yet the simplest. A providential delivery into my hands of that for which I have hungered for forty years. No withdrawal now! It is possible, because scientific; rational, but perilous. If I succeed—*if?* I *shall* succeed. I *will* succeed. . . . And after success—what? . . . Yes; what? Publish the plan and the result? The gallows. . . . So long as *it* shall exist, . . . and *I* exist, the gallows. That much. . . . But how account for its presence? Ah, that pinches hard! I must trust to the future.'

He tore himself from the revery and started.

'I wonder if *she* heard or saw anything.'

With that reflection he cast a glance upon the form on the lounge, and then left the room, locked the door, locked also the door of the outer room, walked down two or three corridors, penetrated to a remote part of the house, and rapped at a door. It was opened by his wife. He, by this time, had regained complete mastery over himself.

'I thought I heard some one in the house just now,' he said, 'but I can find no one.'

'I heard nothing.'

He was greatly relieved.

'I did hear some one knock at the door less than an

hour ago,' she resumed, 'and heard you speak, I think. Did he come in?'

'No.'

The woman glanced at his feet and seemed perplexed.

'I am almost certain,' she said, 'that I heard foot-falls in the house, and yet I see that you are wearing slippers.'

'Oh, I had on my shoes then!'

'That explains it," said the woman, satisfied; 'I think the sound you heard must have been caused by rats.'

'Ah, that was it!' exclaimed the surgeon. Leaving, he closed the door, reopened it, and said, 'I do not wish to be disturbed to-day.' He said to himself, as he went down the hall, 'All is right there.'

He returned to the room in which his visitor lay, and made a careful examination.

'Splendid specimen!' he softly exclaimed; 'every organ sound, every function perfect; fine, large frame; well-shaped muscles, strong and sinewy; capable of wonderful development—if given opportunity. . . . I have no doubt it can be done. Already I have succeeded with a dog,— a task less difficult than this, for in a man the cerebrum overlaps the cerebellum, which is not the case with a dog. This gives a wide range for accident, with but one opportunity in a lifetime! In the cerebrum, the intellect and the affections; in the cerebellum, the senses and the motor forces; in the medulla oblongata, control of the diaphragm. In these two latter lie all the essentials of simple existence. The cerebrum is merely an adornment; that is to say, reason and the affections are almost purely ornamental. I have already proved it. My dog, with its cerebrum removed, was idiotic, but it retained its physical senses to a certain degree.'

While thus ruminating he made careful preparations. He moved the couch, replaced the operating-table under the skylight, selected a number of surgical instruments, prepared certain drug-mixtures, and arranged water, towels, and all the accessories of a tedious surgical operation. Suddenly he burst into laughter.

'Poor fool!' he exclaimed. 'Paid me five thousand dollars to kill him! Didn't have the courage to snuff his own candle! Singular, singular, the queer freaks these madmen have! You thought you were dying, poor idiot! Allow me to inform you, sir, that you are as much alive at this moment as ever you were in your life. But it will be all the same to you. You shall never be more conscious than

you are now; and for all practical purposes, so far as
they concern you, you are dead henceforth, though you
shall live. By the way, how should you feel *without a head?*
Ha, ha, ha! . . . But that's a sorry joke.'

He lifted the unconscious form from the lounge and laid
it upon the operating-table.

                    *   *   *

About three years afterwards the following conversation
was held between a captain of police and a detective:

'She may be insane,' suggested the captain.

'I think she is.'

'And yet you credit her story!'

'I do.'

'Singular!"

'Not at all. I myself have learned something.'

'What?'

'Much, in one sense; little, in another. You have heard
those queer stories of her husband. Well, they are all
nonsensical—probably with one exception. He is generally
a harmless old fellow, but peculiar. He has performed
some wonderful surgical operations. The people in his
neighbourhood are ignorant, and they fear him and wish
to be rid of him; hence they tell a great many lies about
him, and they come to believe their own stories. The one
important thing that I have learned is that he is almost
insanely enthusiastic on the subject of surgery—especially
experimental surgery; and with an enthusiast there is hardly
such a thing as a scruple. It is this that gives me confidence
in the woman's story.'

'You say she appeared to be frightened?'

'Doubly so—first, she feared that her husband would
learn of her betrayal of him; second, the discovery itself
had terrified her.'

'But her report of this discovery is very vague,' argued
the captain. 'He conceals everything from her. She is
merely guessing.'

'In part—yes; in other part—no. She heard the sounds
distinctly, though she did not see clearly. Horror closed
her eyes. What she thinks she saw is, I admit, preposter-
ous; but she undoubtedly saw something extremely frightful. There are many peculiar little circumstances. He has
eaten with her but few times during the last three years,
and nearly always carries his food to his private rooms.

She says that he either consumes an enormous quantity, throws much away, or is feeding something that eats prodigiously. He explains this to her by saying that he has animals with which he experiments. This is not true. Again, he always keeps the door to these rooms carefully locked; and not only that, but he has had the doors doubled and otherwise strengthened, and has heavily barred a window that looks from one of the rooms upon a dead wall a few feet distant.'

'What does it mean?' asked the captain.

'A prison.'

'For animals, perhaps.'

'Certainly not.'

'Why?'

'Because, in the first place, cages would have been better; in the second place, the security that he has provided is infinitely greater than that required for the confinement of ordinary animals.'

'All this is easily explained: He has a violent lunatic under treatment.'

'I had thought of that, but such is not the fact.'

'How do you know?'

'By reasoning thus: He has always refused to treat cases of lunacy; he confines himself to surgery; the walls are not padded, for the woman has heard sharp blows upon them; no human strength, however, could possibly require such resisting strength as has been provided; he would not be likely to conceal a lunatic's confinement from the woman; no lunatic could consume all the food that he provides; so extremely violent mania as these precautions indicate could not continue three years; if there is a lunatic in the case it is very probable that there should have been communication with some one outside concerning the patient, and there has been none; the woman has listened at the keyhole and has heard no human voice within; and last, we have heard the woman's vague description of what she saw.'

'You have destroyed every possible theory,' said the captain, deeply interested, 'and have suggested nothing new.'

'Unfortunately, I cannot; but the truth may be very simple, after all. The old surgeon is so peculiar that I am prepared to discover something remarkable.'

'Have you suspicions?'

'I have.'

'Of what?'

'A crime. The woman suspects it.'

'And betrays it?'

'Certainly, because it is so horrible that her humanity revolts; so terrible that her whole nature demands of her that she hand over the criminal to the law; so frightful that she is in mortal terror; so awful that it has shaken her mind.'

'What do you propose to do?' asked the captain.

'Secure evidence. I may need help.'

'You shall have all the men you require. Go ahead, but be careful. You are on dangerous ground. You would be a mere plaything in the hands of that man.'

Two days afterwards the detective again sought the captain.

'I have a queer document,' he said, exhibiting torn fragments of paper, on which there was writing. 'The woman stole it and brought it to me. She snatched a handful out of a book, getting only a part of each of a few leaves.'

These fragments, which the men arranged as best they could, were (the detective explained) torn by the surgeon's wife from the first volume of a number of manuscript books which her husband had written on one subject,—the very one that was the cause of her excitement. About the time that he began a certain experiment three years ago,' continued the detective, 'he removed everything from the suite of two rooms containing his study and his operating-room. In one of the bookcases that he removed to a room across the passage was a drawer, which he kept locked, but which he opened from time to time. As is quite common with such pieces of furniture, the lock of the drawer is a very poor one; and so the woman, while making a thorough search yesterday, found a key on her bunch that fitted this lock. She opened the drawer, drew out the bottom book of a pile (so that its mutilation would more likely escape discovery), saw that it might contain a clew, and tore out a handful of the leaves. She had barely replaced the book, locked the drawer, and made her escape, when her husband appeared. He hardly ever allows her to be out of his sight when she is in that part of the house.'

The fragments read as follows: '. . . the motory nerves. I had hardly dared to hope for such a result, although inductive reasoning had convinced me of its possibility, my only doubt having been on the score of my lack of skill. Their operation has been only slightly impaired, and even this would not have been the case had the operation been performed in infancy, before the intellect had sought and obtained recognition as an essential part of the whole. Therefore I state, as a proved fact, that the cells of the motory nerves have inherent forces sufficient to the purposes of those nerves. But hardly so with the sensory nerves. These latter are, in fact, an offshoot of the former, evolved from them by natural (though not essential) heterogeneity, and to a certain extent are dependent on the evolution and expansion of a contemporaneous tendency, that developed into mentality, or mental function. Both of these latter tendencies, these evolvements, are merely refinements of the motory system, and not independent entities; that is to say, they are the blossoms of a plant that propagates from its roots. The motory system is the first . . . nor am I surprised that such prodigious muscular energy is developing. It promises yet to surpass the wildest dreams of human strength. I account for it thus: The powers of assimilation had reached their full development. They had formed the habit of doing a certain amount of work. They sent their products to all parts of the system. As a result of my operation the consumption of these products was reduced fully one-half; that is to say, about one-half of the demand for them was withdrawn. But force of habit required the production to proceed. This production was strength, vitality, energy. Thus double the usual quantity of this strength, this energy, was stored in the remaining . . . developed a tendency that did surprise me. Nature, no longer suffering the distraction of extraneous interferences, and at the same time being cut in two (as it were), with reference to this case, did not fully adjust herself to the new situation, as does a magnet, which, when divided at the point of equilibrium, renews itself in its two fragments by investing each with opposite poles; but, on the contrary, being severed from laws that theretofore had controlled her, and possessing still that mysterious tendency to develop into something more potential and complex, she blindly (having lost her lantern) pushed her demands for material that would secure this development, and as blindly used it when it was given her. Hence this marvellous voracity, this insatiable hunger, this wonderful ravenousness; and hence also (there being nothing but the physical part to receive this vast storing of energy) this strength that is becoming almost hourly herculean, almost daily appalling. It is becoming a serious

. . . narrow escape today. By some means, while I was absent, it unscrewed the stopper of the silver feeding-pipe (which I have already herein termed "the artificial mouth"), and, in one of its curious antics allowed all the chyle to escape from its stomach through the tube. Its hunger then became intense—I may say furious. I placed my hands upon it to push it into a chair, when, feeling my touch, it caught me, clasped me around the neck, and would have crushed me to death instantly had I not slipped from its powerful grasp. Thus I always had to be on my guard. I have provided the screw stopper with a spring catch, and . . . usually docile when not hungry; slow and heavy in its movements, which are, of course, purely conscious; any apparent excitement in movement being due to local irregularities in the blood-supply of the cerebellum, which, if I did not have it enclosed in a silver case that is immovable, I should expose and . . .'

The captain looked at the detective with a puzzled air.

'I don't understand it all,' said he.

'Nor I,' agreed the detective.

'What do you propose to do?'

'Make a raid.'

'Do you want a man?'

'Three. The strongest men in your district.'

'Why, the surgeon is old and weak!'

'Nevertheless, I want three strong men; and for that matter, prudence really advises me to take twenty.'

*   *   *

At one o'clock the next morning a cautious, scratching sound might have been heard in the ceiling of the surgeon's operating-room. Shortly afterwards the skylight sash was carefully raised and laid aside. A man peered into the opening. Nothing could be heard.

'That is singular,' thought the detective.

He cautiously lowered himself to the floor by a rope, and then stood for some moments listening intently. There was a dead silence. He shot the slide of a dark-lantern, and rapidly swept the room with the light. It was bare, with the exception of a strong iron staple and ring, screwed to the floor in the centre of the room, with a heavy chain attached. The detective then turned his attention to the outer room; it was perfectly bare. He was deeply perplexed. Returning to the inner room, he called softly to the men to descend. While they were thus occupied he re-entered the outer room and examined the door. A glance sufficed. It was kept closed by a spring attachment, and was locked with a strong spring-lock that could be drawn from the inside.

'The bird has just flown,' mused the detective. 'A singular accident! The discovery and proper use of this thumb-bolt might not have happened once in fifty years, if my theory is correct.'

By this time the men were behind him. He noiselessly drew the spring-bolt, opened the door, and looked out into the hall. He heard a peculiar sound. It was as though a gigantic lobster was floundering and scrambling in some distant part of the old house. Accompanying this sound was a loud, whistling breathing, and frequent rasping gasps.

These sounds were heard by still another person—the surgeon's wife; for they originated very near her rooms, which were a considerable distance from her husband's. She had been sleeping lightly, tortured by fear and harassed by frightful dreams. The conspiracy into which she had recently entered, for the destruction of her husband, was a source of great anxiety. She constantly suffered from the most gloomy forebodings, and lived in an atmosphere of terror. Added to the natural horror of her situation were those countless sources of fear which a fright-shaken mind creates and then magnifies. She was, indeed, in a pitiable state, having been driven first by terror to desperation, and then to madness.

Startled thus out of fitful slumber by the noise at her door, she sprang from her bed to the floor, every terror that lurked in her acutely tense mind and diseased imagination starting up and almost overwhelming her. The idea of flight—one of the strongest of all instincts—seized upon her, and she ran to the door, beyond all control of reason. She drew the bolt and flung the door wide open, and then fled wildly down the passage, the appalling hissing and rasping gurgle ringing in her ears, apparently with a thousandfold intensity. But the passage was in absolute darkness, and she had not taken half-a-dozen steps when she tripped upon an unseen object on the floor. She fell headlong upon it, encountering in it a large, soft, warm substance that writhed and squirmed, and from which came the sounds that had awakened her. Instantly realising her situation, she uttered a shriek such as only an unnamable terror can inspire. But hardly had her cry started the echoes in the empty corridor when it was suddenly stifled. Two prodigious arms had closed upon her and crushed the life out of her.

The cry performed the office of directing the detective and his assistants, and it also aroused the old surgeon, who occupied rooms between the officers and the object of their search. The cry of agony pierced him to the marrow, and a realisation of the cause of it burst upon him with frightful force.

'It has come at last!' he gasped, springing from his bed.

Snatching from a table a dimly-burning lamp and a long knife which he had kept at hand for three years, he dashed into the corridor. The four officers had already started forward, but when they saw him emerge they halted in silence. In that moment of stillness the surgeon paused to listen. He heard the hissing sound and the clumsy floundering of a bulky, living object in the direction of his wife's apartments. It evidently was advancing toward him. A turn in the corridor shut out the view. He turned up the light, which revealed a ghastly pallor in his face.

'Wife!' he called.

There was no response. He hurriedly advanced, the four men following quietly. He turned the angle of the corridor, and ran so rapidly that by the time the officers had come in sight of him again he was twenty steps away. He ran past a huge, shapeless object, sprawling, crawling, and floundering along, and arrived at the body of his wife.

He gave one horrified glance at her face, and staggered away. Then a fury seized him. Clutching the knife firmly, and holding the lamp aloft, he sprang toward the ungainly object in the corridor. It was then that the officers, still advancing cautiously, saw a little more clearly, though still indistinctly, the object of the surgeon's fury, and the cause of the look of unutterable anguish in his face. The hideous sight caused them to pause. They saw what appeared to be a man, yet evidently was not a man; huge, awkward, shapeless; a squirming, lurching, stumbling mass, completely naked. It raised its broad shoulders. *It had no head*, but instead of it a small metallic ball surmounting its massive neck.

'Devil!' exclaimed the surgeon, raising the knife.

'Hold, there!' commanded a stern voice.

The surgeon quickly raised his eye and saw the four officers, and for a moment fear paralysed his arm.

'The police!' he gasped.

Then, with a look of redoubled fury, he sent the knife to the hilt into the squirming mass before him. The wounded monster sprang to its feet and wildly threw its arms about, meanwhile emitting fearful sounds from a silver tube through which it breathed. The surgeon aimed another blow, but never gave it. In his blind fury he lost his caution, and was caught in an iron grasp. The struggling threw the lamp some feet toward the officers, and it fell to the floor, shattered to pieces. Simultaneously with the crash the oil took fire, and the corridor was filled with flame. The officers could not approach. Before them was the spreading blaze, and secure behind it were two forms struggling in a fearful embrace. They heard cries and gasps, and saw the gleaming of a knife.

The wood in the house was old and dry. It took fire at once, and the flames spread with great rapidity. The four officers turned and fled, barely escaping with their lives. In an hour nothing remained of the mysterious old house and its inmates but a blackened ruin.

THE MOTHER OF TURQUOISE

Clotilde Graves

During her lifetime (1863–1932), Clotilde Inez Mary Graves probably was better known for her nom de plume, Richard Dehan, than under her own name. It was in that guise that she wrote The Dop Doctor *(1910), a term commonly used to designate medics of questionable qualifications about whom the timeworn joke was written:*

Patient: *"Doctor, I don't seem to have any energy or pep, I'm tired all the time."*

Doctor: *"The trouble with you is that you drink too much."*

Patient: *"But doctor, I never touch the stuff!"*

Doctor: *"Then that's your problem, a little drink once in a while would do wonders for you."*

Up until a year before her death, in 1931, she was still being published, The Man in the Mask *appearing then. Scholars of the supernatural prize her for her two excellent collections,* Off Sandy Hook and Other Stories *(1915); and* Under the Hermes and Other Stories *(1917).*

She had some success with plays, her earliest, Nitocris, *being produced in 1887 and others of prominence including* A Matchmaker *(1895) and* A Tenement Tragedy *(1907).*

She was a regular contributor to the popular periodicals of the day and The Mother of Turquoise *appeared in the March, 1907, issue of* THE LONDON MAGAZINE *and was the featured short story in the issue, adorned by four illustrations by Charles Sheldon, two of them full-page. The story combines witchcraft with the resurrection of one of the pagan Goddesses of ancient*

153

*Egypt, in a rewarding chiller that never for a word tries
to avoid the fact that a foul and supernatural evil is
underway.*

I SUPPOSE England's dispute with Turkey about Akabah
has induced the reader to rub up his geographical knowledge of that naked, scorching tongue of barren desert and
naked mountain known as the Sinaitic Peninsula. The ancient Egyptians worked turquoise-mines in the Wady Maghara when the Great Pyramid was building. The Bedawy
knew of the mines in Wady Rekhareb, but kept the secret
as only Arabs can, until the Nineteenth Dynasty saw the
departure of the Unclean from Egypt, and the pent-up
waters of the Bitter Lakes swept down from the north-west
upon the hosts of Menephthah, the Pharaoh of the Exodus.
Thenceforward the glory of Egypt reached its climax and
began its decline.

At least, so Majendie told me one day on the journey
out; and he gave one the feeling of being a man who knew.
Majendie and I were the expedition chartered by the direc-
tors of the Sinaitic Turquoise Syndicate, Limited, of Fen-
church Street, London, not counting my fox-terrier, Vic,
and the Arabs and camels we took on at Suez. Majendie
was a well-knit, broad-shouldered, keen-eyed man of
twenty eight or nine, quiet, well-bred, and full of knowledge and information.

Having French, German, Spanish, modern Greek, Hindustani, and Arabic at his tongue's end, acquired in the
spare time of a student of medicine and surgery, this
astonishing young fellow had spent months at the British
Museum in the study of Egyptian hieroglyphics and Chal-
dæan cuneiform inscriptions; and at the period of our meeting had just resigned the berth of surgeon on the steam-
ship "Delta," a vessel employed by the Khedive of Egypt
for lighthouse service in the Red Sea, after two years'
service.

Majendie knew all about the gem we were in search of.
"Half the so-called turquoises on the London, Cairo, and
Suez markets are odontolite," he told me, "fossil bone of
mammoth or dinotherium impregnated with phosphate of
iron. The bony structure may be detected under the microscope by anybody who cares to look, but I have a belief
that people are fond of being swindled."

He lifted his brown, well-shaped left hand to fillip the

ash from his cigar, and I caught a blue gleam from a splendid stone, in a rough, native-worked setting of yellow gold, worn upon the little finger.

"At any rate," said I, "you got your money's worth when you bought that seal."

"This intaglio of Hathor! I did not buy it," said Majendie, quietly glancing at the ring and then at me, in a provoking sort of way. "Nor was it given me," he added, in the same tone, then added: "I found it with several others, where I hope to find some more by and by, luck being with us."

Other travellers have devoted pages to Wady Maghara, the Written Valley. I am not good at descriptions. Briefly, then, let me say that for four miles our caravan defiled through a lofty gorge of sandstone, the smoothed surfaces of whose rocks are literally covered with irregularly carved inscriptions, some larger, others smaller, in characters measuring from a foot high to half an inch. High up upon the towering face of the precipice rising left and right I could distinguish others, and almost every large boulder at our feet bore similar records, less deeply cut, in some instances scratched on the stone.

"Who did them? What are they? Historical records or memorial tablets, or prayers, or what?" I sang out.

"If anybody knew for certain, old man, there wouldn't be much good in our being here," Majendie said, with a dash of triumph in his tone. "When Justinian built the convent of Mount Sinai this character of hieroglyphic was unknown; and since a Teutonic wiseacre, Beer, of Leipzig, published a so-called key to it at Paris in 1840, nobody has managed to decipher them. Lepsius calls them the work of the Shepherd Kings. Layard never saw them; Dr. Flinders Petrie means to come here one day, but he has not got here yet," said Majendie, jerking at his dromedary's heavy, single rein.

And as the desert ship began to pitch fore and aft in preparation for kneeling: "And we have," he added, in that oddly exultant tone. "*A 'iwa*, Musa, we camp here. This is our journey's end, Randolph."

We pitched no tent that night, but had our carpets spread and our wooden native bedsteads set up in a roomy cave that yawned in the face of the sandstone precipice.

That night I had a queer dream. It seemed that a shining figure stood in the entrance of our cave, glowing with radiant light that streamed from her crescent-shaped coronal. Facing us full, she stretched towards me a lotus-flower, and towards my sleeping companion a writhing snake. And my blood was chilled by the look of malice in her brilliant eyes, blue and hard as turquoises, beneath black, bowlike, joined eyebrows, and by the mockery that smiled upon her scarlet lips. And, cold to the very heart, and with an indescribable sensation of suffocation, I awakened.

Next day we unpacked the picks and crowbars; and the sheikh of a tribal family of Bedawy found us out, and sent a message, with a present of dhurra cakes, to ask if we wanted to hire labourers. From him Majendie learned that the gorge was locally called Wady Rekhareb. The sheikh added, with great certainty, that no turquoises had ever been found there within the memory of man. Majendie laughed harshly as he translated the Bedawin's utterance. He pointed to a row of inscriptions baking in the noonday glare on the precipice high above, and began to reel off in English: *"Therefore we bless thee, fecund Hathor, the blue-eyed Mother of the jewel of the Rocks, that thou hast been favourable unto us, Khita the Syrian, Gad the Phœnician, and Tani-hat the Egyptian, sent hither by Menephthah the King, the conqueror, beloved of Amen, Pthah and Harmachis, we duly making oblation of incense and bled sacrifice———"*

"Of a kid," I put in, vaguely reminded of Scriptural passages I had heard droned out on Sundays by our good old vicar at home.

"Of a kid—that's just it," said Majendie, with an awkward-sounding laugh; "and some time or other I'll show you the temple where they offered it." He turned to the Bedawy chief then, whose name was Erbkam, and when the last haggle about the rate of pay (two piastres a day, workmen's bread and dhurra water to be brought by the women) was over, we accompanied Erbkam to the camp. There was nothing to be seen but a group of villainously dirty felt tents, some hobbled camels diligently eating nothing off the bare boulders, a starved mule or two, a ribby horse, a gang of sore-eyed children, and some prematurely aged women. Then out of a tent came a pretty young creature with gazelle eyes, and a gold coin among the silver ones in her black hair, leading a frail little figure bowed into a hoop, and covered with a mass of rags. This was Erbkam's great-grandmother, a lady of ancient family, celebrated through the whole peninsula as a prophetess, the sheikh explained.

"Certainly, if rags and dirt and old age make a prophet-ess, she ought to be one," I said to Majendie. "The young lady, now, is more in my line." And I lifted my hat in my best style to the owner of the gazelle eyes and the gold coin. I could swear she blushed, a manifestation of shyness as unusual with the Arab as with the camel; and I learned that her name was Aissa. The prophetess, who was blind, was called Thorah. Whether she was blind really was not possible to tell. Only, where eyes should have been were folds of wrinkles, shaded by the ragged fringe of her head-cloth, and, being toothless and palsied as well, she mowed and chattered like a rock monkey. Not that she could not get over the ground easily enough: daily she accompanied the pretty Aissa, who was the chief's daughter by his youngest wife but one, down to our camp with the women who brought bread, and I have seen her standing on a boulder near where some of our workmen were quarrying, mowing and mopping; and pointing her stick as if in deri-sion at our futile attempts to strike the turquoise vein. For day by day the "blue jewel of Hathor" eluded us. Neither in the red marl nor the limestone did we come upon a trace, though on either hand of us the living rock testified to the riches the ancient miners had wrung from the place.

"Mistress of Mafkat"—Mafkat means the "copper coun-try"—*"great are thy gifts,"* ran the inscription on another tablet Majendie translated, and which I copied down in my notebook. *"For of copper three hundred ingots, and of the turquoise of the rock three bushels and half a bushel, we have received of thy favour, duly making oblation and sacrifice in thy Temple of Dreams."*

"Why did they call it the Temple of Dreams?" I asked.

"Because, after making oblation and sacrifice, they slept in the precincts of the sacred place," returned Majendie; "and in dreams they were shown where the vein of ore and jewel-matrix were to be found."

"Look here!" I said, getting up from the boulder I had been sitting on. "I want to see that temple now."

A three-mile tramp up the Written Valley brought us to the place; copper was liberally outcropping in the rock, and huge mounds of black slag marked the smelting-places of the ancient miners, just as in old Cornwall. The ruins of the temple were perched on a platform of pinkish sand-stone jutting out from the face of the precipice, about a hundred feet above our heads. Square, bevelled holes in the rock-face showed where the wooden steps of a kind of

ladder had once been fixed, and beside them dangled a
hide rope, securely fastened, as we found by hauling on to
it, to a stone or beam above.

It *was* a stiff climb, but the place was worth it. The front
elevation of the temple had been carved out of the solid
pink sandstone, and the great central chamber went back
into the heart of the mountain, whence it had been hol-
lowed for sixty feet or more. There were altars of the
shape one sees in the Egyptian temple-friezes, great beds
of wood ashes, the fuel for which must have been brought
from great distances, a variety of tanks and basins for
ceremonial washing—one wondered whence they had obtained the water to fill them—and round the central
chamber a honeycomb of cells, each furnished with a stone
bench for the sleeper, a stone pillow for his head, a quantity of lively black beetles, and one or more active scor-
pions.

"You see, the walls are covered with inscriptions of
thanks, and each of the pillars is a memorial of some lucky
find," said Majendie. "When I was here two years ago——"

"I knew you had been here before," I said, sucking my
knuckle, which I had barked rather badly during the ascent, "although your not knowing the real name of the
Wady puzzled me."

"Every wandering desert tribe have their own name for
places," said Majendie; "and on the return journey the
names are changed, as often as not. Historical and geographical purists may suffer; but you can't whack into an
Arab's head that a hill is a hill when he is coming down it.
See, there is the image of the Mother of Turquoise herself,
above the middle altar. Don't go too near."

"Why not?" I queried, staring at Majendie. "You don't
hold that there's any sanctity about the place, do you?"

Then, as he turned away, I went up to the altar, and
was rendered speechless, for the likeness of the profile
figure, carved on a great rock tablet above, to the figure I
had seen in my dream was marvellous. There was the crescent-shaped headdress, there the level brows and the cruel,
sneering smile; and in the outstretched hands of the figure were the lotus-bud and the snake. The altar was
broken, but a deep channel to carry off the blood of the
sacrifice ran round it, and there were little culverts at the
corners. And a long-shaped bundle of stained and weather-
beaten native cloth lay across the stone at the feet of the
inscrutably smiling statue. I could not imagine what the

bundle might contain until, stretching my arm over the edge of the altar, I had touched it lightly with my finger. Then I pulled back my hand—the damaged one—briskly enough, as I shouted to Majendie:

"Why, here is the mummy of a child!"

Majendie made an incoherent sound in answer, and I took another observation of the poor little corpse. Then a dark series of stains upon the altar-stones running to the channel chiselled at the edges enlightened me as to the hideous truth. Now I knew the kind of sacrifice with which those ancient miners—Khita the Syrian, Gad the Phœnician, Tani-hat and Co.—had rewarded the lady of the horned headdress. And I did not admire the lady. But unwittingly I had paid her tribute in the fluid she preferred, for a drop or two of fresh blood from my torn finger was soaking into the surface of the sandstone altar.

I did not fail to express my opinion of Egypt's Semitic deities as Majendie and I scrambled down by the hide rope, which was made fast with a very workmanlike turn and clove-hitch to one of the memorial pillars, and tramped back over the scorching boulders to our camp.

Next day, from a nodule of sandstone, one of our workmen chipped out the first turquoise. A little later I found one myself, a fine and perfect stone. Two others were found, and then the fog of bad luck settled down upon us again. The Arabs chipped and picked and crushed; the supplies got scarcer, and Majendie took to disappearing for hours every day. And, being slightly smitten in that direction myself, I suspected him of carrying on a flirtation with Aissa, and taxed the wearer of the gold coin with giddiness in the broken Arabic which she herself had taught me.

Aissa shook her head, and looked at me out of the corners of her gazelle eyes.

"Aissa say no. She is no fountain for the Anglezi lord to drink at, nor palm-tree to cover him from the sun," she denied energetically; "and if you want know whom the Anglezi make sweet talk, it is Thorah. Thorah always."

Thorah, the blind prophetess, great-grandmother to Erbkam, the sheikh! The notion of Majendie making love to the old lady, and breaking, in the violence of his infatuation, the swords, rusty spears, and wool-tufted muzzle-loading guns of her descendants, tickled me into laughter. But Aissa looked grave.

"Thorah nothing to joke about—great magic woman," she said. I knew that *"es sehr"* means magic of the black or evil description, and certainly the old creature had a witchlike look.

That day we struck a rich vein of matrix, where the stones were of splendid size and quality. The bottom of the cotton-wool-lined tin box that held our finds began to be covered, and the prospects of the Turquoise Syndicate looked up day by day.

We stored away a rich collection of pieces of turquoise-striped matrix on our own account, that being our perquisite, before Fortune deserted us again. Once more Majendie vanished; and some hours after his disappearance two Arab women came down from the camp, looking for the sheikh's youngest child.

"At dawn we saw the child Zelim outside his mother's tent, playing with a jerboa Aissa tamed and gave him. Perhaps it strayed and he followed. The girl Aissa sobs and weeps, for this is an evil place for babes to stray in, as other tribes have learned. Ahi! Awahi! He has been snatched away by evil djinns, as was Nulad, his elder brother, two years ago. Ahi!"

"Why not search for him in the caves?" I asked; "in the cliff-face where the camel-hide rope hangs down from the mouth of the holy place above?"

I designated the Temple of Hathor by the Arabic word for "shrine," because I did not know how otherwise to express myself. The women clapped their hands and shrieked in horror. *That* a holy place, forsooth! Why, it was the home of every devil, literally speaking, in the peninsula; not a man, woman, or child of the Arabs would set foot in the accursed place; and so on.

And yet my thoughts ran continually on the pink temple in the sandstone cliff where the two-year-old mummy of what I guessed to be the child Zelim's older brother lay under the cartouche of Hathor, the Mother of Turquoise. As I drew lines with my stick in the red-hot gravel, and watched the ants running in and out of them, I wondered if the accidental spilling of the blood from my finger on that channelled stone had had anything to do with our first find of turquoise, and also whether Majendie's bandaged arm had had anything to do with later discoveries.

And then, with a horrible leap and sinking of the heart, the new link of evidence joined to the old, and I saw a motive in the abduction of the child Zelim.

"Horrible! Impossible!" I muttered to myself. But Suspicion had fixed her fangs in me. I made an excuse that saved me from breaking bread with Majendie that night. He loomed hideous in the new light that had broken in upon me. Next time he left the camp I would follow him, "heeled," as the Americans say, with my bowie-knife and revolver.

He did not go to bed that night. I was dozing when a long, wailing cry came down the Wady from the Arab camp. I woke up. I saw that Majendie no longer sat by the fire, whose ashes lay dead.

And I rose and slipped on a pair of rubber-soled cricketing-shoes, and set out up the shadowed side of the Written Valley, climbed noiselessly by way of the hide-rope ladder, and, sheltered by a group of sandstone pillars, looked into the pink temple. On a bed of ashes, before the central altar, a fire had been kindled. It roared and blazed as though gum or resin had been smeared upon the fuel.

The mummy had been removed from the altar of the goddess with the crescent tiara; and at the feet of Hathor there lay another bundle, covered with a clean white linen cloth, and the bundle was alive, and wriggling feebly under the covering. Then a face of terror came out of the darkness at the other end of the temple, and it belonged to Majendie. He was bareheaded, wearing only a silk shirt and a pair of flannel trousers. At his elbow actively hobbled the hag Thorah, persuading, entreating, scolding, threatening, persuading him, to what deed I trembled to guess.

"It is nothing, Anglezi. What is the life of a child? A little milk, a few kisses, a little play—then sleep. This one sleeps. I have given him tamarind conserve with '*afiyoon*' [opium]. One touch with a sharp blade across the throat, and the babe awakens in Paradise. Also, She is greatly propitiated. Be bold! Strike, and win the reward!"

"Strike, and win the reward!" I heard Majendie repeat, in a voice very unlike his own.

The withered witch at his elbow gabbled faster:

"Twice twelve months ago, and five beyond twelve, and thou didst prove the truth of my saying. The child Nulad strayed from the tents, and tried to climb the ladder in the rocks, and fell, and then was dying beyond doubt, and I told thee if thou wouldst carry him up the ladder and lay him on the altar of the Mother of the Blue Jewel thou shouldst reap a great reward. One of the jewels thou hast on thy finger, blue as her own eyes, because thou didst bring up the child at my bidding, and lay him here before the breath was out of him, so that She received the oblation of a life. Then thou didst go away, and return with the tall, yellow-haired Anglezi, whom the girl Aissa loves. Think, did not he spill blood upon the stone, and did not She reward? And again, when thou didst creep here in the silence of the night, and open a vein in thine upper arm, and pour the hot blood upon Her stone, the Mother of Turquoise smiled on thee. But now She calls for a complete oblation, and a sacrifice followed by burnt-offering, for She is thirsty and hungry, and incense has been denied Her nostrils for more than three thousand years. Take this and use it, and thou shalt see."

The sorceress loosed her clutch of Majendie's shirt-sleeve, to thrust into his hand a curved, crescent-shaped knife, such a blade as the artists of the Egyptian wall-paintings represented in the hand of the officiating priest. At the same instant she threw something upon the fire, and clouds of bluish, fragrant smoke rose up, and blotted both figures from my sight. When I could see again, the prophetess had disappeared. Majendie, with a deliberate intention expressed in every line of his hitherto nerveless body, was rolling up the sleeve of his silk shirt. And above the level of our heads, upon the broken altar, the drugged child silently squirmed under the linen covering-cloth.

"Majendie! . . . Frank, old man! . . . For Heaven's sake don't do it!" I cried, and seized him as he stepped forward. He was as strong as twenty men . . . I grappled with him for the knife . . . And as our eyes met, I saw that in his stare was no recognition, only the frenzied determination to kill. Twice I tore from him the murderous crescent-blade, twice he wrested it from me, the second time nearly severing the muscles of my left thumb. And as the warm blood jetted, I distinctly heard a woman's laugh. Not the cackle of the accursed Thorah, but the melodious, bell-like laugh of a young woman. . . . A beautiful woman. . . .

I glanced upwards. The bas-relief above the central altar—the oval cartouche tablet with the sculptured image of Hathor—was blotted out. In its place was a living Splendour, a form of terrible beauty, crowned with the new moon, sheathed in tissues of jewel-hues, her beautiful scarlet lips curved into a cruel smile, her jetty arch of eyebrows vaulting the insupportable blue radiance of the eyes I had seen in my dream. In one hand, golden-tinted, with finger-tips of rose, she held a lotus-bud; in the other a writhing snake. And at her bare and lovely feet writhed the child whose innocent blood those red lips thirsted for, the sacrifice by which alone guerdon of her hidden jewels might be won from the Mother of Turquoise.

I saw the vision first, as I and the man who was my comrade struggled between the sacrificial fire and the sacrificial stone. And Majendie must have caught in my dazzled eyes the reflection of that unearthly vision. One moment I reeled, drunken with the wine of the demon's beauty, then I wrenched free my right hand, and with a desperate effort I plucked my Colt's revolver from my hip-pocket and fired. Straight between those blue, gleaming orbs my bullet sped to its mark. There was a shrill, terrible cry, followed by a heavy, rustling fall; and when the smoke cleared off, and the affrighted bats ceased to wheel and dart about my bewildered eyes, I saw that prone upon the altar of Hathor, covering with her dead body the body of the drugged child, the Bedaween sorceress Thorah lay face downwards, her crooked finger-tips almost touching the sandstone floor, upon which in drifts lay the light dust of countless ages.

The child Zelim, beyond a bruise or two, was practically unhurt. I carried him down the hide-rope staircase, and then went back for Majendie. I found *him* delirious and raving, and how I got him down the sheer descent I hardly know.

The Bedawy chief had his youngest-born back again, and, in the rejoicing that followed, the tribe seemed to overlook the absence of its ancestral prophetess. Blind or not, Thorah was a witch of the deepest dye, or else one of the most powerful hypnotists that ever lived. I do not reject either conclusion.

As for Majendie—poor fellow!—whom she had so bewitched, he died of fever at Suez, thanking me gratefully, with almost his last breath, for having saved him from committing an abominable crime. The Turquoise Syndicate were fairly satisfied with the results of their initial venture; but when they wanted me to go out again to the Sinaitic Peninsula, and tap the sandstone rocks for fresh deposits of the "blue jewel of Hathor," I declined, and they sent out another man.

"MAN OVERBOARD!"

Winston Spencer Churchill

There are many who regard the late Winston Leonard
Spencer Churchill as the greatest single man of the
twentieth century so far. While his reputation very heavily leans on the courage and fortitude with which he
guided England victoriously through World War II, and
his clear-sighted anticipation of the world problems to
follow, his books on World War II and the history of
the English-speaking peoples play a part in the great
respect with which he was regarded.

Winston Churchill started out as a journalist and had
been writing continuously all of his life. He was a war
correspondent when captured by the Boers in 1899 and
early in the century had written such highly respected
works as Lord Randolph Churchill (1906), My African
Journey (1908) and Liberalism and the Social Problem
(1909). What is not commonly known was that he was
also a contributor of fiction to the popular magazines.

One of his most effective short stories, a tale of
frightening terror, appeared in the December, 1898, issue
of THE HARMSWORTH MAGAZINE. At that time, the famed
American writer by the name of Winston Churchill had
already published his bestseller The Celebrity and would
go on to such successes as Richard Carvel and The
Crisis. Aware of this, the editor of THE HARMSWORTH
MAGAZINE put a footnote beneath the story which stated,
"As by a very remarkable coincidence there are two
Winston Churchills, both writers, we may mention that
this Mr. Churchill is the son of the late Lord Randolph
Churchill."

The story was titled "Man Overboard!" and subtitled
"An Episode of the Red Sea". The year it appeared,
Winston Churchill would be present at Khartoum with
Kitchener and then would be off to South Africa to
cover the Boer War. The story occupied only three

*pages in the issue in which it was published, but the
editors ran three illustrations with it, one for each page.
It is a grim piece that should strike at a basic fear in
most people.*

IT WAS A LITTLE after half-past nine when the man fell
overboard. The mail steamer was hurrying through the
Red Sea in the hope of making up the time which the currents of the Indian Ocean had stolen. The night was clear,
though the moon was hidden behind clouds. The warm air
was laden with moisture. The still surface of the waters was
only broken by the movement of the great ship, from
whose quarter the long, slanting undulations struck out,
like the feathers from an arrow shaft, and in whose wake
the froth and air bubbles churned up by the propeller
trailed in a narrowing line to the darkness of the horizon.

There was a concert on board. All the passengers were
glad to break the monotony of the voyage, and gathered
around the piano in the companion-house. The decks were
deserted. The man had been listening to the music and
joining in the songs. But the room was hot, and he came
out to smoke a cigarette and enjoy a breath of the wind
which the speedy passage of the liner created. It was the
only wind in the Red Sea that night.

The accommodation-ladder had not been unshipped since
leaving Aden, and the man walked out on to the platform,
as on to a balcony. He leaned his back against the rail and
blew a puff of smoke into the air reflectively. The piano
struck up a lively tune, and a voice began to sing the first
verse of "The Rowdy Dowdy Boys." The measured pulsa-
tions of the screw were a subdued but additional accom-
paniment. The man knew the song. It had been the rage
at all the music halls, when he had started for India seven
years before. It reminded him of the brilliant and busy
streets he had not seen for so long, but was soon to see
again. He was just going to join in the chorus, when the
railing, which had been insecurely fastened, gave way suddenly with a snap, and he fell backwards into the warm
water of the sea amid a great splash.

For a moment he was physically too much astonished
to think. Then he realised that he must shout. He began to
do this even before he rose to the surface. He achieved a
hoarse, inarticulate, half-choked scream. A startled brain
suggested the word "Help!" and he bawled this out lustily

and with frantic effort six or seven times without stopping. Then he listened.

> "Hi! hi! clear the way
>   For the Rowdy Dowdy Boys."

The chorus floated back to him across the smooth water, for the ship had already passed completely by. And as he heard the music a long stab of terror drove through his heart. The possibility that he would not be picked up dawned for the first time on his consciousness. The chorus started again—

> "Then—I—say—boys,
>   Who's for a jolly spree?
> Rum—tum—tiddley—um,
>   Who'll have a drink with me?"

"Help! help! help!" shrieked the man, in desperate fear.

> "Fond of a glass now and then,
>   Fond of a row or noise;
> Hi! hi! clear the way
>   For the Rowdy Dowdy Boys!"

The last words drawled out faint and fainter. The vessel was steaming fast. The beginning of the second verse was confused and broken by the ever-growing distance. The dark outline of the great hull was getting blurred. The stern light dwindled.

Then he set out to swim after it with furious energy, pausing every dozen strokes to shout long wild shouts. The disturbed waters of the sea began to settle again to their rest. The widening undulations became ripples. The aërated confusion of the screw fizzed itself upwards and out. The noise of motion and the sounds of life and music died away.

The liner was but a single fading light on the blackness of the waters and a dark shadow against the paler sky.

At length full realisation came to the man, and he stopped swimming. He was alone—abandoned. With the understanding his brain reeled. He began again to swim, only now instead of shouting he prayed—mad, incoherent prayers, the words stumbling into one another.

Suddenly a distant light seemed to flicker and brighten.

A surge of joy and hope rushed through his mind. They were going to stop—to turn the ship and come back. And with the hope came gratitude. His prayer was answered. Broken words of thanksgiving rose to his lips. He stopped and stared after the light—his soul in his eyes. As he watched it, it grew gradually but steadily smaller. Then the man knew that his fate was certain. Despair succeeded hope. Gratitude gave place to curses. Beating the water with his arms, he raved impotently. Foul oaths burst from him, as broken as his prayers—and as unheeded.

The fit of passion passed, hurried by increasing fatigue. He became silent—silent as was the sea, for even the ripples were subsiding into the glassy smoothness of the surface. He swam on mechanically along the track of the ship, sobbing quietly to himself, in the misery of fear. And the stern light became a tiny speck, yellower but scarcely bigger than some of the stars, which here and there shone between the clouds.

Nearly twenty minutes passed, and the man's fatigue began to change to exhaustion. The overpowering sense of the inevitable pressed upon him. With the weariness came a strange comfort. He need not swim all the long way to Suez. There was another course. He would die. He would resign his existence since he was thus abandoned. He threw up his hands impulsively and sank. Down, down he went through the warm water. The physical death took hold of him and he began to drown. The pain of that savage grip recalled his anger. He fought with it furiously. Striking out with arms and legs he sought to get back to the air. It was a hard struggle, but he escaped victorious and gasping to the surface. Despair awaited him. Feebly splashing with his hands he moaned in bitter misery—

"I can't—I must. O God! let me die."

The moon, then in her third quarter, pushed out from behind the concealing clouds and shed a pale, soft glitter upon the sea. Upright in the water, fifty yards away, was a black triangular object. It was a fin. It approached him slowly.

His last appeal had been heard.

THE BLACK STATUE

Huan Mee

Time has a way of erasing the achievements of many great literary entertainers, among them the record of the works of the author with the strange name of Huan Mee. He was a frequent contributor to the popular magazines of England at the turn of the century, and his stories when they were not detective or mystery, frequently took the form of psychological horror and science fiction.

One of his most popular short stories was The Crystal Bell *in the January, 1902,* PEARSON'S MAGAZINE, *wherein a scientist sets a man in a glass dome and bets a friend that the power of the imagination will have that man thinking he is suffocating, even though air is being permitted to enter.*

The experiment goes as planned and the man in the glass bell collapses as from asphyxiation, when suddenly they realize that the passages for the air have been accidentally closed and that what is happening is not due to the power of suggestion.

The Black Statue *appeared in the February, 1899 issue of* THE HARMSWORTH MAGAZINE, *published by Alfred C. Harmsworth, British newspaper tycoon, as a low-priced competitor to* THE STRAND *and* PEARSON'S MAGAZINE *and as a direct competitor to* THE ROYAL MAGAZINE. *Huan Mee was an occasional contributor and* The Black Statue, *which was subtitled "The Story of a Doctor's Gruesome Discovery," is a horror tale that might also qualify as science fiction.*

"I ALWAYS SED no good could come of it," the woman cries with a choke, and then the little group edges back to the kerb, and gazes open-mouthed at the shuttered windows.

"And you ain't seen your Jim since last Monday, eh?"

"No, I ain't set eyes on 'im. It's just a week to-day. I sed as 'e left in the mornin', 'It would be better for you, Jim, if you slung up your job at Doctor Hazard's, 'cos no good can come of it; and he gives me the creeps every time I looks at 'im.' "

"Wot did Jim say?"

"He says, 'Beggars can't be choosers,' and the doctor paid 'im well."

"And you ain't seen 'im since?"

"No, I ain't, and I b'leve he's a bein' 'sperimented on."

"Well, why don't you tell the pleece?"

"I 'ave, and they're comin' round this mornin'."

The door is pulled to behind the men; the crowd again by a couple of constables, enters the square and pauses before the gloomy house.

"Clear this gaping lot away, Jackson," he says; and the crowd, by dint of physical persuasion, and repeated injunctions to "pass along," is hustled to the corner, where it awaits events. "Now, Smith, just knock a rat-tat."

Neither the first, second, nor third knock has the slightest effect, except to bring back the crowd, strongly reinforced, until it hangs around the railings.

"Force it," the man quietly remarks; and in a few minutes the door is open, and the excited idlers almost encroach on to the doorstep. "Jackson, clear this mob out of the square; Smith, follow me."

The doors is pulled to behind the men; the crowd again retreats in disorder to the corner, and the constable walks to and fro in front of the house.

The two who have entered glance into the front room; it is empty, while the back room and the upper part of the house are the same.

"Try the basement, Smith."

They descend the stairs, and come to a sudden stop as they are met by an unexpected door.

"Sounds like iron," the chief exclaims, as he raps his knuckles against it.

"That's what it is," the constable agrees.

"Knock on it with that bar, and see if anyone's alive in the house or not."

As soon as the first blow has fallen the door is thrown open, and a man clad in his shirt and trousers confronts them; a man tall and dark, with his face clean shaven, his hair cut closely to his head, and his shirt sleeves rolled tightly to his shoulders.

"Well, what is it, eh?" he asks. "Come in"; and as they enter he closes the door behind them.

The whole place seems weird and uncanny. The further end is draped by a long curtain, hanging from the ceiling to the floor; the walls are covered with shelves and cases, filled with glass vessels and polished instruments that vividly suggest their own uses, while in a corner alcove stands a life-sized statue, a Greek god, in black marble.

"What is the meaning of this instrusion? What do you want? Am I in London, or is this some part of the world where men's homes can be broken into, their scientific researches disturbed by strangers?"

"This house has been without a sign of life for a week, and your servant, who entered then, has never left it."

"You mean the man who used to do odd jobs for me. I discharged him ten days ago, and have not seen him since."

"He came here on Monday."

"He did not. I see you don't believe me—maybe you go so far as to think I have murdered him, eh? Of course, you've searched the house. This is my laboratory, and there's only the room through the curtains, there."

The officers step forward; the man draws back the curtains.

"Now, then, look! You see there's no one there, and if you're quite satisfied, I prefer to be left alone. You found your way in, so now you can find it out."

*   *   *

For three years the gloomy house in the square has been vacant—not to let, but simply vacant, for Dr. Hazard is touring on the Continent. The missing servant has not been seen in London since the day he so suddenly and mysteriously disappeared, and the little gossiping group which once took such a morbid interest in his whereabouts has forgotten him in the excitement of other nine-day wonders, which have flourished and withered in their turn.

But now a change has suddenly come about; for the master is returning.

Brisk, business-like men measure floors and windows, energetic British workmen sit on planks and smoke, and all is ostentatious bustle and activity. At last the day comes when the final workman grudgingly and reluctantly takes his leave. Pantechnicons arrive and disgorge their contents, which shall transform the dismal dwelling into a habitation fit for a man and woman—for it is rumoured that Dr. Hazard is bringing home a wife.

That she is beautiful, the few loungers who are privileged to see the couple descend from the carriage cannot but admit; but still there is something chilling and repellent in that beauty. There is so much of the doctor's cold, insolent sneer reflected in her face, that it seems to them that like has chosen like.

Dr. Hazard assists his wife to alight, and she passes up the steps, and then turns and glances back in icy astonishment, as a young woman darts across the road, and lays a detaining arm upon her husband's sleeve.

"'Ave you found 'im, doctor?"

"Found whom?"

"My brother—Jim, you know—'im as used to work for you."

"No, no, my good woman. Go away. How should I have found him?"

The woman still retains her hold of his sleeve, as he tries to shakes her off.

"You know where 'e is, Dr. Hazard," she cries, fiercely. "You know where 'e is."

"Tut, tut, my good woman. How should I know?"

Without further parley, he thrusts her on one side and passes in.

"You do know, 'cos you knows as I knows 'e's in there," and she points to the house.

His wife, moving from the window, turns towards him as he enters.

"Some of your friends seem to have good memories for you," she says.

"Yes. It's nonsense. Her brother disappeared three years ago, and she thinks I had something to do with it."

"And had you?"

"You're jesting."

"I never jest; I know life is nothing to you."

"On the contrary, life is a great deal to me. I have studied it; it interests me. I shall be able to show you some remarkable experiments, now we are home. I have everything to my hand in my laboratory—everything to aid me in my study of life and death."

"And I, to my horror, have found how little you think of either."

"You speak truly," the doctor answers. "I think nothing of either; but it is your home-coming. Forget these trifles, and let me show you the house."

"I wonder why I married you," she says, as she glares into his eyes.

"Out of gratitude for my service to your father."

"I wonder why I did not sooner kill myself."

"Tush! you talk like a child."

"The first time I saw you I shuddered, for you were as a blight in the very air; and then, slowly and viciously, you plotted in silence, until you had broken my heart and bought me from my father—until you held him bound hand and foot, and I was the price of your silence."

"You have said this so many times before," he mockingly interjects.

"And I say it for the last time now," she cried; "for in this house I see death written, and it is yours. A death worthy of such a devil."

"Loud applause from the gallery," the man cynically interjects; "now for the tour of inspection."

"My laboratory," Dr. Hazard exclaims, as they pause at length before the iron door, "or what you would perhaps call my torture chamber. Do you care to see it before science resumes her researches?"

She inclines her head, enters as he switches on the light, and gazes coldly round the room, aware that her husband's eye is upon her to catch a tremor of the lips that would show a spark of fear, and then with a gasp she falls back, and points with a trembling hand to the corner, where a curtain on a brass rod cuts off a portion of the room.

"Who is behind there?" she cries. "Who is behind there?"

He crosses the room, pulls back the curtain, and faces her.

"You are frightened at nothing," he chuckles. "A statue in black marble is sufficient to set you trembling; come nearer and examine it. Come and see with what marvellous accuracy every vein, every muscle and tendon is carved upon the stone."

"Who did it?"

"I, from life. You did not know I excelled in sculpture as well as other arts."

"It's a wonderful piece of work," she whispers, attracted in spite of herself, struggling to regain her composure, and not knowing why an icy fear still seems to grip her heart. "Very true to life."

"Very true indeed. Give me your hand."

He takes her hand, and places it upon the arm of the statue.

"There," he says, quietly, "you can almost fancy you feel the muscles beneath the skin, almost fancy that arm once moved. It is, as you say, very true to life."

With a cry of terror she drags her hand away, and, clutching the table for support, leans back against it, utterly unnerved, a nameless horror in her eyes.

"Is he—it—like the missing man?" she gasps at last.

Dr. Hazard purses his lips, and eyes the statue critically.

"Hum! it is strange," he answers, after a moment of silence. "But now you mention it, there is a likeness."

He offers her his arm.

"Don't come near me."

"As you please."

"Do you experiment with that in the room?"

"Certainly; for that is the result of my greatest experiment. You heard of the missing man they're still worrying me about?" He jerked his head meaningly towards the statue.

"It is not true; you are trying to drive me mad."

"Nonsense! It's true enough. That's the man, and I defy the world to find it out!"

His face flushes with a dull blaze of passion, and he catches her by the wrist and twists her round until her eyes look into his.

"And remember this, Beatrice: let there be no more of this childish folly and foolish threats, or as sure as you stand before me I'll kill you, and you shall be the companion statue on the opposite pedestal."

* * *

"What do you think of the port, Hertz?"

"Splendid wine; '47, eh?" the man replies, holding his glass to the light.

"No, quite a modern vintage. Treated by my own process."

"What a wonderful chap you are, Hazard—always doing something to astound people; always inventing something."

"Pooh! You can't call an artificial maturing of wine an invention; but I have one or two inventions with which I mean to surprise the world. The illumination of this room is one of my secrets; those electric lights will burn for years without renewal or attention. Electricity as men understand it now is nothing. As I know it, it is a power that can control the world, that can prolong man's life beyond his wildest dreams, and then preserve his body unalterable for all time. The height of the ambition of the ancients was embalming.

"What progress! They embalmed their departed dead, that they might keep them even at their feasts. Death at their feasts," repeats Dr. Hazard, frowning under his eyebrows at his wife, who sits opposite to him at the table.

Throughout the dinner, the doctor's scorn of his wife has been so obvious that his guests gladly seize upon the new tenour of the conversation for relief.

"Then you have invented a process to arrest decay?" Dr. Hertz asks.

"Yes."

The doctor's wife rests her arms upon the table and leans towards her husband.

"You own you have invented a process to arrest decay in a body?" she says, coldly. "You own it, before your friends?"

"Certainly," he exclaims, carelessly flicking the ash from his cigar.

"It is wonderful!" Dr. Hertz remarks.

"Mrs. Hazard, your husband is a remarkable man. You must be proud of him."

"Proud of him!" she exclaims, twisting her fingers in the tablecloth, and bending towards the visitor. "Proud of him! I hate him. I loathe him. He is right; he speaks truly; he has invented such a process—a process that permits him to slay men with impunity, and change them into black and shining marble. He is, as you say, a remarkable man."

The two guests gaze in astonishment at the woman who has risen from her seat, and with dilated eyes points at her husband, who sits back in his chair smoking his cigar.

"My dear Beatrice," he coldly exclaims at last, "you have another of your hysterical fits coming on. I am afraid I have erred in allowing you to hear so much of my discoveries. You are overwrought and excited. If you would rather retire, we will excuse you."

"I denounce you," she cries, "denounce you before your guests as a murderer—the murderer of the man who was in your employ three years ago. They searched London for him, and he was never found, and why? Because he never left this house; because he is here now. I dare you, I defy you, to take your friends, scientists like yourself, to your laboratory and show them the black statue—the body of the man you murdered, as you would murder me—if you dared."

The doctor frowns and looks perplexedly at his guests.

"I am sorry, my friends," he exclaims, rising and laying a hand on the shoulder of each. "It is very unfortunate, poor girl. You understand, of course. Would you mind humouring her? Will you come and see the statue that frightens her? It's a magnificent piece of work, a Greek god I bought in Florence."

The doctor and his colleagues descend to the laboratory, and his wife follows.

With eyes that keenly appreciate, the two men glance around the room at the various appliances and delicate instruments that fill the cases lining the walls, at the strange-looking coils and other apparatus that even they cannot give names to.

"Here," cries the doctor, walking to the alcove screened by the curtain, "is the statue. Life-like I confess, startlingly life-like; but that is all. Behold!"

With a flourish almost melodramatic, he flings back the curtain, and the lights gleam upon the polished figure—the Greek god with his arms folded upon his breast. The men stand rooted to the spot in admiration.

"Well, what do you think of my statue?"

"Your victim!"

"Hush, Beatrice. You alarm my friends."

"It is magnificent!"

"Yes," the doctor continues, "it is life itself. Look how the muscles stand out upon the arms, the veins in the hands and temples. Observe the folds of the girdle. Is it not superb?"

"Perfection!"

"And yet it is marble. Only marble, Beatrice," he continues, picking up a tiny pestle from the table. "Test it, Hertz."

"My dear Hazard——"

"To gratify her. Perhaps it will soothe her."

Dr. Hertz places his hand upon the smooth, cold surface of the statue, and then lightly taps it.

"It's a body," the woman cries. "Can't you see it is a body, or are you fools?"

"My dear Mrs. Hazard, no. You must forget all about that; it's only a beautiful piece of work in marble."

"You fool!"

"Beatrice, how dare you?"

"Now, my dear Hazard, don't excite her. It's very unfortunate."

"It's marble, Beatrice, don't you understand? Marble! marble! marble!" and the doctor strikes the figure with his fist as he shouts and glares at his wife. "I'm expecting a companion to it, Beatrice—a Venus. I've waited too long for it. I've been too lenient, but I will have it within a week."

There are hidden meanings, for his wife alone, in all that Dr. Hazard says during the remainder of the evening, and she answers back, scorn for scorn, hate for hate, and contempt for his contempt.

He has received the half-suggested, half-expressed commiserations of his friends with the quiet dignity suitable to the circumstances, and now he bolts the door and descends direct to the laboratory.

"It's a good thing for me that some scientists are fools, or I should have been in a bad way to-night," he mutters. "Curse the spitfire, she's too dangerous."

He passes into the inner room, there is a sound of basket work creaking as a big jar is dragged across the room, and then a running and splashing as liquid pours into the bath. The furnace throws out a ruddy glow, and the doctor takes off his coat, and works in a red light as the heat of the room increases.

Then wires are attached to one of the strange instruments at which his guests had marvelled, the opposite ends to plates of metal which are cast into the bath, and, lighting a cigar, he starts the battery and waits.

In a quarter of an hour he dips a rod into the liquid, and, withdrawing it, gazes with a sigh of satisfaction at the black, shining glaze with which it has become coated. Then, placing it on one side, he re-enters the outer room.

For a moment he stands listening at the door of the laboratory, and then stealthily moves up the stairs. The house is silent. Through the long oval fanlight over the hall door a struggling moonbeam throws a narrow ribbon of light upon the polished floor. Outside, a distant footstep approaches, passes, and fades away. The clock strikes two.

Slowly he ascends towards his wife's room. No doubt she is sleeping, and the task will be easier. And then, in the blackness of the staircase, he becomes conscious of another person, hears the faint suppressed breathing of someone hiding, lurking in the darkest corner and fearful of discovery.

He takes a phial from his pocket, and holding it well away from his face, pours the contents upon a handkerchief and listens again. Yes, there is someone. It is Beatrice. Perhaps creeping down to him as he is creeping up to her; coming by stealth to kill him as he works.

Suddenly he springs forward, and grips her by the throat. There is an instant's struggle as he holds the handkerchief over her mouth—a moan, stifled in its birth, and she drops limply to the floor—dead.

Half carrying, half dragging the body, he descends to the laboratory. The light has gone out.

"Curse it," he mutters; "at this time, above all others—and I boasted it was infallible."

He passes into the inner room, where the crimson glow from the furnace gives just sufficient light to enable him to discern the outline of the bath, and then gradually and carefully he lowers his burden, until it lies full length upon the bottom and the liquid rises almost to the edge.

He returns to the outer chamber, and by the flare of a spirit-lamp sets himself to remedy the defect in the light. As he works in the shadow, a woman glides round the half-open door, glances at him, then at the knife she carries; but, as he slightly shifts his position, passes swiftly across the room and conceals herself behind the curtain of the empty alcove.

The doctor holds the lamp above his head, and looks anxiously around. The curtains sway as though someone moved behind them, and he holds his breath and takes a step backwards; then the half-open door catches his eye, and with a sneer at his own nerves he pushes it to and turns again to his work.

A little longer, and the rooms blaze with light once more, and he walks into the inner chamber and gazes into the bath.

At the bottom there lies a figure seemingly cut from black polished marble. There is a long-drawn sigh behind him, and he turns with an involuntary cry of terror.

"Beatrice!"

He must be mad, haunted; he grips the side of the bath and stares down into it.

Yes, there lies the woman—not Beatrice, but the sister

of the man standing behind the curtain—the two now
turned to everlasting stone.

He knows that his wife is walking towards him, and yet
he cannot move; his limbs seem paralysed. In a moment
she will clutch him, and force him down beside his victim.

He must break the spell of horror that roots him to the
spot, and with a supreme effort he takes a step towards
her; but the gleam of frenzy in her eyes unnerves him.
He blindly retreats, then stumbles against the bath, and,
falling backwards, meets the doom he had prepared for her.

THE SEAL OF SOLOMON THE GREAT

Wardon Allan Curtis

Wardon Allan Curtis was rescued from literary oblivion when his remarkable short story The Monster of Lake Lametrie *from the September, 1899,* PEARSON'S MAGAZINE *was included in the anthology* Science Fiction By Gaslight: A History and Anthology of Science Fiction in the Popular Magazines 1891 to 1911. *A skilled writer with an excellent sense of humor, he wrote relatively little, but what he did write showed immense promise.*

Though humor was his forte, The Seal of Solomon the Great *which originally appeared in* THE ARGOSY *for February, 1901, is an especially effective serious handling of the concept of the Genii, and aimed more to evoke horror than humor. The "Seal of Solomon" recurs again in his only book* The Strange Adventures of Mr. Middleton *published by Herbert S. Stone, Chicago, in 1903. Though linked together by the device of a story teller Emir Achmed Ben Daoud, the book is actually a group of separate stories, many of them science fiction and fantasy. One that will call for further investigation is* The Adventure of Norah Sullivan and the Student of Heredity. *It deals with a scientist who learns of an elixir which greatly accelerates growth and succeeds in making a guinea pig as big as an elephant. In a desperate search for food to sustain its bulk, the animal knocks down buildings, upsets traffic until it is finally destroyed by a poisoned cabbage.*

In the early years of science fiction magazines one of the more popular authors was Miles J. Breuer, M. D. A story which enhanced his reputation and which was reprinted several times was The Hungry Guinea-Pig

179

in AMAZING STORIES, *January, 1930. The story dealt with a scientist who through selective breeding and a special elixir, raised a guinea-pig as big as a house. The animal breaks loose and driven by hunger, knocks down buildings, tramples people and disrupts a city in a search for food. It is lured by truck loads of cabbages into an open space where it is blown up.*

Wardon Allan Curtis, on a number of counts, thereby proves a very interesting early fantasy and science fiction author who might reward further research.

WE ALL RESENTED having a civil engineer appointed as the head of our archeological expedition in lower Chaldea— a man ignorant of Chaldee, Hebrew, even modern Arabic, archeology, and history.

But we had asked certain favors of the government, among them the services of an engineer. The government replied that the granting of these favors would constitute us a quasi government expedition, and therefore stipulated that the government officer who accompanied us—the engineer—should be in command.

Now this was something we had not contemplated, and which we realized was entirely due to the requests at head-quarters by the engineer himself, a member of the British corps of irrigating engineers in Egypt possessed of a "pull" in inverse proportion to his ability, his geniality, and his civility.

But we needed these government favors; there was no way to get them without McGear, and so we submitted to be governed by McGear.

In addition to merely adding to the world's knowledge of Chaldean civilization, we wished to establish certain dates in Chaldean and Biblical history. By establishing these dates, we could reckon the correct dates of other events which we knew occurred at certain stated lengths of time before or after them.

We knew that "Ur of the Chaldees," whence Abraham led his followers forth to the conquest of Canaan, was a seaport town when that event occurred. Its ruins are now over one hundred miles inland.

By ascertaining the rate the coast is annually extended by the deposits brought down by the united currents of the Tigris and Euphrates, we could very closely approximate how long ago it was that Abraham flourished.

To determine the rate of deposit was to be McGear's duty, a small enough task, too, since a previous expedition had all but determined it.

So for three long months McGear lounged in idleness in his tent, while the rest of us dug in the ruins all day, and spent our evenings deciphering inscriptions.

Lounged I say, save when, to show his authority, he came out and interfered with our labors, set our diggers at work upon other tasks, and appropriated to himself whatsoever of our finds pleased his fancy. A signet ring of King Urukh, 1800 B. C., to an archeologist more priceless than any diamond, he confiscated, and wore upon his fat second finger. A little cylinder of sard—inscribed in bas relief with the portrait and name of a high priest, used to impress a signature upon the damp clay of a brick before baking—he seized and transformed into a watch charm.

We meditated getting these treasures back when we returned to civilization, but in the meantime we submitted to the seizures, submitted to his gobbling all the best food and three times as much as any one else had; submitted to his coarse wit and practical jokes; submitted to his constant run of loud talk and singing in the evening when we were endeavoring to concentrate our attention upon the arduous task of deciphering inscriptions.

Daily he became more domineering. Daily he more and more broke down our authority with our Arab laborers, and daily he more and more demoralized them.

That we disliked him need hardly be said, and finally we came to the conclusion that either he must leave, or the expedition return home.

As a means to get rid of him, we decided to give over our excavations for a while, and turn to studying the rate of deposit on the coast line. We thought that, perhaps, when his duty with the expedition had been performed, he would quit, especially as he had somewhat complained of late, and declared our life very monotonous.

So we took the boat down river, and in due time arrived at the Persian Gulf.

On the morning after our arrival, Deming, Horton, McGear, and myself, put forth along the coast in a small fishing sloop manned by three Arabs, having various dredging and measuring apparatus aboard.

At ten o'clock the wind dropped dead, and at the same time we made the pleasing discovery that the food and water we had prepared to bring with us had been left behind. Though near the coast, there was no water nearer than our point of departure, fifteen miles away.

Rowing our heavy, unwieldy craft was to the last degree onerous, but so great was the uncertainty of a breeze that we began taking our turns at the two oars, all but Mc-Gear; thirsty, hungry, all but McGear. He sat calmly in the bow.

Simultaneously with the discovery that our provisions were left behind, he had discovered that the sailors had aboard a loaf of bread and a small jug of water. He at once ate all of the bread and drank half of the water.

"Self-preservation is the first law of nature," said he, as he watched the rest of us row, and now and then pulled at the jug, which he declined to pass to us in response to our requests.

The fierce sun that beat down upon our labors was fast extracting the moisture from us, and we grew pitiably thirsty.

Our progress was at a snail's pace. We would actually be suffering before we got back to camp, even be in danger of heat prostration, all but McGear.

As we proceeded, some one of us occasionally cast a drag net overboard to while away the dismal tedium. Marine plants, a few fishes, came up and were examined.

Afternoon arrived. The net was going all the time now, and we watched the results with a sort of desperate eagerness. We must do all that we could to distract out minds from our torturing thirst.

Suddenly there was a cry from Horton. A dark mass came up over the side in the net.

When we had cleared the weeds and slime from it, we saw that it was a leaden casket, a foot and a half long by a foot wide and eight inches high. There was no joint to be seen in it.

If its weight had not told us, we might have thought it a solid block of lead. But it was comparatively light.

Turn about, those of us not rowing, we sawed at the casket with our knives. It was tedious work, and the zest of our curiosity slackened as the gratifying of it was deferred.

The tortures of thirst grew so great that it was impossible to keep our minds from them. Even McGear began to be uncomfortable, for he had drunk the last water in his jug some time before.

At last my knife sank to its hilt. It had passed through the wall of the casket. A few more cuts, and we had the thing open.

From a mass of thickly wadded wool, from the midst of heavy swathings of green silk, as bright as if just from the loom, there emerged, brilliantly flashing in the sun, a great flask of burnished copper.

"A flask of ancient Cypriote wine!" cried McGear.

"I hope it is," said Horton. "I hope it is something that will help allay our thirst."

"I know it is wine," added McGear. "I was at Famagusta when they dug up those ten bottles, and I had a taste."

He referred to the famous find of English archeologists shortly after Britain took possession of Cyprus, when ten earthenware bottles encased in an outer sheathing of copper, bearing the name of Bragadino, governor when the Turks finally wrested the island from the Venetians in 1571, had been unearthed.

Wine over four hundred years old, realizing as nearly as will ever be realized the dream of many a drinker as set forth in the novel of Petronius Arbiter, where at Trimalchio's feast, that supposed contemporary of Nero serves his guests with "Opimian Falernian, one thousand years old!"

"I saw those bottles in the British Museum," said Horton, "but they were inscribed in Cypriote Greek, while this bears a legend in Arabic. Besides, how would a Cypriote flask get into the Persian Gulf?"

On the side of the flask, an inscription had been deeply etched and then inlaid with silver. Horton read from the silver letters:

" 'This contains the Genii Sacar, imprisoned by Sulieman.' "

"Suleiman?" asked Deming.

"The Arabic for Solomon, of course. What does it mean?"

"What does this mean?" said I, pointing to our crew, who, with every appearance of extreme alarm, had fled to the other end of the boat.

"Oh, masters, masters," cried the skipper, "do not release that evil spirit to kill us."

"What is this balderdash?" said Deming.

"Have you not read in the tales of the Thousand and One Nights, O effendim, the tale of the fisherman who found a copper bottle in his net, and opening it, let out a vapor that became a vast cloud, which at length shrunk and took shape, and was a huge genii? And, O effendim, cannot you recall that it was a copper bottle, and that the genii told him that he was one of *two* rebellious genii imprisoned in bottles with the seal of Sulieman upon the mouth, and, O effendim"—and here the man's voice sank to a horrified, hoarse, gasping croak—"the other genii's name was Sacar."

"Over the mouth of the bottle is a leaden seal," announced Horton slowly, "and there I read, 'Solomon, King of Kings.' And, gentlemen, it is not in Arabic, but Hebrew."

"Which proves," said Deming, "that no Arab went to the trouble to get up this strange joke, throwing this thing into the sea on the wild chance that somebody would find it, and that that somebody would remember the tale of the fisherman. It was some foreigner who knew Hebrew as well as Arabic, and took care to make his joke plausible."

"Which proves," said McGear, snatching the bottle from Horton—"which proves," he continued after he had sprung away from us amidships with his prize, "that you are telling a long fool story to keep me from getting hold of this wine."

He began to pry off the leaden seal.

"You were getting ready suddenly to pull out the plug and drink it before I could get any. It's Cypriote wine."

He had almost dug out the pitch covered plug.

"You said it was an Arabic inscription. I can tell Arabic from Greek. It's Greek."

Horton sprang forward, the plug flew out, and with his right hand extended to ward off Horton, with his left McGear thrust the bottle into his mouth.

It was all in a moment, but I saw his little piggy eyes look disappointed, as if the wine he expected had not flowed, then saw them start and bulge, saw his face swell and empurple, as if at last the whole contents of the flask had burst forth down his gullet, choking him, then saw his frame puff and bloat and bloat, as if he were a hollow thing filled with gas; then, then, with a horrible rending and bursting, McGear was no more, nothing but a mist of blood, a diaphanous cloud of infinitesimal bits of flesh that floated across the sun like a haze of red dust, and was gone.

But what was that other awful white mist that took

shape, now a cloud, now a mass like a pelt of thick driving snow, shrinking, darkening, until a huge, monstrous sky towering giant swayed over our boat for a moment, then with a paean of joy that filled the whole circle of the horizon, soared away.

The authorities at London, in their investigations of the affair of McGear's death, have seen fit to disregard the affidavits of the members of our expedition and of the three Arab sailors.

But all their endeavors to bring evidence to disprove or even discredit our statements proving vain, they have made this one concession. They have entered McGear as having come to his death by apoplexy and dropsy.

THE DREAMS
IN THE WITCH-HOUSE

H. P. Lovecraft

One of the paradoxes of Lovecraft's admirers is the annoyance they have felt when that talented author was referred to as a major science fiction writer as well as a master of the supernatural. Despite the undeniable evidence of The Colour Out of Space, The Whisperer in Darkness, The Shadow Out of Time, *to name three major works, they have particularly rankled when shown how much closer to science fiction such masterpieces by him as* The Dunwich Horror, The Call of Cthulhu, The Shunned House *and even* The Temple *were than to the supernatural.*

The paradox rests in the strong efforts some of these same people have made to show that The Dreams in the Witch-House *is as much science fiction as it is supernatural. They received no small assistance in this effort from H. P. Lovecraft who in the context of the story referred to Einstein's theories, the space-time continuum, "the elements of high atomic weight which chemistry was absolutely powerless to identify." The possibility of stepping from the third into the fourth dimension and back again, extra-dimensional geometry was considered, and finally the statement "the alien curves and spirals of some ethereal vortex which obeyed laws unknown to the physics and mathematics of any conceivable universe," sounded a note of frustration.*

The truth was that H. P. Lovecraft did not believe in the supernatural. Never did and never would to the day of his death and felt that many of his readers didn't and attempted to offer the possibility that there was some scientific rather than supernatural explanation for witchcraft to make his stories more convincing.

In this he succeeded, for though The Dreams in the Witch-House *cannot be said to be a "forgotten" masterpiece of horror, it is certainly far too infrequently encountered in anthologies of the genre.*

WHETHER THE DREAMS brought on the fever or the fever brought on the dreams Walter Gilman did not know. Behind everything crouched the brooding, festering horror of the ancient town, and of the moldy, unhallowed garret gable where he wrote and studied and wrestled with figures and formulæ when he was not tossing on the meager iron bed. His ears were growing sensitive to a preternatural and intolerable degree, and he had long ago stopped the cheap mantel clock whose ticking had come to seem like a thunder of artillery. At night the subtle stirring of the black city outside, the sinister scurrying of rats in the wormy partitions, and the creaking of hidden timbers in the centuried house, were enough to give him a sense of strident pandemonium. The darkness always teemed with unexplained sound—and yet he sometimes shook with fear lest the noises he heard should subside and allow him to hear certain other, fainter noises which he suspected were lurking behind them.

He was in the changeless, legend-haunted city of Arkham, with its clustering gambrel roofs that sway and sag over attics where witches hid from the King's men in the dark, olden days of the Province. Nor was any spot in that city more steeped in macabre memory than the gable room which harbored him—for it was this house and this room which had likewise harbored old Keziah Mason, whose flight from Salem Jail at the last no one was ever able to explain. That was in 1692—the jailer had gone mad and babbled of a small white-fanged furry thing which scuttled out of Keziah's cell, and not even Cotton Mather could explain the curves and angles smeared on the gray stone walls with some red, sticky fluid.

Possibly Gilman ought not to have studied so hard. Non-Euclidean calculus and quantum physics are enough to stretch any brain; and when one mixes them with folklore, and tries to trace a strange background of multidimensional reality behind the ghoulish hints of the Gothic tales and the wild whispers of the chimney-corner, one can hardly expect to be wholly free from mental tension. Gilman came from Haverhill, but it was only after he had entered college in Arkham that he began to connect his mathematics with the fantastic legends of elder magic. Something in the air of the hoary town worked obscurely on his imagination. The professors at Miskatonic had urged him to slacken up, and had voluntarily cut down his course at several points. Moreover, they had stopped him from consulting the dubious old books on forbidden secrets that were kept under lock and key in a vault at the university library. But all these precautions came late in the day, so that Gilman had some terrible hints from the dreaded *Necronomicon* of Abdul Al-hazred, the framentary *Book of Eibon*, and the suppressed *Unaussprechlichen Kulten* of von Junzt to correlate with his abstract formulæ on the properties of space and the linkage of dimensions known and unknown.

He knew his room was in the old Witch-House—that, indeed, was why he had taken it. There was much in the Essex County records about Keziah Mason's trial, and what she had admitted under pressure to the Court of Oyer and Terminer had fascinated Gilman beyond all reason. She had told Judge Hathorne of lines and curves that could be made to point out directions leading through the walls of space to other spaces beyond, and had implied that such lines and curves were frequently used at certain midnight meetings in the dark valley of the white stone beyond Meadow Hill and on the unpeopled island in the river. She had spoken also of the Black Man, of her oath, and of her new secret name of Nahab. Then she had drawn those devices on the walls of her cell and vanished.

Gilman believed strange things about Keziah, and had felt a queer thrill on learning that her dwelling was still standing after more than 235 years. When he heard the hushed Arkham whispers about Keziah's persistent presence in the old house and the narrow streets, about the irregular human tooth-marks left on certain sleepers in that and other houses, about the childish cries heard near May-Eve and Hallowmass, about the stench often noted in the old house's attic just after those dreaded seasons, and about the small, furry, sharp-toothed thing which haunted the moldering structure and the town and nuzzled people curiously in the black hours before dawn, he resolved to live in the place at any cost. A room was easy to secure; for the house was unpopular, hard to rent, and long given over to cheap lodgings. Gilman could not have told what he expected to find there, but he knew he wanted to be in the building where some circumstance had more or less suddenly given a mediocre old woman of the Seventeenth Century an insight into mathematical depths perhaps beyond the utmost modern delvings of Planck, Heisenberg, Einstein, and de Sitter.

He studied the timber and plaster walls for traces of cryptic designs at every accessible spot where the paper had peeled, and within a week managed to get the eastern attic room where Keziah was held to have practised her spells. It had been vacant from the first—for no one had ever been willing to stay there long—but the Polish landlord had grown wary about renting it. Yet nothing whatever happened to Gilman till about the time of the fever. No ghostly Keziah flitted through the somber halls and chambers, no small furry thing crept into his dismal eyrie to nuzzle him, and no record of the witch's incantations rewarded his constant search. Sometimes he would take walks through shadowy tangles of unpaved musty-smelling lanes where eldritch brown houses of unknown age leaned and tottered and leered mockingly through narrow, small-paned windows. Here he knew strange things had happened once, and there was a faint suggestion behind the surface that everything of that monstrous past might not—at least in the darkest, narrowest, and most intricately crooked alleys—have utterly perished. He also rowed out twice to the ill-regarded island in the river, and made a sketch of the singular angles described by the moss-grown rows of gray standing stones whose origin was so obscure and immemorial.

Gilman's room was of good size but queerly irregular shape; the north wall slanting perceptibly inward from the outer to the inner end, while the low ceiling slanted gently downward in the same direction. Aside from an obvious rat-hole and the signs of other stopped-up ones, there was no access—nor any appearance of a former avenue of access—to the space which must have existed between the slanting wall and the straight outer wall on the house's north side, though a view from the exterior showed where a window had been boarded up at a very remote date. The loft above the ceiling—which must have had a slanting floor—was likewise inaccessible. When Gilman climbed up a ladder to the cobwebbed level loft above the rest of the attic he found vestiges of a bygone aperture tightly and heavily covered with ancient planking and secured by the stout wooden pegs common in Colonial carpentry. No amount of persuasion, however, could induce the stolid landlord to let him investigate either of these two closed spaces.

As time wore along, his absorption in the irregular wall and ceiling of his room increased; for he began to read into the odd angles a mathematical significance which seemed to offer vague clues regarding their purpose. Old Keziah, he reflected, might have had excellent reasons for living in a room with peculiar angles; for was it not through certain angles that she claimed to have gone outside the boundaries of the world of space we know? His interest gradually veered away from the unplumbed voids beyond the slanting surfaces, since it now appeared that the purpose of those surfaces concerned the side he was already on.

The touch of brain-fever and the dreams began early in February. For some time, apparently, the curious angles of Gilman's room had been having a strange, almost hypnotic effect on him; and as the bleak winter advanced he had found himself staring more and more intently at the corner where the down-slanting ceiling met the inward-slanting wall. About this period his inability to concentrate on his formal studies worried him considerably, his apprehensions about the mid-year examinations being very acute. But the exaggerated sense of hearing was scarcely less annoying. Life had become an insistent and almost unendurable cacophony, and there was that constant, terrifying impression of *other* sounds—perhaps from regions beyond life—trembling on the very brink of audibility. So far as concrete noises went, the rats in the ancient partitions were the worst. Sometimes their scratching seemed not only furtive but deliberate. When it came from beyond the slanting north wall it was mixed with a sort of dry rattling; and when it came from the century-closed loft above the slanting ceiling Gilman always braced himself as if expecting some horror which only bided its time before descending to engulf him utterly.

The dreams were wholly beyond the pale of sanity, and Gilman felt that they must be a result, jointly, of his studies in mathematics and in folklore. He had been thinking too much about the vague regions which his formulæ told him must lie beyond the three dimensions we know, and about the possibility that old Keziah Mason—guided by some influence past all conjecture—had actually found the gate to those regions. The yellowed county records containing her testimony and that of her accusers were so damnably suggestive of things beyond human experience—and the descriptions of the darting little furry object which served as her familiar were so painfully realistic despite their incredible details.

That object—no larger than a good-sized rat and quaintly called by the townspeople "Brown Jenkin"—seemed to have been the fruit of a remarkable case of sympathetic herd-delusion, for in 1692 no less than eleven persons had testified to glimpsing it. There were recent rumors, too, with a baffling and disconcerting amount of agreement. Witnesses said it had long hair and the shape of rat, but that its sharp-toothed, bearded face was evilly human while its paws were like tiny human hands. It took messages betwixt old Keziah and the devil, and was nursed on the witch's blood, which it sucked like a vampire. Its voice was a kind of loathsome titter, and it could speak all languages. Of all the bizarre monstrosities in Gilman's dreams, nothing filled him with greater panic and nausea than this blasphemous and diminutive hybrid, whose image flitted across his vision in a form a thousandfold more hateful than anything his waking mind had deduced from the ancient records and the modern whispers.

Gilman's dreams consisted largely in plunges through limitless abysses of inexplicably colored twilight and bafflingly disordered sound; abysses whose material and gravitational properties, and whose relation to his own entity, he could not even begin to explain. He did not walk or climb, fly or swim, crawl or wriggle; yet always experienced a mode of motion partly voluntary and partly involuntary. Of his own condition he could not well judge, for sight of his arms, legs, and torso seemed always cut off by some odd disarrangement of perspective; but he felt that his physical organization and faculties were somehow marvelously transmuted and obliquely projected—though not without a certain grotesque relationship to his normal proportions and properties.

The abysses were by no means vacant, being crowded with indescribably angled masses of alien-hued substance, some of which appeared to be organic while others seemed inorganic. A few of the organic objects tended to awake vague memories in the back of his mind, though he could form no conscious idea of what they mockingly resembled or suggested. In the later dreams he began to distinguish separate categories into which the organic objects appeared to be divided, and which seemed to involve in each case a radically different species of conduct-pattern and basic motivation. Of these categories one seemed to him to include objects slightly less illogical and irrelevant in their motions than the members of the other categories.

All the objects—organic and inorganic alike—were totally beyond description or even comprehension. Gilman sometimes compared the inorganic matter to prisms, labyrinths, clusters of cubes and planes, and cyclopean buildings; and the organic things struck him variously as groups of bubbles, octopi, centipedes, living Hindoo idols, and intricate arabesques roused into a kind of ophidian animation. Everything he saw was unspeakably menacing and horrible; and whenever one of the organic entities appeared by its motions to be noticing him, he felt a stark, hideous fright which generally jolted him awake. Of how the organic entities moved, he could tell no more than of how he moved himself. In time he observed a further mystery—the tendency of certain entities to appear suddenly out of empty space, or to disappear totally with equal suddenness. The shrieking, roaring confusion of sound which permeated the abysses was past all analysis as to pitch, timber or rhythm; but seemed to be synchronous with vague visual changes in all the indefinite objects, organic and inorganic alike. Gilman had a constant sense of dread that it might rise to some unbearable degree of intensity during one or another of its obscure, relentlessly inevitable fluctuations.

But it was not in these vortices of complete alienage that he saw Brown Jenkin. That shocking little horror was reserved for certain lighter, sharper dreams which assailed him just before he dropped into the fullest depths of sleep. He would be lying in the dark fighting to keep awake when a faint lambent glow would seem to shimmer around the centuried room, showing in a violet mist the convergence of angled planes which had seized his brain so insidiously. The horror would appear to pop out of the rat-hole in the corner and patter toward him over the sagging, wide-planked floor with evil expectancy in its tiny, bearded human face; but mercifully, this dream always melted away before the object got close enough to nuzzle him. It had hellishly long, sharp, canine teeth. Gilman tried to stop up the rat-hole every day, but each night the real tenants of the partitions would gnaw away the obstruction, whatever it might be. Once he had the landlord nail tin over it, but the next night the rats gnawed a fresh hole, in making which they pushed or dragged out into the room a curious little fragment of bone.

Gilman did not report his fever to the doctor, for he knew he could not pass the examinations if ordered to the college infirmary when every moment was needed for cramming. As it was, he failed in Calculus D and Advanced General Psychology, though not without hope of making up lost ground before the end of the term.

It was in March when the fresh element entered his lighter preliminary dreaming, and the nightmare shape of Brown Jenkin began to be companioned by the nebulous blur which grew more and more to resemble a bent old woman. This addition disturbed him more than he could account for, but finally he decided that it was like an ancient crone whom he had twice actually encountered in the dark tangle of lanes near the abandoned wharves. On those occasions the evil, sardonic, and seemingly unmotivated stare of the beldame had set him almost shivering—especially the first time, when an overgrown rat darting across the shadowed mouth of a neighboring alley had made him think irrationally of Brown Jenkin. Now, he reflected, those nervous fears were being mirrored in his disordered dreams.

That the influence of the old house was unwholesome he could not deny, but traces of his early morbid interest still held him there. He argued that the fever alone was responsible for his nightly fantasies, and that when the touch abated he would be free from the monstrous visions. Those visions, however, were of absorbing vividness and convincingness, and whenever he awaked he retained a vague sense of having undergone much more than he remembered. He was hideously sure that in unrecalled dreams he had talked with both Brown Jenkin and the old woman, and that they had been urging him to go somewhere with them and to meet a third being of greater potency.

Toward the end of March he began to pick up in his mathematics, though other studies bothered him increasingly. He was getting an intuitive knack for solving Riemannian equations, and astonished Professor Upham by his comprehension of fourth-dimensional and other problems which had floored all the rest of the class. One afternoon there was a discussion of possible freakish curvatures in space, and of theoretical points of approach or even contact between our part of the cosmos and various other regions as distant as the farthest stars or the trans-galactic gulfs themselves—or even as fabulously remote as the tentatively conceivable cosmic units beyond the whole Einsteinian space-time continuum. Gilman's handling of this theme filled every one with admiration, even though some of his hypothetical illustrations caused an increase in the always plentiful gossip about his nervous and solitary eccentricity. What made the students shake their heads was his sober theory that a man might—given mathematical knowledge admittedly beyond all likelihood of human acquirement—step deliberately from the earth to any other celestial body which might lie at one of an infinity of specific points in the cosmic pattern.

Such a step, he said, would require only two stages; first, a passage out of the three-dimensional sphere we know, and second, a passage back to the three-dimensional sphere at another point, perhaps one of infinite remoteness. That this could be accomplished without loss of life was in many cases conceivable. Any being from any part of three-dimensional space could probably survive in the fourth dimension; and its survival of the second stage would depend upon what alien part of three-dimensional space it might select for its re-entry. Denizens of some planets might be able to live on certain others—even planets belonging to other galaxies, or to similar dimensional phases of other space-time continua—though of course there must be vast numbers of mutually uninhabitable even though mathematically juxtaposed bodies or zones of space.

It was also possible that the inhabitants of a given dimensional realm could survive entry to many unknown and incomprehensible realms of additional or indefinitely multiplied dimensions—be they within or outside the given space-time continuum—and that the converse would be likewise true. This was a matter for speculation, though one could be fairly certain that the type of mutation involved in a passage from any given dimensional plane to the next higher plane would not be destructive of biological integrity as we understand it. Gilman could not be very clear about his reasons for this last assumption, but his haziness here was more than overbalanced by his clearness on other complex points. Professor Upham especially liked his demonstration of the kinship of higher mathematics to certain phases of magical lore transmitted down the ages from an ineffable antiquity—human or pre-human—whose knowledge of the cosmos and its laws was greater than ours.

Around the first of April Gilman worried considerably because his slow fever did not abate. He was also troubled by what some of his fellow-lodgers said about his sleep-walking. It seemed that he was often absent from his bed, and that the creaking of his floor at certain hours of the night was remarked by the man in the room below. This fellow also spoke of hearing the tread of shod feet in the night; but Gilman was sure he must have been mistaken in this, since shoes as well as other apparel were always precisely in place in the morning. One could develop all sorts of aural delusions in this morbid old house—for did not Gilman himself, even in daylight, now feel certain that noises other than rat-scratching came from the black voids beyond the slanting wall and above the slanting ceiling? His pathologically sensitive ears began to listen for faint foot-falls in the immemorially sealed loft overhead, and some-times the illusion of such things was agonizingly realistic.

However, he knew that he had actually become a som-nambulist; for twice at night his room had been found vacant, though with all his clothing in place. Of this he had been assured by Frank Elwood, the one fellow-student whose poverty forced him to room in this squalid and unpopular house. Elwood had been studying in the small hours and had come up for help on a differential equation, only to find Gilman absent. It had been rather presump-tuous of him to open the unlocked door after knocking had failed to rouse a response, but he had needed the help very badly and thought that his host would not mind a gentle prodding awake. On neither occasion, though, had Gilman been there; and when told of the matter he wondered where he could have been wandering, barefoot and with only his nightclothes on. He resolved to investi-gate the matter if reports of his sleep-walking continued, and thought of sprinkling flour on the floor of the corridor to see where his footsteps might lead. The door was the only conceivable egress, for there was no possible foothold outside the narrow window.

As April advanced, Gilman's fever-sharpened ears were disturbed by the whining prayers of a superstitious loom-fixer named Joe Mazurewicz, who had a room on the ground floor. Mazurewicz had told long, rambling stories about the ghost of old Keziah and the furry, sharp-fanged, nuzzling thing, and had said he was so badly haunted at times that only his silver crucifix—given him for the purpose by Father Iwanicki of St. Stanislaus' Church—could bring him relief. Now he was praying because the Witches' Sabbath was drawing near. May Eve was Walpurgis Night, when hell's blackest evil roamed the earth and all the slaves of Satan gathered for nameless rites and deeds. It was always a very bad time in Arkham, even though the fine folks up in Miskatonic Avenue and High and Saltonstall Streets pretended to know nothing about it. There would be bad doings, and a child or two would probably be missing. Joe knew about such things, for his grandmother in the old country had heard tales from her grandmother. It was wise to pray and count one's beads at this season. For three months Keziah and Brown Jenkin had not been near Joe's room, nor near Paul Choynski's room, nor anywhere else—and it meant no good when they held off like that. They must be up to something.

Gilman dropped in at the doctor's office on the 16th of the month, and was surprised to find his temperature was not as high as he had feared. The physician questioned him sharply, and advised him to see a nerve specialist. On reflection, he was glad he had not consulted the still more inquisitive college doctor. Old Waldron, who had curtailed his activities before, would have made him take a rest—an impossible thing now that he was so close to great results in his equations. He was certainly near the boundary between the known universe and the fourth dimension, and who could say how much farther he might go?

But even as these thoughts came to him he wondered at the source of his strange confidence. Did all of this perilous sense of imminence come from the formulæ on the sheets he covered day by day? The soft, stealthy, imaginary footsteps in the sealed loft above were unnerving. And now, too, there was a growing feeling that somebody was constantly persuading him to do something terrible which he could not do. How about the somnambulism? Where did he go sometimes in the night? And what was that faint suggestion of sound which once in a while seemed to trickle though the confusion of identifiable sounds even in broad daylight and full wakefulness? Its rhythm did not correspond to anything on earth, unless perhaps to the cadence of one or two unmentionable Sabbat-chants, and sometimes he feared it corresponded to certain attributes of the vague shrieking or roaring in those wholly alien abysses of dream.

The dreams were meanwhile getting to be atrocious. In the lighter preliminary phase the evil old woman was now of fiendish distinctness, and Gilman knew she was the one who had frightened him in the slums. Her bent back, long nose, and shrivelled chin were unmistakable, and her shapeless brown garments were like those he remembered. The expression on her face was one of hideous malevolence and exultation, and when he awaked he could recall a croaking voice that persuaded and threatened. He must meet the Black Man, and go with them all to the throne of Azathoth at the center of ultimate chaos. That was what she said. He must sign the book of Azathoth in his own blood and take a new secret name now that his independent delvings had gone so far. What kept him from going with her and Brown Jenkin and the other to the throne of Chaos where the thin flutes pipe mindlessly was the fact that he had seen the name "Azathoth" in the *Necronomicon*, and knew it stood for a primal evil too horrible for description.

The old woman always appeared out of thin air near the corner where the downward slant met the inward slant. She seemed to crystallize at a point closer to the ceiling than to the floor, and every night she was a little nearer and more distinct before the dream shifted. Brown Jenkin, too, was always a little nearer at the last, and his yellowish-white fangs glistened shockingly in that unearthly violet phosphorescence. Its shrill loathsome tittering stuck more and more in Gilman's head, and he could remember in the morning how it had pronounced the words "Azathoth" and "Nyarlathotep."

In the deeper dreams everything was likewise more distinct, and Gilman felt that the twilight abysses around him were those of the fourth dimension. Those organic entities whose motions seemed least flagrantly irrelevant and unmotivated were probably projections of life-forms from our own planet, including human beings. What the others were in their own dimensional sphere or spheres he dared not try to think. Two of the less irrelevantly moving things—a rather large congeries of iridescent, prolately spheroidal bubbles and a very much smaller polyhedron of unknown colors and rapidly shifting surface angles—

seemed to take notice of him and follow him about or float ahead as he changed position among the titan prisms, labyrinths, cube-and-plane clusters and quasi-buildings; and all the while the vague shrieking and roaring waxed louder and louder, as if approaching some monstrous climax of utterly unendurable intensity.

During the night of April 19-20th the new development occurred. Gilman was half involuntarily moving about in the twilight abysses with the bubble-mass and the small polyhedron floating ahead, when he noticed the peculiarly regular angles formed by the edges of some gigantic neighboring prism-clusters. In another second he was out of the abyss and standing tremulously on a rocky hillside bathed in intense, diffused green light. He was barefooted and in his nightclothes, and when he tried to walk discovered that he could scarcely lift his feet. A swirling vapor hid everything but the immediate sloping terrain from sight, and he shrank from the thought of the sounds that might surge out of that vapor.

Then he saw the two shapes laboriously crawling toward him—the old woman and the little furry thing. The crone strained up to her knees and managed to cross her arms in a singular fashion, while Brown Jenkin pointed in a certain direction with a horribly anthropoid fore-paw which it raised with evident difficulty. Spurred by an impulse he did not originate, Gilman dragged himself forward along a course determined by the angle of the old woman's arms and the direction of the small monstrosity's paw, and before he had shuffled three steps he was back in the twilight abysses. Geometrical shapes seethed around him, and he fell dizzily and interminably. At last he woke in his bed in the crazily angled garret of the eldritch old house.

He was good for nothing that morning, and stayed away from all his classes. Some unknown attraction was pulling his eyes in a seemingly irrelevant direction, for he could not help staring at a certain vacant spot on the floor. As the day advanced, the focus of his unseeing eyes changed position, and by noon he had conquered the impulse to stare at vacancy. About two o'clock he went out for lunch, and as he treaded the narrow lanes of the city he found himself turning always to the southeast. Only an effort halted him at a cafeteria in Church Street, and after the meal he felt the unknown pull still more strongly.

He would have to consult a nerve specialist after all

—perhaps there was a connection with his somnambu-lism—but meanwhile he might at least try to break the morbid spell himself. Undoubtedly he could still manage to walk away from the pull; so with great resolution he headed against it and dragged himself deliberately north along Garrison Street. By the time he had reached the bridge over the Miskatonic he was in a cold perspiration, and he clutched at the iron railing as he gazed upstream at the ill-regarded island whose regular lines of ancient standing stones brooded sullenly in the afternoon sunlight.

Then he gave a start. For there was a clearly visible living figure on that desolate island, and a second glance told him it was certainly the strange old woman whose sinister aspect had worked itself so disastrously into his dreams. The tall grass near her was moving, too, as if some other living thing were crawling close to the ground. When the old woman began to turn toward him he fled precip-itately off the bridge and into the shelter of the town's labyrinthine waterfront alleys. Distant though the island was, he felt that a monstrous and invincible evil could flow from the sardonic stare of that bent, ancient figure in brown.

The southeastward pull still held, and only with tremen-dous resolution could Gilman drag himself into the old house and up the rickety stairs. For hours he sat silent and aimless, with his eyes shifting gradually westward. About six o'clock his sharpened ears caught the whining prayers of Joe Mazurewicz two floors below, and in desperation he seized his hat and walked out into the sunset-golden streets, letting the now directly southward pull carry him where it might. An hour later darkness found him in the open fields beyond Hangman's Brook, with the glimmering spring stars shining ahead. The urge to walk was gradually chang-ing to an urge to leap mystically into space, and suddenly he realized just where the source of the pull lay.

It was in the sky. A definite point among the stars had a claim on him and was calling him. Apparently it was a point somewhere between Hydra and Argo Navis, and he knew that he had been urged toward it ever since he had awaked soon after dawn. In the morning it had been un-derfoot, and now it was roughly south but stealing toward the west. What was the meaning of this new thing? Was he going mad? How long would it last? Again mustering his resolution, Gilman turned and dragged himself back to the sinister old house.

Mazurewicz was waiting for him at the door, and seemed both anxious and reluctant to whisper some fresh bit of superstition. It was about the witch-light. Joe had been out celebrating the night before—it was Patriots' Day in Massachusetts—and had come home after midnight. Looking up at the house from outside, he had thought at first that Gilman's window was dark, but then he had seen the faint violet glow within. He wanted to warn the gentleman about that glow, for everybody in Arkham knew it was Keziah's witch-light which played near Brown Jenkin and the ghost of the old crone herself. He had not mentioned this before, but now he must tell about it because it meant that Keziah and her long-toothed familiar were haunting the young gentleman. Sometimes he and Paul Choynski and Landlord Dombrowski thought they saw that light seeping out of cracks in the sealed loft above the young gentleman's room, but they had all agreed not to talk about that. However, it would be better for the gentleman to take another room and get a crucifix from some good priest like Father Iwanicki.

As the man rambled on, Gilman felt a nameless panic clutch at his throat. He knew that Joe must have been half drunk when he came home the night before; yet the mention of a violet light in the garret window was of frightful import. It was a lambent glow of this sort which always played about the old woman and the small furry thing in those lighter, sharper dreams which prefaced his plunge into unknown abysses, and the thought that a wakeful second person could see the dream-luminance was utterly beyond sane harborage. Yet where had the fellow got such an odd notion? Had he himself talked as well as walked around the house in his sleep? No, Joe said, he had not—but he must check up on this. Perhaps Frank Elwood could tell him something, though he hated to ask.

Fever—wild dreams—somnambulism—illusions of sounds—a pull toward a point in the sky—and now a suspicion of insane sleep-talking! He must stop studying, see a nerve specialist, and take himself in hand. When he climbed to the second story he paused at Elwood's door but saw that the other youth was out. Reluctantly he continued up to his garret room and sat down in the dark. His gaze was still pulled to the southward, but he also found himself listening intently for some sound in the closed loft above, and half imagining that an evil violet light seeped down through an infinitesimal crack in the low, slanting ceiling.

That night as Gilman slept, the violet light broke upon him with heightened intensity, and the old witch and small furry thing, getting closer than ever before, mocked him with inhuman squeals and devilish gestures. He was glad to sink into the vaguely roaring twilight abysses, though the pursuit of that iridescent bubble-congeries and that kaleidoscopic little polyhedron was menacing and irritating. Then came the shift as vast converging planes of a slippery-looking substance loomed above and below him—a shift which ended in a flash of delirium and a blaze of unknown, alien light in which yellow, carmine, and indigo were madly and inextricably blended.

He was half lying on a high, fantastically balustraded terrace above a boundless jungle of outlandish, incredible peaks, balanced planes, domes, minarets, horizontal disks poised on pinnacles, and numberless forms of still greater wildness—some of stone and some of metal—which glittered gorgeously in the mixed, almost blistering glare from a polychromatic sky. Looking upward he saw three stupendous disks of flame, each of a different hue, and at a different height above an infinitely distant curving horizon of low mountains. Behind him tiers of higher terraces towered aloft as far as he could see. The city below stretched away to the limits of vision, and he hoped that no sound would well up from it.

The pavement from which he easily raised himself was of a veined, polished stone beyond his power to identify, and the tiles were cut in bizarre-angled shapes which struck him as less asymmetrical than based on some unearthly symmetry whose laws he could not comprehend. The balustrade was chest-high, delicate, and fantastically wrought, while along the rail were ranged at short intervals little figures of grotesque design and exquisite workmanship. They, like the whole balustrade, seemed to be made of some sort of shining metal whose color could not be guessed in the chaos of mixed effulgences, and their nature utterly defied conjecture. They represented some ridged barrel-shaped object with thin horizontal arms radiating spoke-like from a central ring and with vertical knobs or bulbs projecting from the head and base of the barrel. Each of these knobs was the hub of a system of five long, flat, triangularly tapering arms arranged around it like the arms of a starfish—nearly horizontal, but curving slightly away from the central barrel. The base of the bottom knob was fused to the long railing with so delicate a point of contact that several figures had been broken off and were missing. The figures were about four and a half inches in height, while the spiky arms gave them a maximum diameter of about two and a half inches.

When Gilman stood up, the tiles felt hot to his bare feet. He was wholly alone, and his first act was to walk to the balustrade and look dizzily down at the endless, cyclopean city almost two thousand feet below. As he listened he thought a rhythmic confusion of faint musical pipings covering a wide tonal range welled up from the narrow streets beneath, and he wished he might discern the denizens of the place. The sight turned him giddy after a while, so that he would have fallen to the pavement had he not clutched instinctively at the lustrous balustrade. His right hand fell on one of the projecting figures, the touch seeming to steady him slightly. It was too much, however, for the exotic delicacy of the metal-work, and the spiky figure snapped off under his grasp. Still half dazed, he continued to clutch it as his other hand seized a vacant space on the smooth railing.

But now his over-sensitive ears caught something behind him, and he looked back across the level terrace. Approaching him softly though without apparent furtiveness were five figures, two of which were the sinister old woman and the fanged, furry little animal. The other three were what sent him unconscious; for they were living entities about eight feet high, shaped precisely like the spiky images on the balustrade, and propelling themselves by a spider-like wriggling of their lower set of starfish-arms.

Gilman awaked in his bed, drenched by a cold perspiration and with a smarting sensation in his face, hands and feet. Springing to the floor, he washed and dressed in frantic haste, as if it were necessary for him to get out of the house as quickly as possible. He did not know where he wished to go, but felt that once more he would have to sacrifice his classes. The odd pull toward that spot in the sky between Hydra and Argo had abated, but another of even greater strength had taken its place. Now he felt that he must go north—infinitely north. He dreaded to cross the bridge that gave a view of the desolate island in the Miskatonic, so went over the Peabody Avenue bridge. Very often he stumbled, for his eyes and ears were chained to an extremely lofty point in the blank blue sky.

After about an hour he got himself under better control,

and saw that he was far from the city. All around him stretched the bleak emptiness of salt marshes, while the narrow road ahead led to Innsmouth—that ancient, half-deserted town which Arkham people were so curiously unwilling to visit. Though the northward pull had not diminished, he resisted it as he had resisted the other pull, and finally found that he could almost balance the one against the other. Plodding back to town and getting some coffee at a soda fountain, he dragged himself into the public library and browsed aimlessly among the lighter magazines. Once he met some friends who remarked how oddly sunburned he looked, but he did not tell them of his walk. At three o'clock he took some lunch at a restaurant, noting meanwhile that the pull had either lessened or divided itself. After that he killed the time at a cheap cinema show, seeing the inane performance over and over again without paying any attention to it.

About nine at night he drifted homeward and shuffled into the ancient house. Joe Mazurewicz was whining unintelligible prayers, and Gilman hastened up to his own garret chamber without pausing to see if Elwood was in. It was when he turned on the feeble electric light that the shock came. At once he saw there was something on the table which did not belong there, and a second look left no room for doubt. Lying on its side—for it could not stand up alone—was the exotic spiky figure which in his monstrous dream he had broken off the fantastic balustrade. No detail was missing. The ridged, barrel-shaped center, the thin radiating arms, the knobs at each end, and the flat, slightly outward-curving starfish-arms spreading from those knobs—all were there. In the electric light the color seemed to be a kind of iridescent gray veined with green; and Gilman could see amidst his horror and bewilderment that one of the knobs ended in a jagged break, corresponding to its former point of attachment to the dream-railing.

Only his tendency toward a dazed stupor prevented him from screaming aloud. This fusion of dream and reality was too much to bear. Still dazed, he clutched at the spiky thing and staggered downstairs to Landlord Dombrowski's quarters. The whining prayers of the superstitious loom-fixer were still sounding through the moldy halls, but Gilman did not mind them now. The landlord was in, and greeted him pleasantly. No, he had not seen that thing before and did not know anything about it. But his wife had said she found a funny tin thing in one of the beds when she fixed the rooms at noon, and maybe that was it. Dombrowski called her, and she waddled in. Yes, that was the thing. She had found it in the young gentleman's bed—on the side next the wall. It had looked very queer to her but of course the young gentleman had lots of queer things in his room—books and curios and pictures and markings on paper. She certainly knew nothing about it.

So Gilman climbed upstairs again in mental turmoil, convinced that he was either still dreaming or that his somnambulism had run to incredible extremes and led him to depredations in unknown places. Where had he got this outré thing? He did not recall seeing it in any museum in Arkham. It must have been somewhere, though; and the sight of it as he snatched it in his sleep must have caused the odd dream-picture of the balustraded terrace. Next day he would make some very guarded inquiries—and perhaps see the nerve specialist.

Meanwhile he would try to keep track of his somnambulism. As he went upstairs and across the garret hall he sprinkled about some flour which he had borrowed—with a frank admission as to its purpose—from the landlord. He had stopped at Elwood's door on the way, but had found all dark within. Entering his room, he placed the spiky thing on the table, and lay down in complete mental and physical exhaustion without pausing to undress. From the closed loft above the slanting ceiling he thought he heard a faint scratching and padding, but he was too disorganized even to mind it. That cryptical pull from the north was getting very strong again, though it seemed now to come from a lower place in the sky.

In the dazzling violet light of dream the old woman and the fanged, furry thing came again and with a greater distinctness than on any former occasion. This time they actually reached him, and he felt the crone's withered claws clutching at him. He was pulled out of bed and into empty space, and for a moment he heard a rhythmic roaring and saw the twilight amorphousness of the vague abysses seething around him. But that moment was very brief, for presently he was in a crude, windowless little space with rough beams and planks rising to a peak just above his head, and with a curious slanting floor underfoot. Propped level on that floor were low cases full of books of every degree of antiquity and disintegration, and in the center were a table and bench, both apparently fastened in place. Small objects of unknown shape and nature were ranged on the tops of the cases, and in the flaming violet light Gilman thought he saw a counterpart of the spiky image which had puzzled him so horribly. On the left the floor fell abruptly away, leaving a black triangular gulf out of which, after a second's dry rattling, there presently climbed the hateful little furry thing with the yellow fangs and bearded human face.

The evilly grinning beldame still clutched him, and beyond the table stood a figure he had never seen before—a tall, lean man of dead black coloration but without the slightest sign of negroid features; wholly devoid of either hair or beard, and wearing as his only garment a shapeless robe of some heavy black fabric. His feet were indistinguishable because of the table and bench, but he must have been shod, since there was a clicking whenever he changed position. The man did not speak, and bore no trace of expression on his small, regular features. He merely pointed to a book of prodigious size which lay open on the table, while the beldame thrust a huge gray quill into Gilman's right hand. Over everything was a pall of intensely maddening fear, and the climax was reached when the furry thing ran up the dreamer's clothing to his shoulders and then down his left arm, finally biting him sharply in the wrist just below his cuff. As the blood spurted from this wound Gilman lapsed into a faint.

He awaked on the morning of the 22nd with a pain in his left wrist, and saw that his cuff was brown with dried blood. His recollections were very confused, but the scene with the black man in the unknown space stood out vividly. The rats must have bitten him as he slept, giving rise to the climax of that frightful dream. Opening the door, he saw that the flour on the corridor floor was undisturbed except for the huge prints of the loutish fellow who roomed at the other end of the garret. So he had not been sleepwalking this time. But something would have to be done about those rats. He would speak to the landlord about them. Again he tried to stop up the hole at the base of the slanting wall, wedging in a candlestick which seemed of about the right size. His ears were ringing horribly, as if with the residual echoes of some horrible noise heard in dreams.

As he bathed and changed clothes he tried to recall what he had dreamed after the scene in the violet-litten space, but nothing definite would crystallize in his mind.

That scene itself must have corresponded to the sealed loft overhead, which had begun to attack his imagination so violently, but later impressions were faint and hazy. There were suggestions of the vague, twilight abysses, and of still vaster, blacker abysses beyond them—abysses in which all fixed suggestions were absent. He had been taken there by the bubble-congeries and the little polyhedron which always dogged him; but they, like himself, had changed to wisps of mist in this farther void of ultimate blackness. Something else had gone on ahead—a larger wisp which now and then condensed into nameless approximations of form—and he thought that their progress had not been in a straight line, but rather along the alien curves and spirals of some ethereal vortex which obeyed laws unknown to the physics and mathematics of any conceivable cosmos. Eventually there had been a hint of vast, leaping shadows, of a monstrous, half-acoustic pulsing, and of the thin, monotonous piping of an unseen flute—but that was all. Gilman decided he had picked up that last conception from what he had read in the *Necronomicon* about the mindless entity Azathoth, which rules all time and space from a curiously environed black throne at the center of Chaos.

When the blood was washed away the wrist wound proved very slight, and Gilman puzzled over the location of the two tiny punctures. It occurred to him that there was no blood on the bedspread where he had lain—which was very curious in view of the amount on his skin and cuff. Had he been sleep-walking within his room, and had the rat bitten him as he sat in some chair or paused in some less rational position? He looked in every corner for brownish drops or stains, but did not find any. He had better, he thought, sprinkle flour within the room as well as outside the door—though after all no further proof of his sleep-walking was needed. He knew he did walk—and the thing to do now was to stop it. He must ask Frank Elwood for help. This morning the strange pulls from space seemed lessened, though they were replaced by another sensation even more inexplicable. It was a vague, insistent impulse to fly away from his present situation, but held not a hint of the specific direction in which he wished to fly. As he picked up the strange spiky image on the table he thought the older northward pull grew a trifle stronger; but even so, it was wholly overruled by the newer and more bewildering urge.

He took the spiky image down to Elwood's room, steel-

ing himself against the whines of the loom-fixer which
welled up from the ground floor. Elwood was in, thank
heaven, and appeared to be stirring about. There was time
for a little conversation before leaving for breakfast and
college; so Gilman hurriedly poured forth an account of
his recent dreams and fears. His host was very sympathetic,
and agreed that something ought to be done. He was
shocked by his guest's drawn, haggard aspect, and noticed
the queer, abnormal-looking sunburn which others had
remarked during the past week. There was not much,
though, that he could say. He had not seen Gilman on any
sleep-walking expedition, and had no idea what the curious
image could be. He had, though, heard the French-Cana-
dian who lodged just under Gilman talking to Mazurewicz
one evening. They were telling each other how badly they
dreaded the coming of Walpurgis Night, now only a few
days off; and were exchanging pitying comments about the
poor, doomed young gentleman. Desrochers, the fellow
under Gilman's room, had spoken of nocturnal footsteps
shod and unshod, and of the violet light he saw one night
when he had stolen fearfully up to peer through Gilman's
keyhole. He had not dared to peer, he told Mazurewicz,
after he had glimpsed that light through the cracks around
the door. There had been soft talking, too—and as he began to describe it his voice had sunk to an inaudible
whisper.

Elwood could not imagine what had set these superstitious creatures gossiping, but supposed their imaginations
had been roused by Gilman's late hours and somnolent
walking and talking on the one hand, and by the nearness
of traditionally-feared May-Eve on the other hand. That
Gilman talked in his sleep was plain, and it was obviously
from Desrochers' keyhole-listenings that the delusive notion
of the violet dream-light had got abroad. These simple
people were quick to imagine they had seen any odd thing
they had heard about. As for a plan of action—Gilman
had better move down to Elwood's rooms and avoid sleeping alone. Elwood would, if awake, rouse him whenever
he began to talk or rise in his sleep. Very soon, too, he
must see the specialist. Meanwhile they would take the
spiky image around to the various museums and to certain
professors; seeking identification and stating that it had
been found in a public rubbish-can. Also, Dombrowski
must attend to the poisoning of those rats in the walls.

Braced up by Elwood's companionship, Gilman attended classes that day. Strange urges still tugged at him, but he could sidetrack them with considerable success. During a free period he showed the queer image to several professors, all of whom were intensely interested, though none of them could shed any light upon its nature or origin. That night he slept on a couch which Elwood had had the landlord bring to the second-story room, and for the first time in weeks was wholly free from disquieting dreams. But the feverishness still hung on, and the whines of the loom-fixer were an unnnerving influence.

During the next few days Gilman enjoyed an almost perfect immunity from morbid manifestations. He had, Elwood said, showed no tendency to talk or rise in his sleep; and meanwhile the landlord was putting rat-poison everywhere. The only disturbing element was the talk among the superstitious foreigners, whose imaginations had become highly excited. Mazurewicz was always trying to make him get a crucifix, and finally forced one upon him which he said had been blessed by the good Father Iwanicki. Desrochers, too, had something to say; in fact, he insisted that cautious steps had sounded in the now vacant room above him on the first and second nights of Gilman's absence from it. Paul Choynski thought he heard sounds in the halls and on the stairs at night, and claimed that his door had been softly tried, while Mrs. Dombrowski vowed she had seen Brown Jenkin for the first time since All-Hallows. But such naïve reports could mean very little, and Gilman let the cheap metal crucifix hang idly from a knob on his host's dresser.

For three days Gilman and Elwood canvassed the local museums in an effort to identify the strange spiky image, but always without success. In every quarter, however, interest was intense; for the utter alienage of the thing was a tremendous challenge to scientific curiosity. One of the small radiating arms was broken off and subjected to chemical analysis. Professor Ellery found platinum, iron and tellurium in the strange alloy; but mixed with these were at least three other apparent elements of high atomic weight which chemistry was absolutely powerless to classify. Not only did they fail to correspond with any human element, but they did not even fit the vacant places reserved for probable elements in the periodic system. The mystery remains unsolved to this day, though the image is on exhibition at the museum of Miskatonic University.

On the morning of April 27th a fresh rat-hole appeared in the room where Gilman was a guest, but Dombrowski tinned it up during the day. The poison was not having much effect, for scratchings and scurryings in the walls were virtually undiminished.

Elwood was out late that night, and Gilman waited up for him. He did not wish to go to sleep in a room alone—especially since he thought he had glimpsed in the evening twilight the repellent old woman whose image had become so horribly transferred to his dreams. He wondered who she was, and what had been near her rattling the tin cans in a rubbish-heap at the mouth of a squalid courtyard. The crone had seemed to notice him and leer evilly at him—though perhaps this was merely his imagination.

The next day both youths felt very tired, and knew they would sleep like logs when night came. In the evening they drowsily discussed the mathematical studies which engrossed Gilman, and speculated about the linkage with ancient magic and folklore which seemed so darkly probable. They spoke of old Keziah Mason, and Elwood agreed that Gilman had good scientific grounds for thinking she might have stumbled on strange and significant information. The hidden cults to which these witches belonged often guarded and handed down surprising secrets from elder, forgotten eons; and it was by no means impossible that Keziah had actually mastered the art of passing through dimensional gates. Tradition emphasizes the uselessness of material barriers in halting a witch's motions, and who can say what underlies the old tales of broomstick rides through the night?

Whether a modern student could ever gain similar powers from mathematical research alone, was still to be seen. Success, Gilman added, might lead to dangerous and unthinkable situations; for who could foretell the conditions pervading an adjacent but normally inaccessible dimension? On the other hand, the picturesque possibilities were enormous. Time could not exist in certain belts of space, and by entering and remaining in such a belt one might preserve one's life and age indefinitely; never suffering organic metabolism or deterioration except for slight amounts incurred during visits to one's own or similar planes. One might, for example, pass into a timeless dimension and emerge at some remote period of the earth's history as young as before.

Whether anybody had ever managed to do this, one could

hardly conjecture with any degree of authority. Old legends are hazy and ambiguous, and in historic times all attempts at crossing forbidden gaps seem complicated by strange and terrible alliances with beings and messengers from outside. There was the immemorial figure of the deputy or messenger of hidden and terrible powers—the "Black Man" of the witch-cult, and the "Nyarlathotep" of the *Necronomicon*. There was, too, the baffling problem of the lesser messengers or intermediaries—the quasi-animals and queer hybrids which legend depicts as witches' familiars. As Gilman and Elwood retired, too sleepy to argue further, they heard Joe Mazurewicz reel into the house half drunk, and shuddered at the desperate wildness of his whining prayers.

That night Gilman saw the violet light again. In his dream he had heard a scratching and gnawing in the partitions, and thought that some one fumbled clumsily at the latch. Then he saw the old woman and the small furry thing advancing toward him over the carpeted floor. The beldame's face was alight with inhuman exultation, and the little yellow-toothed morbidity tittered mockingly as it pointed at the hearty-sleeping form of Elwood on the other couch across the room. A paralysis of fear stifled all attempts to cry out. As once before, the hideous crone seized Gilman by the shoulders, yanking him out of bed and into empty space. Again the infinitude of the shrieking abysses flashed past him, but in another second he thought he was in a dark, muddy, unknown alley of fetid odors with the rotting walls of ancient houses towering up on every hand.

Ahead was the robed black man he had seen in the peaked space in the other dream, while from a lesser distance the old woman was beckoning and grimacing imperiously. Brown Jenkin was rubbing itself with a kind of affectionate playfulness around the ankles of the black man, which the deep mud largely concealed. There was a dark open doorway on the right, to which the black man silently pointed. Into this the grinning crone started, dragging Gilman after her by his pajama sleeves. There were evil-smelling staircases which creaked ominously, and on which the old woman seemed to radiate a faint violet light; and finally a door leading off a landing. The crone fumbled with the latch and pushed the door open, motioning to Gilman to wait, and disappearing inside the black aperture.

The youth's over-sensitive ears caught a hideous strangled

cry, and presently the beldame came out of the room bearing a small, senseless form which she thrust at the dreamer as if ordering him to carry it. The sight of this form, and the expression on its face, broke the spell. Still too dazed to cry out, he plunged recklessly down the noisome staircase and into the mud outside; halting only when seized and choked by the waiting black man. As consciousness departed he heard the faint, shrill tittering of the fanged, rat-like abnormality.

On the morning of the 29th Gilman awaked into a maelstrom of horror. The instant he opened his eyes he knew something was terribly wrong, for he was back in his old garret room with the slanting wall and ceiling, sprawled on the now unmade bed. His throat was aching inexplicably, and as he struggled to a sitting posture he saw with growing fright that his feet and pajama bottoms were brown with caked mud. For the moment his recollections were hopelessly hazy, but he knew at least that he must have been sleep-walking. Elwood had been lost too deeply in slumber to hear and stop him. On the floor were confused muddy prints, but oddly enough they did not extend all the way to the door. The more Gilman looked at them, the more peculiar they seemed; for in addition to those he could recognize as his there were some smaller, almost round markings—such as the legs of a large chair or a table might make, except that most of them tended to be divided into halves. There were also some curious muddy rat-tracks leading out of a fresh hole and back into it again. Utter bewilderment and the fear of madness racked Gilman as he staggered to the door and saw that there were no muddy prints outside. The more he remembered of his hideous dream the more terrified he felt, and it added to his desperation to hear Joe Mazurewicz chanting mournfully two floors below.

Descending to Elwood's room he roused his still-sleeping host and began telling of how he had found himself; but Elwood could form no idea of what might really have happened. Where Gilman could have been, how he got back to his room without making tracks in the hall, and how the muddy, furniture-like prints came to be mixed with his in the garret chamber, were wholly beyond conjecture. Then there were those dark, livid marks on his throat, as if he had tried to strangle himself. He put his hands up to them, but found that they did not even approximately fit. While they were talking, Desrochers dropped in to say that he had heard a terrific clattering overhead in the dark small hours. No, there had been no one on the stairs after midnight, though just before midnight he had heard faint footfalls in the garret, and cautiously descending steps he did not like. It was, he added, a very bad time of year for Arkham. The young gentleman had better be sure to wear the crucifix Joe Mazurewicz had given him. Even the daytime was not safe, for after dawn there had been strange sounds in the house—especially a thin, childish wail hastily choked off.

Gilman mechanically attended classes that morning, but was wholly unable to fix his mind on his studies. A mood of hideous apprehension and expectancy had seized him, and he seemed to be awaiting the fall of some annihilating blow. At noon he lunched at the University Spa, picking up a paper from the next seat as he waited for dessert. But he never ate that dessert; for an item on the paper's first page left him limp, wild-eyed, and able only to pay his check and stagger back to Elwood's room.

There had been a strange kidnapping the night before in Orne's Gangway, and the two-year-old child of a clod-like laundry worker named Anastasia Wolejko had completely vanished from sight. The mother, it appeared, had feared the event for some time; but the reasons she assigned for her fear were so grotesque that no one took them seriously. She had, she said, seen Brown Jenkin about the place now and then ever since early in March, and knew from its grimaces and titterings that little Ladislas must be marked for sacrifice at the awful Sabbat on Walpurgis Night. She had asked her neighbor Mary Czanek to sleep in the room and try to protect the child, but Mary had not dared. She could not tell the police, for they never believed such things. Children had been taken that way every year ever since she could remember. And her friend Pete Stowacki would not help because he wanted the child out of the way.

But what threw Gilman into a cold perspiration was the report of a pair of revellers who had been walking past the mouth of the gangway just after midnight. They admitted they had been drunk, but both vowed they had seen a crazily dressed trio furtively entering the dark passageway. There had, they said, been a huge robed negro, a little old woman in rags, and a young white man in his nightclothes. The old woman had been dragging the youth, while around the feet of the negro a tame rat was rubbing and weaving in the brown mud.

Gilman sat in a daze all the afternoon, and Elwood—who had meanwhile seen the papers and formed terrible conjectures from them—found him thus when he came home. This time neither could doubt but that something hideously serious was closing in around them. Between the fantasms of nightmare and the realities of the objective world a monstrous and unthinkable relationship was crystallizing, and only stupendous vigilance could avert still more direful developments. Gilman must see a specialist sooner or later, but not just now, when all the papers were full of this kidnapping business.

Just what had really happened was maddeningly obscure, and for a moment both Gilman and Elwood exchanged whispered theories of the wildest kind. Had Gilman unconsciously succeeded better than he knew in his studies of space and its dimensions? Had he actually slipped outside our sphere to points unguessed and unimaginable? Where—if anywhere—had he been on those nights of demoniac alienage? The roaring twilight abysses—the green hillside—the blistering terrace—the pulls from the stars—the ultimate black vortex—the black man—the muddy alley and the stairs—the old witch and the fanged, furry horror—the bubble-congeries and the little polyhedron—the strange sunburn—the wrist wound—the unexplained image—the muddy feet—the throat-marks—the tales and fears of the superstitious foreigners—what did all this mean? To what extent could the laws of sanity apply to such a case?

There was no sleep for either of them that night, but next day they both cut classes and drowsed. This was April 30th, and with the dusk would come the hellish Sabbat-time which all the foreigners and the superstitious old folk feared. Mazurewicz came home at six o'clock and said people at the mill were whispering that the Walpurgis-revels would be held in the dark ravine beyond Meadow Hill where the old white stone stands in a place queerly devoid of all plant life. Some of them had even told the police and advised them to look there for the missing Wolejko child, but they did not believe anything would be done. Joe insisted that the poor young gentleman wear his nickel-chained crucifix, and Gilman put it on and dropped it inside his shirt to humor the fellow.

Late at night the two youths sat drowsing in their chairs, lulled by the praying of the loom-fixer on the floor below. Gilman listened as he nodded, his preternaturally sharpened hearing seeming to strain for some subtle, dreaded murmur beyond the noises in the ancient house. Unwholesome recollections of things in the *Necronomicon* and the *Black Book* welled up, and he found himself swaying to infandous rhythms said to pertain to the blackest ceremonies of the Sabbat and to have an origin outside the time and space we comprehend.

Presently he realized what he was listening for—the hellish chant of the celebrants in the distant black valley. How did he know so much about what they expected? How did he know the time when Nahab and her acolyte were due to bear the brimming bowl which would follow the black cock and the black goat? He saw that Elwood had dropped asleep, and tried to call out and waken him. Something, however, closed his throat. He was not his own master. Had he signed the black man's book after all?

Then his fevered, abnormal hearing caught the distant, wind-borne notes. Over miles of hill and field and alley they came, but he recognized them none the less. The fires must be lit, and the dancers must be starting in. How could he keep himself from going? What was it that had enmeshed him? Mathematics—folklore—the house—old Keziah—Brown Jenkin . . . and now he saw that there was a fresh rat-hole in the wall near his couch. Above the distant chanting and the nearer praying of Joe Mazurewicz came another sound—a stealthy, determined scratching in the partitions. He hoped the electric lights would not go out. Then he saw the fanged, bearded little face in the rat-hole—the accursed little face which he at last realized bore such a shocking, mocking resemblance to old Keziah's —and heard the faint fumbling at the door.

The screaming twilight abysses flashed before him, and he felt himself helpless in the formless grasp of the iridescent bubble-congeries. Ahead raced the small, kaleidoscopic polyhedron, and all through the churning void there was a heightening and acceleration of the vague tonal pattern which seemed to foreshadow some unutterable and unendurable climax. He seemed to know what was coming —the monstrous burst of Walpurgis-rhythm in whose cosmic timbre would be concentrated all the primal, ultimate space-time seethings which lie behind the massed spheres of matter and sometimes break forth in measured reverberations that penetrate faintly to every layer of entity and give hideous significance throughout the worlds to certain dreaded periods.

But all this vanished in a second. He was again in the cramped, violet-litten peaked space with the slanting floor, the low cases of ancient books, the bench and table, the queer objects, and the triangular gulf at one side. On the table lay a small white figure—an infant boy, unclothed and unconscious—while on the other side stood the monstrous, leering old woman with a gleaming, grotesque-hafted knife in her right hand, and a queerly proportioned pale metal bowl covered with curiously chased designs and having delicate lateral handles in her left. She was intoning some croaking ritual in a language which Gilman could not understand, but which seemed like something guardedly quoted in the *Necronomicon*.

As the scene grew clear he saw the ancient crone bend forward and extend the empty bowl across the table—and unable to control his own motions, he reached far forward and took it in both hands, noticing as he did so its comparative lightness. At the same moment the disgusting form of Brown Jenkin scrambled up over the brink of the triangular black gulf on his left. The crone now motioned him to hold the bowl in a certain position while she raised the huge, grotesque knife above the small white victim as high as her right hand could reach. The fanged, furry thing began tittering a continuation of the unknown ritual, while the witch croaked loathsome responses. Gilman felt a gnawing, poignant abhorrence shoot through his mental and emotional paralysis, and the light metal shook in his grasp. A second later the downward motion of the knife broke the spell completely, and he dropped the bowl with a resounding bell-like clangor while his hands darted out frantically to stop the monstrous deed.

In an instant he had edged up the slanting floor around the end of the table and wrenched the knife from the old woman's claws; sending it clattering over the brink of the narrow triangular gulf. In another instant, however, matters were reversed; for those murderous claws had locked themselves tightly around his own throat, while the wrinkled face was twisted with insane fury. He felt the chain of the cheap crucifix grinding into his neck, and in his peril wondered how the sight of the object itself would affect the evil creature. Her strength was altogether superhuman, but as she continued her choking he reached feebly in his shirt and drew out the metal symbol, snapping the chain and pulling it free.

At sight of the device the witch seemed struck with panic, and her grip relaxed long enough to give Gilman a chance to break it entirely. He pulled the steel-like claws from his neck, and would have dragged the beldame over the edge of the gulf had not the claws received a fresh access of strength and closed in again. This time he resolved to reply in kind, and his own hands reached out for the creature's throat. Before she saw what he was doing he had the chain of the crucifix twisted about her neck, and a moment later he had tightened it enough to cut off her breath. During her last struggle he felt something bite at his ankle, and saw that Brown Jenkin had come to her aid. With one savage kick he sent the morbidity over the edge of the gulf and heard it whimper on some level far below.

Whether he had killed the ancient crone he did not know, but he let her rest on the floor where she had fallen. Then, as he turned away, he saw on the table a sight which nearly snapped the last thread of his reason. Brown Jenkin, tough of sinew and with four tiny hands of demoniac dexterity, had been busy while the witch was throttling him, and his efforts had been in vain. What he had prevented the knife from doing to the victim's chest, the yellow fangs of the furry blasphemy had done to a wrist—and the bowl so lately on the floor stood full beside the small lifeless body.

In his dream-delirium Gilman heard the hellish alien-rhythmed chant of the Sabbat coming from an infinite distance, and knew the black man must be there. Confused memories mixed themselves with his mathematics, and he believed his subconscious mind held the *angles* which he needed to guide him back to the normal world alone and unaided for the first time. He felt sure he was in the immemorially sealed loft above his own room, but whether he could ever escape through the slanting floor or the long-stopped egress he doubted greatly. Besides, would not an escape from a dream-loft bring him merely into a dream-house—an abnormal projection of the actual place he sought? He was wholly bewildered as to the relation betwixt dream and reality in all his experiences.

The passage through the vague abysses would be frightful, for the Walpurgis-rhythm would be vibrating, and at last he would have to hear that hitherto-veiled cosmic pulsing which he so mortally dreaded. Even now he could detect a low, monstrous shaking whose tempo he suspected all too well. At Sabbat-time it always mounted and reached through to the worlds to summon the initiate to nameless rites. Half the chants of the Sabbat were patterned on this faintly overheard pulsing which no earthly ear could endure in its unveiled spatial fullness. Gilman wondered, too, whether he could trust his instincts to take him back to the right part of space. How could he be sure he would not land on that green-litten hillside of a far planet, on the tessellated terrace above the city of tentacled monsters somewhere beyond the galaxy, or in the spiral black vortices of that ultimate void of Chaos where reigns the mindless demon-sultan Azathoth?

Just before he made the plunge the violet light went out and left him in utter blackness. The witch—old Keziah—Nahab—that must have meant her death. And mixed with the distant chant of the Sabbat and the whimpers of Brown Jenkin in the gulf below he thought he heard another and wilder whine from unknown depths. Joe Mazurewicz—the prayers against the Crawling Chaos now turning to an inexplicably triumphant shriek—worlds of sardonic actuality impinging on vortices of febrile dream—Iä! Shub-Niggurath! The Goat with a Thousand Young. . . .

They found Gilman on the floor of his queerly-angled old garret room long before dawn, for the terrible cry had brought Desrochers and Choynski and Dombrowski and Mazurewicz at once, and had even wakened the soundly sleeping Elwood in his chair. He was alive, and with open, staring eyes, but seemed largely unconscious. On his throat were the marks of murderous hands, and on his left ankle was a distressing rat-bite. His clothing was badly rumpled, and Joe's crucifix was missing. Elwood trembled, afraid even to speculate on what new form his friend's sleep-walking had taken. Mazurewicz seemed half dazed because of a "sign" he said he had had in response to his prayers, and he crossed himself frantically when the squealing and whimpering of a rat sounded from beyond the slanting partition.

When the dreamer was settled on his couch in Elwood's room they sent for Doctor Malkowski—a local practitioner who would repeat no tales where they might prove embarrassing—and he gave Gilman two hypodermic injections which caused him to relax in something like natural drowsiness. During the day the patient regained consciousness at times and whispered his newest dream disjointedly to Elwood. It was a painful process, and at its very start brought out a fresh and disconcerting fact.

Gilman—whose ears had so lately possessed an abnormal sensitiveness—was now stone-deaf. Doctor Malkowski, summoned again in haste, told Elwood that both eardrums were ruptured, as if by the impact of some stupendous sound intense beyond all human conception or endurance. How such a sound could have been heard in the last few hours without arousing all the Miskatonic Valley was more than the honest physician could say.

Elwood wrote his part of the colloquy on paper, so that a fairly easy communication was maintained. Neither knew what to make of the whole chaotic business, and decided it would be better if they thought as little as possible about it. Both, though, agreed that they must leave this ancient and accursed house as soon as it could be arranged. Evening papers spoke of a police raid on some curious revellers in a ravine beyond Meadow Hill just before dawn, and mentioned that the white stone there was an object of age-long superstitious regard. Nobody had been caught, but among the scattering fugitives had been glimpsed a huge negro. In another column it was stated that no trace of the missing child Ladislas Wolejko had been found.

The crowning horror came that very night. Elwood will never forget it, and was forced to stay out of college the rest of the term because of the resulting nervous breakdown. He had thought he heard rats in the partitions all the evening, but paid little attention to them. Then, long after both he and Gilman had retired, the atrocious shrieking began. Elwood jumped up, turned on the lights, and rushed over to his guest's couch. The occupant was emitting sounds of veritably inhuman nature, as if racked by some torment beyond description. He was writhing under the bedclothes, and a great red stain was beginning to appear on the blankets.

Elwood scarcely dared to touch him, but gradually the screaming and writhing subsided. By this time Dombrowski, Choynski, Desrochers, Mazurewicz, and the top-floor lodger were all crowding into the doorway, and the landlord had sent his wife back to telephone for Doctor Malkowski.

Everybody shrieked when a large rat-like form suddenly jumped out from beneath the ensanguined bedclothes and scuttled across the floor to a fresh, open hole close by. When the doctor arrived and began to pull down those frightful covers Walter Gilman was dead.

It would be barbarous to do more than suggest what had killed Gilman. There had been virtually a tunnel through his body—something had eaten his heart out. Dombrowski, frantic at the failure of his rat-poisoning efforts, cast aside all thought of his lease and within a week had moved with all his older lodgers to a dingy but less ancient house in Walnut Street. The worst thing for a while was keeping Joe Mazurewicz quiet; for the brooding loom-fixer would never stay sober, and was constantly whining and muttering about spectral and terrible things.

It seems that on that last hideous night Joe had stooped to look at the crimson rat-tracks which led from Gilman's couch to the near-by hole. On the carpet they were very indistinct, but a piece of open flooring intervened between the carpet's edge and the baseboard. There Mazurewicz had found something monstrous—or thought he had, for no one else could quite agree with him despite the undeniable queerness of the prints. The tracks on the flooring were certainly vastly unlike the average prints of a rat, but even Choynski and Desrochers would not admit that they were like the prints of four tiny human hands.

The house was never rented again. As soon as Dombrowski left it the pall of its final desolation began to descend, for people shunned it both on account of its old reputation and because of the new fetid odor. Perhaps the ex-landlord's rat-poison had worked after all, for not long after his departure the place became a neighborhood nuisance. Health officials traced the smell to the closed spaces above and beside the eastern garret room, and agreed that the number of dead rats must be enormous. They decided, however, that it was not worth their while to hew open and disinfect the long-sealed spaces; for the fetor would soon be over, and the locality was not one which encouraged fastidious standards. Indeed, there were always vague local tales of unexplained stenches upstairs in the Witch-House just after May-Eve and Hallowmass. The neighbors acquiesced in the inertia—but the fetor none the less formed an additional count against the place.

Toward the last the house was condemned as a habitation by the building inspector.

Gilman's dreams and their attendant circumstances have never been explained. Elwood, whose thoughts on the entire episode are sometimes almost maddening, came back to college the next autumn and graduated in the following June. He found the spectral gossip of the town much diminished, and it is indeed a fact that—notwithstanding certain reports of a ghostly tittering in the deserted house which lasted almost as long as that edifice itself—no fresh appearances either of Old Keziah or of Brown Jenkin have been muttered of since Gilman's death. It is rather fortunate that Elwood was not in Arkham in that later year when certain events abruptly renewed the local whispers about elder horrors. Of course he heard about the matter afterward and suffered untold torments of black and bewildered speculation; but even that was not as bad as actual nearness and several possible sights would have been.

In March, 1931, a gale wrecked the roof and great chimney of the vacant Witch-House, so that a chaos of crumbling bricks, blackened, moss-grown shingles, and rotting planks and timbers crashed down into the loft and broke through the floor beneath. The whole attic story was choked with debris from above, but no one took the trouble to touch the mess before the inevitable razing of the decrepit structure. That ultimate step came in the following December, and it was when Gilman's old room was cleared out by reluctant, apprehensive workmen that the gossip began.

Among the rubbish which had crashed through the ancient slanting ceiling were several things which made the workmen pause and call in the police. Later the police in turn called in the coroner and several professors from the university. There were bones—badly crushed and splintered but clearly recognizable as human—whose manifestly modern date conflicted puzzlingly with the remote period at which their only possible lurking place, the low, slant-floored loft overhead, had supposedly been sealed from all human access. The coroner's physician decided that some belonged to a small child, while certain others—found mixed with shreds of rotten brownish cloth—belonged to a rather undersized, bent female of advanced years. Careful sifting of debris also disclosed many tiny bones of rats caught in the collapse, as well as older rat-bones gnawed by small fangs in a fashion now and then highly productive of controversy and reflection.

Other objects found included the mangled fragments of many books and papers, together with a yellowish dust left from the total disintegration of still older books and papers. All, without exception, appeared to deal with black magic in its most advanced and horrible forms; and the evidently recent date of certain items is still a mystery as unsolved as that of the modern human bones. An even greater mystery is the absolute homogeneity of the crabbed, archaic writing found on a wide range of papers whose conditions and watermarks suggest age differences of at least 150 to 200 years. To some, though, the greatest mystery of all is the variety of utterly inexplicable objects —objects whose shapes, materials, types of workmanship, and purposes baffle all conjecture—found scattered amidst the wreckage in evidently diverse states of injury. One of these things—which excited several Miskatonic professors profoundly—is a badly damaged monstrosity plainly resembling the strange image which Gilman gave to the college museum, save that it is larger, wrought of some peculiar bluish stone instead of metal, and possessed of a singularly angled pedestal with undecipherable hieroglyphics.

Archeologists and anthropologists are still trying to explain the bizarre designs chased on a crushed bowl of light metal whose inner side bore ominous brownish stains when found. Foreigners and credulous grandmothers are equally garrulous about the modern nickel crucifix with broken chain mixed in the rubbish and shiveringly identified by Joe Mazurewicz as that which he had given poor Gilman many years before. Some believe this crucifix was dragged up to the sealed loft by rats, while others think it must have been on the floor in some corner of Gilman's old room all the time. Still others, including Joe himself, have theories too wild and fantastic for sober credence.

When the slanting wall of Gilman's room was torn out, the once sealed triangular space between that partition and the house's north wall was found to contain much less structural debris, even in proportion to its size, than the room itself; though it had a ghastly layer of older materials which paralyzed the wreckers with horror. In brief, the floor was a veritable ossuary of the bones of small children —some fairly modern, but others extending back in infinite gradations to a period so remote that crumbling was almost complete. On this deep bony layer rested a knife of great size, obvious antiquity, and grotesque, ornate, and exotic design—above which the debris was piled.

In the midst of this debris, wedged between a fallen plank and a cluster of cemented bricks from the ruined chimney, was an object destined to cause more bafflement, veiled fright, and openly superstitious talk in Arkham than anything else discovered in the haunted and accursed building. This object was the partly crushed skeleton of a huge diseased rat, whose abnormalities of form are still a topic of debate and source of singular reticence among the members of Miskatonic's department of comparative anatomy. Very little concerning this skeleton has leaked out, but the workmen who found it whisper in shocked tones about the long, brownish hairs with which it was associated.

The bones of the tiny paws, it is rumored, imply prehensile characteristics more typical of a diminutive monkey than of a rat, while the small skull with its savage yellow fangs is of the utmost anomalousness, appearing from certain angles like a miniature, monstrously degraded parody of a human skull. The workmen crossed themselves in fright when they came upon this blasphemy, but later burned candles of gratitude in St. Stanislaus' Church because of the shrill, ghostly tittering they felt they would never hear again.

If you have enjoyed this book, you will want to read other inexpensive Pyramid best-sellers listed in the back of this book. You will find them wherever paperbacks are sold or you can order them direct from the publisher. *Yours For The Asking:* a free, illustrated catalogue listing more than 700 books published by Pyramid. Write the publisher: PYRAMID BOOKS, Dep't. K-99, 444 Madison Avenue, New York, N.Y. 10022.